THE GIRL BEYOND FOREVER

ADAM LOXWOOD

PENDULUM BOOKS

For all the people who have never given up

CHAPTER 1

I wasn't in the car.

I was somewhere else.

The last place I'd ever been happy.

The sun shines through the trees. Leaves cast dappled shadows on the dry grass as branches sway in the gentle breeze. I am barefoot, and my feet crunch the brittle summer earth into dust as I move stealthily towards the big oak at the bottom of our garden.

She's hiding there.

She always hides there.

A flutter of purple flowers on pink cotton. A small, perfectly formed cheek. She can't resist peeking, but I know the rules and pretend I haven't seen her. I know her stomach will be churning with the excitement of the chase, anticipating that sudden moment of discovery.

The roar.

The run.

The hug. The rush of adrenaline giving way to the relief that it's all pretend. That she's safe, wrapped in my arms. That I'm never going to let her go.

I forced myself to relive the memory every single day, so that my recollection was always perfect and my pain raw. So I never forgot her. My little girl, running through the sunlit garden. Sweet. Innocent. Beautiful. Forever just out of reach.

The plastic bites into my left foot, and I look down to see a blue shard, a relic of some old garden toy chewed up by the mower. I move, swiftly now; I can hear her tittering with excitement. She takes another peek, this time from the right side of the tree. I pretend I haven't seen and swing to the left. As I round the gnarly old tree, I see her.

Amber.

Ten years old.

Ten years of innocent perfection.

I growl.

Amber jumps and squeals, 'Monster!'

She runs across the lawn, and I pursue, growling and roaring with every step. Halfway to the house she turns to make a stand, trying to intimidate me with her sapphire blue eyes. I scoop her up, burying my face in her platinum blonde hair and roaring with renewed fury.

'Stop it, Daddy,' Amber squeals. 'It tickles!'

'Of course it tickles,' I say. 'I'm the tickle monster.'

'You cheated,' she tells me. 'You didn't count properly. You're supposed to count like this.'

She holds up her right hand and taps her thumb over her four fingers.

'One,' she says, as her thumb returns to her index finger and repeats its bounce over the other digits. 'Two.'

I'd taught her a way to count out seconds properly, something I'd learnt in the field, and she never let me forget it.

'I'll count properly next time, I promise,' I say.

'Hey, you two, lunch is ready!' Sarah yells from the patio.

Sarah.

Beautiful Sarah.

Our love died that night.

Withered in the face of horror.

Amber wriggles free and runs towards her rotund mother. Sarah can't pick her up because of the baby in her belly: the boy is seven months along and puts enough of a strain on her back. I watch her stroke Amber's head. I don't know how much this mundane moment will come to mean to me. It's just another day. Just another game of hide and seek. I cannot guess at the number of nights my eyes will run dry at this memory. Blissfully ignorant of the future, I join my family for lunch.

CHAPTER 2

'You with us, Schaefer?' Jean asked, bringing my wandering mind back to the car. 'Schaefer?'

Detective Sergeant Peterson Jean. Family originally from Haiti, tall, thin, late-thirties, wide eyes. He'd helped me on some cases and we'd struck up an uneasy alliance. I looked past him, through the windscreen at a hooded figure walking our way.

'That's him,' I said.

'You sure?' Noel asked.

Detective Sergeant David Noel. Yorkshireman. Army veteran, like me. Short, wiry like a terrier, face pockmarked and scarred from a roadside bomb near Kabul. More to my taste than Jean, but still police and not to be completely trusted.

I couldn't see the hooded figure's face, but the clothes matched my informant's description. Noel scanned my face for doubt and found none.

'Let's call it,' Noel told his partner.

Jean grabbed the radio. 'Visual on the suspect. Everyone stand by.'

I sank a little further into the back seat. The hooded figure wasn't cagey, even though he must have known he was being hunted. He wasn't using any counter-surveillance techniques. He wasn't even checking the street. But I'd learnt to be cautious. I peered over Jean's shoulder and watched the hooded figure go into a front garden and walk up the short path towards one of the red brick terrace houses. He didn't even look round when he put the key in the lock. This was a confident man, afraid of nothing. The hooded figure stepped inside and shut the door behind him.

Noel and Jean both looked at me. Were they expecting me to say something? It wasn't my place to order the raid.

'You sure that's him?' Noel asked.

'It's him,' I replied.

'Okay. Let's go.'

Jean radioed the news. 'We're moving.'

I was the first to get out of the car. Up ahead I saw a squad of six SCO19 officers exit a battered, old, unmarked van. Their matt black Heckler & Koch submachine guns were deadly shadows clasped close to their chests. I felt a gentle tug at my arm. It was Noel.

'You know the deal: stay back,' he instructed.

I was certain I'd seen more action than Noel or Jean, but I wasn't police, so they wanted me well clear of any danger.

We quickly crossed Chapel Street, which was otherwise deserted. It was the middle of September and the first chill of autumn was in the air. I pictured all the families living on this quiet South London street, sat in front of their televisions, or sleeping in their beds, unaware of the darkness just outside their own front doors.

As we reached the other side of the street, Noel signalled the armed officers, and the squad split in two. Three of the SCO19 officers followed Noel towards the front of the house. The other three joined Jean and followed him down a dark alleyway that cut between two of the houses. I went with them, plunging into a narrow strip of darkness as the houses either side blocked the sulphur glow of the street lamps. A few steps further and I was back in the yellow haze of London at night. I could see Jean ahead of me, moving well: deliberate and silent. He led the SCO19 squad right, along a service road that ran behind the terrace. I followed, and was ten yards behind Jean when the landmine exploded.

CHAPTER 3

The battlefield had taught me how time plays tricks. It slows and you can pick out the most exquisite details, but you still find yourself longing for more time to avoid the knife, bullet or blast.

Light travels faster than sound, and I saw the flash of the fireball first, and then felt the shockwave pick me up and toss me against a garden wall. I felt the intense heat of the inferno that broiled two of the police officers ahead of me. They were still alive and screamed like children as they burnt. Jean and another officer were knocked to the ground not far from me.

The world went muffled and distant and for a moment I thought I might lose consciousness. A loud hum pushed my eardrums into my head, creating an uncomfortable pressure, but I stayed with the world. My arms and legs weren't responsive and moved wildly when I tried to stand, like a marionette tangled in its own strings. My body trembled and my aching muscles were unable to coordinate their way upright.

Jean and the other officer groaned and floundered, and as my hearing returned, I realised their radios were alive with chatter.

'Bravo, what's your status?' It was Noel, speaking from the front of the house. 'Jean, are you okay? What just happened?'

Neither man could reply, so I crawled towards them.

'Open it,' I heard Noel say.

His officers would be going in through the front door, and I wanted to warn them this was no normal raid.

The radio broadcast some thuds and crashes and the sound of glass shattering. Then shouts and gunshots.

'Officers down, officers down,' Noel yelled over the radio. 'Get them out of there. We need immediate medical assistance.'

There was a pause. Then, 'Jean, I don't know if you can hear me, mate, but the suspect is coming your way. He's armed and very dangerous.'

Peering through the flames, over the bodies of the fallen police officers, I saw the back door open. I lay motionless the moment I saw Leon Yates step out, gun in hand. A gun that told me he wouldn't hesitate to put a bullet in my head. I could see his pasty skin, dark hair and angry, shadowed eyes beneath his hood.

He stumbled down the back steps and ran through the flaming ruins of the garden, past the dead policemen and Jean and the other cop, who were both out of it. He turned left and ran past me. As he neared the end of the alley, I took a deep breath. If I lost Yates now, there was a real chance of losing him for good. I had no idea what had happened to Noel's team, but there was no sign of them. I would have to go after the man myself. I took another deep breath and forced myself to my feet. I was unsteady and dazed, maybe even concussed, but I could move. I took a couple of unsteady steps, and built up speed, gradually remembering how everything worked. It all hurt, but it functioned, and I was running now. I chased Yates to the end of the alleyway.

Ahead of me, he turned left onto Galton Street and I went after him.

CHAPTER 4

I burst out of the alley to see Yates pulling a driver out of his BMW 3-series at gun point. The locals knew better than to break London's cardinal rule: *don't get involved*. As they hurried into one of the half-dozen shops on a small parade I saw a couple of them make hurried phone calls. They weren't to know the police were just down the road, in no state to help. An old lady at the bus stop suddenly found a reason to return to the convenience store, while two teenagers simply watched Yates with wry smiles on their faces, like a couple of theatre goers enjoying a West End show.

The BMW driver saw me run onto the street, and Yates followed the man's gaze. There was an unmistakable flash of recognition – how did he know me?

I ducked behind the bus stop as Yates started shooting. Thick glass sprayed me as he peppered the panels with bullets. The smiling teenagers weren't such fans of lawlessness now, and joined me on the other side of a low metal balustrade that offered some protection against the gunfire. I noticed they were both still smiling, exhilarated rather than afraid, and wondered what kind of wrong turns their lives had taken.

The bullets stopped, and I heard the roar of an engine. I broke cover to look down the street and saw the tail lights of the stolen BMW recede into the distance.

I saw a suited man standing beside his new Mercedes E-Class. The upright citizen was on the phone to the police and didn't notice me slip into his driver's seat and start the engine until it was too late.

'Hey!' Upright yelled, as I gunned the engine. He carried on shouting, but I didn't hear what he said. I could only see the man's jerky, angry gestures shrink in the rear view mirror.

I saw Yates just miss an oncoming van as he overtook a bus. The van driver went white, and his vehicle took out Yates's wing mirror as the BMW roared onto the correct side of the street. The van driver stopped immediately, shaking, preventing me from copying Yates's manoeuvre.

Beyond the bus, I caught sight of Yates entering a roundabout. He was driving like a demon shot straight from Hell. I knew I'd lose Yates if I didn't track his exit, so I swung the car left, and felt the traction control kick in as the Mercedes mounted the pavement. The Merc smashed through an advertising hoarding, and then tore up the metal railings that lined the approach to the roundabout as I returned to the road. The bonnet was badly damaged and the engine started smoking, but I caught sight of Yates taking the third exit onto Walworth Road towards Elephant & Castle, and decided to try to gain some ground by cutting the wrong way round.

The drivers on the roundabout were so shocked to see a car coming towards them that I didn't get a single angry blast from a horn. I narrowly avoided colliding with a small Renault, whose driver was on the phone, and mounted the roundabout, trashing the Merc's undercarriage in the process. I felt the tyres bite as they reconnected with tarmac. The

Merc swung in front of a lorry, smoking and steaming, and I followed Yates up Walworth Road.

The car wasn't going to last much longer, and I'd need help if I was going to get Yates. I pulled my phone from my pocket and dialled a number.

'Noel,' the detective answered.

'It's Schaefer. I'm following Yates. We're approaching Elephant and Castle. The Norris Estate.'

I heard him say to someone, 'It's Schaefer. He's got eyes on the target. I want another SCO19 unit en route now.'

The steering wheel started fighting me. I'd done catastrophic damage to the Merc.

'I've got to go,' I said, pulling at the wheel.

Noel managed to say, 'Stay clear of this guy, Schaefer,' before I hung up.

CHAPTER 5

I saw the BMW make a left onto one of the side streets that wound into the Norris Estate, and followed, but the Mercedes died a few yards beyond the junction, so I got out and ran. I was carrying injuries from the blast and my body lit up with pain, but there was no way I was losing Yates.

I tracked the bend in the road and found the BMW about a hundred yards further up. A crowd of teenagers surrounded it like hungry vultures. Norris was one of London's most notorious sink estates, and the high-rise blocks were feeder schools for Britain's prisons. Two young gangsters jumped inside the car and started stripping out the radio and speakers. I ignored the hostile looks I got from the rest of the gang as I passed, and kept my eyes fixed on Yates, who was about thirty yards ahead.

Further on, two hard-eyed, hooded youths sat on a low, graffiti-covered wall, and watched me approach. I pretended not to notice as they hopped off the wall and fell in behind me, but it was clear I was in hostile territory. Up ahead, Yates passed two tower blocks and entered the third. I used my mobile to send Noel a text: *Block 3.*

I opened the heavy security door with its ancient broken lock, and smashed glass panel, and stepped inside the dark hallway.

My heart skipped when Yates stepped out of the shadows and pressed a Browning pistol into my neck. He was twisted and cruel and the air of death hung upon him. His paper-white skin was slick with grease and sweat and his eyes were windows into a soul tormented by drug abuse.

'Seek and ye shall find,' Yates rasped. His breath stank of decay. 'You known to me, brother.'

I realised the hard-eyed youths were at my shoulders, penning me in.

This is bad, I thought, *I've walked straight into a trap.*

'Yeah, you are known. The Dolor Man. Is beautiful thing, the darkness he make,' Yates said.

He was high, unhinged or most likely both.

'I don't want any trouble. I'm here to see a friend,' I tried, playing up my growing sense of fear.

He didn't buy it.

'Lie!' Yates yelled. Then quietly, 'Let me be a friend, brother. Let me taste your path. We serve the same master.'

'I have no idea what you're talking about,' I replied honestly.

He eyed me as though I was prey. If I hadn't spent the past decade swimming in a sea of human filth, I might have been scared of a man talking spiritualism and magic, but as it was, all I saw was a crazed, gun-toting maniac in the grip of delusion.

'I help you see,' Yates hissed. He paused for a moment, staring directly into my eyes, goading me, and then said a single word, 'Amber.'

I went rigid at the name, but my body came alive with a storm of almost unbearable emotions. Red anger flared hot, blue sorrow tugged from the pit of despair that had almost consumed me, incandescent hatred for the man who had just said a word so sweet and yet so, so foul.

ADAM LOXWOOD

Amber.
My daughter.
My lost little girl.

CHAPTER 6

I tried not to betray my swirling emotions, but yellow fear gripped me too, and my mind filled with doubt. How did he know about Amber? What did he know about her? Why did he even know her name? Who was Yates working for? Why did I no longer feel in control?

My natural response to hearing my daughter's name would have been to beat the answers out of this foul man, but there was the practical problem of the gun at my throat.

'Ah,' Yates continued. 'Now your eyes open. Now you know we brethren.'

He thought we were alike, but I was nothing like him. My mission was just. My goal pure. I ignored the rest of the emotional spectrum and focused on my red rage and let it build. That this foul excuse of a man knew anything about my daughter. That her name had even passed his lips. That he might know something about what had happened to her.

The gun discharged as I stepped back, but I was fast and clear of the muzzle, so the bullet flew past my face and hit the ceiling as the gunshot set my ears ringing. Filled with righteous fury, I grabbed Yates's wrist, and twisted it violently. He howled and dropped the gun. Both Hard Eyes snatched at me, and I vaguely felt their attempts to hold me, but I focused on Yates, who was backing towards the stairs.

'You're going to tell me what you know,' I vowed. 'And then I'm going to kill you.'

I turned and head-butted the larger of the Hard Eyes, breaking his nose. I grabbed the smaller man and drove his head into the rutted concrete wall. Two more forceful blows, and the man was unconscious. The larger man had composed himself and pulled a knife, which he waved menacingly. He looked like an experienced blademan and probably expected me to run at the sight of the shining edge, but I had faced down far worse, and instead of backing off, I surprised the man by moving forward. He fumbled a slash, but I caught his arm, directed the momentum and forced it down towards his thigh. Hard Eye screamed as he stabbed himself in the leg, but I spared him any enduring pain by knocking him out with two potent jabs.

I picked up the Browning and ran after Yates, who was already two flights above me. I took the stairs two at a time, matching him step for step. By the fifth floor, my lungs burnt and my heart jack-hammered, but I knew pain passed. Sorrow. Regret. Failure. These were the things that stayed, and they could only be relieved by one thing, so I kept running.

As I reached the eighth floor, I looked up and saw Yates leave the stairwell on the tenth floor. The steel fire door clattered shut behind him. I raced up the final two flights and burst into a deserted corridor. As I caught my breath I sent Noel another message: *10th floor*.

I pocketed my phone and moved along the dimly lit corridor. The grimy walls and the dozen or so flaking apartment doors were all covered in graffiti. Among the conventional street tags were Latin words, pentagrams and other occult symbols that were exactly the sorts of things I'd expected of Yates. I was on alert, moving silently, tense as a catgut cello string and had made it halfway along the corridor, when I heard one of the doors open behind me. I turned to see a kid half my edge holding a sawn-off shotgun, the black barrels holding nothing but oblivion. The door opposite opened and an even younger kid stepped out. This one held an Uzi submachine gun.

'This our nest, friend.' I heard Yates's voice coming from behind me, and turned to see my target standing in the last doorway. 'Outsiders, they not welcome.'

Every single unopened door along the corridor opened at once, and Yates's young acolytes stepped out, brandishing a variety of weapons. Guns, swords, knives and axes were all on display, and even I couldn't help but feel intimidated. If this was to be my end, I'd meet it standing up, fighting for the only thing that still mattered.

'Tell me what you know about Amber.'

I aimed the Browning at Yates, and cocked it to make a point. I couldn't kill them all, but I could kill him.

Yates flashed a shark's smile. 'You won't kill me, friend. He seen to that. You blessed and cursed.'

I looked at the dead-eyed kids who surrounded me. 'You think death scares me?'

'Death ain't waiting for you, friend.' Yates smiled. 'There something much, much worse.'

I held his stare, unafraid of what was to come. My index finger pressed against the trigger. One bullet for him and it would all end for me.

'Drop your weapons! Drop your weapons!'

A chorus of deep voices boomed off the walls as a squad of heavily armed SCO19 officers rushed the corridor.

I saw all the kids look to Yates for guidance, as the machine gun-wielding police officers closed on them. Yates gave an almost imperceptible nod, and all his acolytes complied, dropping their weapons and filling the corridor as they surrendered. More and more of them appeared from inside the flats, and the corridor was soon dangerously overcrowded. He was a wily fox, using the unquestioning devotion he inspired in his followers to execute a simple escape through the fire exit at the other end of the corridor. The cops couldn't even see him through the crush of bodies, and even if they had, there was virtually no chance of pursuit.

I forced my way through the throng of acolytes, and where I met resistance, cleared it with the butt of my pistol. After the first couple of cracked heads and limp, fallen bodies, I found the going easier as the last of the crowd parted for me.

I pushed my way onto the emergency stairwell and looked up and down. There was no sign of Yates in either direction, but I could see another SCO19 squad five flights below.

'Drop your gun!' the lead officer yelled.

No chance.

I started towards the roof, because Yates would not have risked an encounter with the police by heading down.

Shots echoed around the stairwell and bullets pocked the concrete around me as I sprinted up the final two flights of stairs. I burst onto the roof, slamming the heavy door behind me. I'd expected an attack, a fight with gun or blade or hand, so I was taken aback to meet no resistance and to find Yates standing on the lip of the roof, contemplating the drop.

'Tell me what you know,' I demanded.

I hadn't met anyone who'd know anything about Amber for years. This man might be a gateway to a new line of inquiry. Hope, so long an enemy corroding my soul, rose again, but I tried to tell myself not to let it build. The darkness that followed its extinction had taken me to bleak places and I wasn't sure how much more disappointment I could bear.

Yates turned to face me slowly, a wry smile on his face. 'The truth is always hidden in plain sight, Thomas,' he said in the finest English. He reverted to his usual patois. 'That the river card. Show he face.'

My gut lurched as Yates took a small step back. 'Stop right there!'

'This your pain, friend,' he said. 'Time for a new beginning.'

As the second squad of SCO19 officers burst through the stairwell door, Leon Yates stepped off the roof and fell to his death twelve storeys below.

I ignored the warning cries from the police officers behind me and ran to the edge of the roof. Far below I could see Yates's mangled, contorted body. The world became stiflingly distant as I realised my first proper lead in years was gone. I began my descent into the pit of sorrow, and hardly felt the heavy hands on my shoulders as police officers pulled me roughly away from the edge.

CHAPTER 7

'You okay?' Noel asked, hurrying towards me.

I was leaning through the doors of one of the many ambulances that now filled the courtyard outside the tower block, and resting my backside on the lip of the vehicle. The paramedics had insisted on checking me over after the explosion, but had found nothing that a whisky and a good night's sleep wouldn't cure. They'd gone off to look for business in the scrum of cops and gangsters at the foot of the block.

Noel had the shell-shocked expression of a rookie who'd seen battle for the first time, but he was an experienced detective, and his troubled demeanour signalled what a rough night he'd had.

'I'm fine,' I replied. 'You?'

Noel rubbed his face with his palm. 'Rough. We lost two officers. Another four in hospital. He shot two of my boys at the front of the house.'

'And Jean?' I asked. Jean had looked in bad shape the last time I'd seen him.

'He's one of the four,' Noel replied. 'They say his injuries are superficial.'

'Sorry. I had no idea it would go down like this. It was supposed to be a spiritual group, not some kind of gang.'

'You weren't to know,' Noel said, but I had no idea whether he was just trying to make me feel better. 'We didn't have any intelligence on him or whatever this gang is.' He nodded at the crowd by the building.

'Yates is on the other side of the block. He jumped off the roof.'

Noel spat at the mention of the man. 'I hope he's burning.'

I looked at the scrum by the building, where thirty or so young men were being penned in and processed by a twenty-strong squad of uniformed officers. Paramedics loitered nearby, but the only one of the men who'd been injured was Yates, and he couldn't be cured. His acolytes were searched, identified and cuffed before being loaded into one of four police vans. What started as the simple snatch-and-grab of one suspect for questioning had turned into a major criminal incident.

Pope, a wiry detective I didn't know so well, approached. I got the sense Pope disapproved of me. His narrow, untrusting eyes always thinned when I was around, and I'd never seen him smile. He seemed even less enamoured with me than usual, possibly because Yates had been a lead I'd brought them. My plan had been simple; have Yates arrested and use him to find the boy I'd been hired to locate.

'Any of these yours?' Pope asked.

I studied the acolytes more closely and saw a face I recognised.

'Him,' I replied, getting to my feet. I pointed out a tall, muscular young man whose eyes were like suns burning bright with hatred. 'That's Derek Liddle.'

CHAPTER 8

The guy slumped on the bench seat stank like the bins behind an East End kebab shop. Bins that hadn't been emptied for a week. I tried to guess his age, but it was difficult. His bushy, long beard obscured half his face, and the other half was covered in thick grime. I stepped away from the drunk who was sleeping in a badly stained, thin purple raincoat, and slowly paced the lobby. Police stations were all the same. The notice board displaying public service messages, a homeless drunk sleeping one off, teenagers arrested for booze-fuelled assault, tired police officers slowly rotting from within as their daily exposure to the worst of humanity turns them into dark cynics.

Not the worst, I corrected myself. *Even the police don't see the real darkness.*

Ron and Sandra Liddle entered like cattle into a slaughterhouse. They knew bad things happened in this unfamiliar place, but weren't sure what. Ron's father had come to London from Jamaica in the sixties. Sandra's family had been here longer. I like to be thorough, and had traced her lineage back to a great-grandfather who worked in the Liverpool dockyards. Both Afro-Caribbean, both in their fifties, both slightly overweight. Law-abiding, hardworking, nothing to suggest any involvement in Derek's disappearance. They seemed smaller than the last time I'd seen them, shrinking into themselves with the shame of being in a police station. I saw dismay and bewilderment in their eyes. When they engaged me to find their son, they never expected the trail to lead to a violent cult led by a dangerously unbalanced, ruthless and, as it turned out, suicidal criminal.

'Mr and Mrs Liddle,' I said as pleasantly as I could. This didn't need to be any worse for them than it already was. 'We found Derek.'

Sandra clasped my arm and asked, 'Where is he?'

'Inside,' I said, nodding towards a door that led to the custody suite. 'We found him with a man calling himself Leon Yates. You ever hear of him?'

Sandra shook her head. 'I used to know all Derek's friends. But in the last couple of years he became a stranger.'

'I should've been stronger with the boy,' Ron started.

'I've seen kids run away from the most perfect homes,' I cut him off with the truth. There was no pattern, and parents often drove themselves to the brink of insanity, questioning history and doubting everything they'd ever done. 'Doesn't matter how strong or weak you are with them. If the need is there, someone like Yates will come along and exploit it.'

Ron and Sandra's faces registered surprise. I turned to see Pope leading Derek Liddle out of the custody suite. Derek's eyes narrowed when he caught sight of his parents. They weren't sure whether to be angry or relieved.

'What you here for!' Derek yelled. 'You nothing to me but dead.'

'Derek, please don't say that,' Sandra responded, her voice thick with hurt, her eyes shimmering with sadness.

'Don't talk to me, ghost,' her son shouted back. 'Begone!'

'Calm down, or I'll put you back inside,' Pope warned. He turned to me. 'He wasn't carrying, so we've got nothing to hold him on. He's all yours.'

Pope uncuffed Derek, who smiled slyly. 'Police always gonna lose the game,' he observed. 'We ain't got no rules.'

'Me neither,' I said as I grabbed Derek's hands and bound them together with a cable tie.

'What the fuck!' he objected.

'Mr and Mrs Liddle, are you happy for me to continue as discussed?' I asked.

Sandra looked away, and Ron glanced at his son sadly before nodding.

'Derek Liddle, you have been sectioned under the Mental Health Act. For your own safety, I am authorised to use such force as is necessary to restrain you for your own wellbeing.' I pulled him close and looked him right in the eye. 'So I'm ready anytime you want to start playing.'

CHAPTER 9

Derek treated me to brooding silence for most of the drive out of London. The trip, which usually took forty minutes, had taken almost an hour because I had to make sure I didn't lose Ron and Sandra, who followed in their own car. In light of Derek's hostility towards them, I thought it would be wise to keep them apart. I almost lost them in the one-way system around Croydon, and was forced to stay in the slow lane on the A22 down to Sussex. I turned off the A22 roundabout and headed towards Perry Wood. My trips to Milton House were troubling. The psychiatric hospital was full of too many young, broken people, and a visit usually meant I was adding another poor soul to the population. The road to Perry Wood was one of my favourites, however, and it always took my mind off my destination. The trees arched together to form an unbroken canopy above the winding country lane, and cracks of moonlight danced between the densely packed leaves.

'Seigneur said you'd come for me,' Derek said.

I looked in the rear view mirror and saw him giving me a cold stare. I stared right back.

'You suffering, bro. He say you carry your burden well, for a weak man.'

'You keep talking, and I'll show you just how weak I really am.'

Derek didn't say anything else, as I turned off the road and drove between the grand sandstone pillars that marked the start of a private driveway.

Milton House was a double-fronted four-storey Regency stately home that had been converted into a specialist psychiatric hospital with the addition of two large wings. The walls of the main house were formed of large, heavy stones that always made me think of a mausoleum, but maybe that was my own darkness tarnishing the place. It was one of the finest psychiatric institutions in the country and specialised in mending broken young minds.

I parked by the main entrance and jumped out of my eleven-year-old BMW 5-series. It was dependable, but like me it was showing the hard grind of the past ten years and was covered in scratches, dents and rust patches. But Amber had loved the car and I'd always pictured myself bringing her home in it.

When I opened the back door Derek just glared at me. I wasn't in the mood for bolshiness, so I pulled him from the car. Ron and Sandra arrived as I was leading Derek towards the building. They parked behind me, got out and followed us up the broad stone steps to the main door, which was flanked by wide columns.

Ron and Sandra's heads were bowed like supplicants about to make an offering in an ancient temple, a posture I'd seen in other parents. Many felt a profound sense of shame and failure as they climbed these stone steps. I always tried to find ways to help parents understand it wasn't their fault, and in truth, it rarely was. Few of the kids I recovered were ever driven into the hands of cultists by abuse or neglect. Most were middle-class youngsters who lost their way and went on a dangerous quest for answers.

I pressed the buzzer, and a voice crackled from the intercom by the front door, 'Yes?'

'It's Thomas Schaefer.'

I glanced up at the CCTV camera bolted to the wall so the security guard could see my face. Moments later the buzzer sounded, and I pushed the door open.

I led Derek into the cavernous marble lobby. Ken, the lone security guard, sat behind a desk and gave me a nod of recognition. The lobby of Milton House looked as though it had been decorated by IKEA. There was a lot of wood and glass and warm tones, and it was designed to make people feel this was a place for safe, modern psychiatric care. I knew the décor deteriorated the deeper one went into the building.

The inner security door buzzed open and one of the nurses approached. I'd seen her around the hospital but couldn't remember her name. She was young, maybe nineteen or twenty, and slight, with pinned-up blonde hair. She was followed by two orderlies who looked like a couple of rugby full-backs.

'My name's Charlie Simmons,' the nurse said. 'You must be Mr Schaefer.'

'Derek Liddle, on a twenty-eight-day assessment,' I replied, pushing him forward.

'We've been expecting you, Mr Liddle,' Charlie said, as the two orderlies took him into their custody.

'Let me go,' Derek protested.

'Derek, these people want to help you,' Ron said.

Charlie turned her attention to Ron and Sandra. 'Mr and Mrs Liddle, if you'll follow me, we'll complete the admissions paperwork.'

As the orderlies led Derek away, Ron clasped my hand and shook it gratefully. 'Thank you, Mr Schaefer. You don't know what it means to have our son back.'

I wasn't sure they had their son back. At least not yet.

Across the lobby, Derek struggled against the orderlies' restraining hands. 'It's not me who needs help, old man! It's all you shadows. You and the old bitch will die in pain!' He yelled wildly, spraying the floor with spittle. 'When the darkness comes, who will feel your pain?'

The orderlies redoubled their efforts to pull Derek through the security door, but he pushed forward for one final pronouncement.

'And you, old Mr,' he shouted, directing his anger towards me, 'Seigneur told me you on a dark path. Papa Boya got you. You worse than dead! You feel that cold hand of time running…'

Derek's rant was cut short when the security door slammed shut, but I could see him shouting and straining against the orderlies as they dragged him down the corridor.

Tears filled Sandra Liddle's eyes. I felt sorry for her, but I knew there were worse things than seeing your child raving. At least the Liddles had a chance of getting their child back.

I turned over Derek's words. Seigneur was probably Leon Yates, but who was Papa Boya, and why were they talking about me? Was he just trying to get inside my head? I couldn't shake the feeling there was more to it. How had Yates known about Amber?

Charlie placed a reassuring hand on Sandra's shoulder.

'We'll look after him,' she said softly. 'If you'd like to follow me, we'll get the paperwork done.'

Ron comforted his distraught wife, as Charlie led them into the administrative offices that flanked the lobby. I watched them go, feeling none of the satisfaction I should have felt at the end of an investigation, because I knew it wasn't the end. I'd found their boy, but others now had to try to undo the psychological damage and repair their relationship with him. And besides, too much had gone wrong: the deaths of at least two police officers and the suicide of a man who had known something about Amber. There was no success to celebrate this night.

I walked over to the reception desk.

'Is Dr Gilmore here?' I asked Ken.

'Yes. He's taking the women's group.'

The women's group, I thought. The bland name failed to convey the misery. Gilmore would be in Hell.

'Can you buzz me through?' I asked.

'Sure.'

He pressed one of the buttons on a panel on the desk, and a side door that led to the upper floors clicked open.

'You have a good night,' Ken called out, as I walked away.

It couldn't get any worse.

CHAPTER 10

The women's group was held three times a week in a recreation room on the second floor. There were no touches of IKEA here. The 1980s institutional décor had been given a fresh coat of paint recently, but other than that it was as soulless and uninspiring as when it had been fitted. Heavy wooden doors with wire mesh picture windows to ensure no one would get hurt if the glass was shattered, bars on the windows (horizontal rather than vertical to make them seem like safety rather than security measures), and black linoleum floor that sent the sound of squeaking shoes echoing along the corridors.

I stood outside the rec room, peering through a panel of reinforced windows. The steel mesh crisscrossed the women's faces and bodies, parcelling them into manageable cubes. Perhaps that's what they needed, something to cut up their problems and make them digestible. Was that what Gilmore was doing? I could see him now, talking softly, as though speaking a lullaby to the women. There were six of them. The longest residents of Milton House, each with more than three years served, the saddest collection of souls in the building. They sat on plastic chairs arranged in a circle, under the watchful gaze of Russell, one of the orderlies.

Farah, in her late twenties, voluptuous and bawdy like a lustful Earth mother, always trying to touch Gilmore. Jane, still and silent, prim and proper like a new book on a library shelf that had never been opened, never wanted. She looked as though she'd lived three hard decades without joy. Anna with her striking red hair and brown eyes, perhaps eighteen or nineteen, bag o' bones-thin, with shadows like bruises under her haunted eyes. She never spoke, and always just looked at me pleadingly as though I of all people could rescue her. Haley, another teenager, tattooed and muscular, insolent as though she knew better than Gilmore and was just going through the motions. Hodda, in her mid-twenties, wearing the same lost expression as Anna, would often be found crying. And finally, Jenny, early forties, dirty tangled hair and shoulders hunched as though she was carrying the weight of the world. She was the most unnerving of the group because she'd lost an eye and made no effort to cover up the scarred remains that marred the left side of an otherwise beautiful face. I'd once asked Gilmore about it, but even he didn't know when the terrible injury had occurred.

Years in the shadows had honed my ability to judge a person's true intentions, but I always struggled around Dr Alvin Gilmore. The gaunt, seventy-four-year-old psychiatrist who ran Milton House never betrayed anything other than empathy and warmth. I hadn't met anyone else who was as consistently happy and well-balanced as the genial man that sat in the rec room. Perhaps it was good manners, the result of breeding, education, and a way of life that died with the birth of the attention deficit, narcissistic new century. Or maybe Gilmore, one of the country's most accomplished psychiatrists, was simply untroubled by the fears and doubts that blighted the hearts of the people he treated. He caught sight of me now and nodded and smiled.

I shuffled around the empty corridor for a few minutes, watching Gilmore trade wisdom for misery, and when the women's group had made whatever progress they were supposed to have made, he ended the session and got to his feet. The women were aimless, until Russell stepped forward and gave them directions.

Gilmore emerged from the room looking a little drained, but he pinned a smile to his face the moment he saw me and made me feel my presence was welcome, even though it was the very end of what I'm sure had been a tiring day.

'Thomas,' he said enthusiastically. 'Why don't you come up for a drink?'

'That would be very kind, Dr Gilmore,' I replied.

'Thomas.' Gilmore's eyes twinkled as he smiled. 'How many times do I have to ask you to call me Alvin?'

'At least one more.'

He scoffed.

'Anna!' Russell shouted, and I turned to see the damaged teenager coming straight for me.

Her eyes were blazing with hatred, and she was trying to talk, but made incomprehensible grunts and growls. I felt nothing but pity, but Russell was too big and slow for the wispy girl, and I got ready to restrain her myself.

Gilmore stepped between us and raised his hand.

'Stop, Anna,' he said quietly. 'This isn't how we behave.'

She froze and bowed her head like a pack animal that had been shamed by an alpha. Gilmore closed on her and took her hands gently.

'You must learn to let go of your fears,' he said. 'If you hold on to the past you will never be free.'

Anna eyeballed him and for a moment I saw rebellion, but it faded quickly. She didn't nod or do anything much, but she didn't resist when Russell took her arm.

'Russell will see you all back to your rooms,' Gilmore told them. 'I'm sorry, Thomas,' he said, turning to me. 'I'm not quite sure what happened there.'

'She was horny,' Haley said, and she and Farah giggled as the women were led away.

Their laughter echoed along the corridor, but it wasn't contagious and the others followed Russell in silence. It was an unsettling scene, but such episodes had become part of my life and I was perhaps a little too numb to them.

'Come on,' Gilmore said. 'Let me get you that drink.'

CHAPTER 11

Gilmore lived in lodgings on the fourth floor of Milton House. He was devoted to his work, and his presence meant he was available at all times for any emergencies. He unlocked the double doors at the top of the main staircase and led me inside his grand, spacious apartment. We walked along the high-ceilinged hall, which was filled with vibrant pot plants and priceless antiques. Fine oil paintings, mostly baroque nudes, lined the walls. The masterful use of light and shadow in the oils gave the hall a depth that imbued the apartment with an even greater sense of grandeur.

Gilmore was an old traditionalist in every sense, but there was something about him that was also very youthful. Maybe it was the way he moved. He carried his lithe frame with no hint of burden. It certainly wasn't his appearance. Gilmore's close-cropped grey hair hadn't changed in the eleven years we'd known each other, and I was willing to bet that, like most men who reach a certain age, it hadn't changed in the eleven years before that. The doctor favoured tailored suits and tweeds, and considered a cravat casual. He was sporting one now. The overall effect was of a man out of time, a throwback to the 1930s. I liked it, but could never have carried it off. A leather jacket, T-shirt, jeans and boots were my business casual. And my formal, come to think of it.

I followed Gilmore into his study. Inexplicably, the room always made me think of mulled wine and Christmas, and I always felt as though there was a roaring fire, even when, like tonight, the forty-inch stone fireplace was empty.

The red shade on the brass banker's lamp on Gilmore's large, oak partners' desk gave the room a crimson tint, which made it feel even warmer and more welcoming. Purpose-built shelves lined three walls from floor to ceiling, and each carried unimaginable riches in parchment and paper: Gilmore had one of the finest collections of rare books in the country. His appreciation of history, ancient art and long-forgotten cultures was unrivalled.

Gilmore went to a small cabinet and poured two drinks.

'Single malt okay?' he asked.

'Yes, thanks.'

'Water?'

'Ice, if you've got any,' I replied.

'There are those who believe a good malt can be destroyed by rocks,' Gilmore said as he took an ice tray from a small freezer compartment in a drinks fridge built into the cabinet. 'But the head of Glengyle Distillery once told me that's complete poppycock. It's your dram, he said, you put what you damned well like in it.'

Gilmore popped a couple of cubes into the glass, and handed me the crystal tumbler.

'Your health,' he proposed.

I raised his glass in salute, and took a sip. It was a fine whisky.

'So, Thomas, what can I do for you?' he asked.

'I found Derek Liddle,' I replied.

'Excellent. His parents will be relieved.' Gilmore sat in one of two leather wingbacks, and gestured for me to take the other.

I sat down, and swirled the ice cubes around my glass.

'What's on your mind, Thomas?'

'Does the name Leon Yates mean anything to you?'

Gilmore shook his head.

'He ran the Area Boys,' I said. 'It's a street gang that seems to use cult techniques to indoctrinate members. The mysticism helps ensure their loyalty. That's where I found Liddle.'

I paused for a moment, trying to recall exactly what Yates had said.

'I had a chance to talk to Leon Yates before he threw himself off a tower block. He mentioned a name.'

I worried the tumbler, pressing my fingers into the crystal ridges. I didn't want to say the name. I didn't want to admit my first lead in years had died a few hours ago.

'What did he say?' Gilmore pressed.

'Amber.'

Gilmore sighed and studied me with a look of pity I'd seen him use on his patients. He was probably trying to gauge exactly just how unbalanced his most reliable investigator was.

'I see,' he said. 'And after all these years rescuing unfortunates from charismatic cult leaders, you have finally chanced upon something that you cannot explain.'

I knew what Gilmore thought about the supernatural: mysticism was the preserve of the ignorant. As far as he was concerned, there was nothing in mind or body that could not be explained by science and logic; the spiritual world did not exist. I wilted slightly under his withering gaze.

'What did he say exactly?' he probed.

'He said that I was the Dollar Man, and that someone had done something beautiful. He said that we served the same master,' I replied. 'And he said the name Amber.'

'The Dollar Man?' he asked. 'How odd. And there's no chance you misheard "Amber?"'

I shook my head.

'And this was just before he threw himself off the building?'

I caught more than a hint of scepticism in Gilmore's voice.

'These Area Boys, they sell drugs?'

I could already see where Gilmore was going: Yates was a deranged, drugged-up lunatic who stumbled upon something that mattered to me.

'I don't think Yates was high,' I replied.

'But you can't be sure,' he countered. 'There is a chance that this man was not only deranged, but intoxicated.'

'How would he know her name?' I asked. I was a little irritated by his reticence.

'You have a reputation, Thomas,' Gilmore replied, diplomatically. 'Know thy enemy, isn't that what they say? It is possible he read about your case.'

'Maybe,' I conceded, but there had been something in Yates's eyes that suggested more than just a passing knowledge of my situation.

'There's someone I'd like you meet, Thomas,' Gilmore said. 'A mother. Her daughter went missing a week ago.'

He paused. I knew I wouldn't like what came next.

'She's ten,' he continued.

'No kids,' I countered immediately.

'You should—'

'No kids. You know that. No one under sixteen.'

'You should meet her,' Gilmore persisted. 'She gave me a copy of a symbol she found in her daughter's room.'

He produced a small piece of card from his breast pocket and handed it to me. The white card was marked with a mandala, a spiritual symbol common in parts of Asia. Usually mandalas were formed of geometric shapes within a circle. This particular mandala contained three overlapping triangles, their points touching the edge of the circumference. I felt a little sick; I had seen this design before. I looked at Gilmore in disbelief.

'This was in her daughter's room?' I asked.

'On her bed.' Gilmore nodded gravely. 'Now you understand why I feel you must see her.'

I studied the mandala that had come to symbolise all the evil and darkness in my life. This same symbol had been left in Amber's room the night she'd been taken.

'Her number is on the back,' Gilmore said.

I turned the card over and saw a telephone number and a name: Penny Blake.

CHAPTER 12

Noel looked around nervously as he ferreted in his pocket for a pack of cigarettes. One of the last few warriors braving lung cancer for that nicotine high.

'The nobs won't be happy if they find out I'm talking to you,' he said.

There wasn't much I could say to that. I wasn't going to crawl under a rock, however badly things had gone last night, and I knew no matter how much Noel might complain, he needed me. I wasn't bound by rules or procedures, and every now and again he and Jean found it useful to ask me to follow up a lead or interrogate a suspect. I went to places they couldn't, and I was quite happy to do their dirty work as long as they threw a few favours my way.

We moved away from Kennington Police Station, a modern, brown brick building that rose like a rotten tooth into London's lunchtime sky. Noel shrank into his coat as he lit a cigarette. There wasn't much wind. Had last night made me toxic? Was he trying to avoid being seen with me? Kennington Road was busy with people and traffic, but I didn't recognise any of the faces.

'Two officers dead, another four injured; this is an official clusterfuck,' Noel said, drawing on his cigarette. 'They want heads, and I've got to put yours on a plate, Schaefer. Until you came along, Intelligence hadn't even heard of the Area Boys.'

I wondered whether I'd misjudged the man; perhaps they didn't need me after all. Or maybe the blowback from the botched operation was just too intense.

'Stack the paperwork however you like, Noel,' I replied. 'I don't care. I'm not police. The only way they can punish me is with prison, and I haven't done anything illegal. Not on this one.'

'I don't want to know,' Noel remarked. 'I'm sorry, but they want details of who gave us the intel and why we launched the operation.'

'I understand.' But I didn't really. I did what was right, no matter the cost. These people did what they needed to do to protect their jobs.

Noel relaxed slightly. He had obviously been concerned about how I would handle the news I was to be the fall guy. I couldn't care less about the police. They were useful but not essential, and as long as they stayed out my way, there wouldn't be a problem.

'Did you find anything?' I asked.

'It was like Aladdin's cave at the flats. Guns, money, drugs, stolen goods. But since the principal is dead, we're just reeling in minnows,' Noel said with more than a hint of accusation. 'You got your man though.'

I ignored the pointed dig. 'What about the house?'

'Nothing.'

'Nothing? Why the landmine?'

'Maybe it was an alarm to warn him when someone was coming,' Noel suggested. 'Or a deterrent.'

I wasn't so sure.

'And when I say nothing,' Noel continued, 'I mean nothing. The place is stripped bare. A couple of the minnows say it was a shrine for devotions. Personally I reckon it's where Yates used to do his banging. These cult guys have always got hard-ons, and he'd want to keep any tarts clear of the young bucks at the flats.'

Noel's half-baked theory made me realise just how much I'd learnt about the dark world of cults. If Yates had left one of his 'tarts' naked in the corridor and gone on a round-the-world cruise, she would have been untouched upon his return. Such was the power of these cult leaders. People like Noel, who had never experienced the devastating hold of these charismatic men and women, failed to see that mundane values didn't apply. The way cults operated was so far removed from normality that I didn't even bother responding to Noel. I didn't have time to school him.

'You get anything on him?' I asked.

Noel shook his head.

'Looks like his real name wasn't Leon Yates. He had an *Érinn go Brách* tattoo. Ireland till doomsday. We'll get Dublin to check prints and dental records.'

'Do you know how long he's been in the country?' I asked.

'No idea. Not until we find out who he really is.'

'Thanks,' I said. 'How's Jean?'

'OK,' Noel replied. 'Few cuts and bruises, but he's getting discharged this afternoon. I'm going to pick him up.'

'You're a sweetheart,' I teased him.

'It's what good partners do,' he replied. 'But you wouldn't know about playing nicely with others.'

I didn't smile and he shifted uncomfortably when he realised his attempt at a joke had fallen flat.

'Make sure you stick around,' he said. 'We're going to want an official statement.'

I nodded. 'I'll be here.'

As I walked away, Noel called after me, 'And, Schaefer, do me a favour. Don't bring us any more cases for a while.'

CHAPTER 13

I'd spent the past couple of hours parked on Chapel Street, watching Yates's house from my car. The last members of the forensics team and their uniformed escort had left half an hour ago, but I sat in the car and waited just to make sure there weren't any foot patrols. Over the years I'd learnt the value of patience, and wanted to be sure Noel or his superiors hadn't posted a roving guard. Thirty minutes later, I was certain there were no uniforms in the area. The house was empty and no one was coming back.

I guess there's one reason to be thankful for the cuts, I thought to myself as I stepped out of the car.

The alley was cordoned off at the street, and there were signs advising members of the public they would be prosecuted if they breached the cordon. I slipped under a length of police tape and retraced my steps of the previous night.

I emerged from the darkest section of the alley, and immediately saw the imprint of the previous day's carnage: scorch marks on the walls, a small crater etched into the ground at the epicentre of the blast, and dark patches on the concrete paving where someone had pressure-washed the bloodstains. Two men had died in that small backyard, and I refused to believe that it was because Yates did not want them to catch him in his love nest. There had to be something more important inside. Noel had said the police had found nothing, but Yates wouldn't booby-trap this place for no reason.

I walked through the ragged blast hole in the garden wall and climbed the small steps to the back door. I used a pocket knife to slice through the police tape and pulled out a small case that contained my lock-picking tools. In addition to the locks built into the door, the police had affixed a heavy-duty padlock. It took me less than two minutes to crack them all.

The late afternoon sunlight shone through the open door, illuminating the remains of a kitchen. There were no curtains or blinds; the windows had been painted black. I flipped a light switch next to the door, but nothing happened. The fitting was missing a bulb. I stepped inside, shut the door and pulled a small torch from my pocket. A narrow beam of light cut into the darkness. I shone the torch around the room and realised that the entire place had been painted black: the windows, the walls, the floorboards. The room had been stripped; crooked gas and water pipes jutted into the room, and electrical wiring hung loose from painted plaster.

I moved through the kitchen and went into the hallway and found it in a similar state. The floorboards, walls and narrow windows had been covered in thick black paint, and there was no bulb in the light fitting. I walked carefully and slowly, trying to fight the growing feeling I was somewhere very dangerous. The thin blade of light from my torch lit up a doorway and I peered into what must have once been a living room, and saw the same black walls, windows and floor. This was no love nest; Yates was using this place for something.

I climbed the stairs, the beam of the torch leading my eyes as they searched for something – anything – the police had missed. Forensics might not have found anything, but they weren't as desperate as me. And yet, as I moved through the house, I found nothing. I couldn't even begin to think what the forensics team might have missed.

I paused halfway up the staircase and reflected on the last ten years of failure. I'd let my daughter down in the most profound way possible, and my catalogue of errors grew thicker with each year that passed. Allowing Yates to die was the latest in a long list of failings. I should have stopped him, taken him into custody. I had to correct that mistake. I needed to find out how he knew about Amber. I told myself what I always said when I felt I couldn't go on: *Amber is counting on you.*

I climbed the rest of the stairs, crossed the landing and peered into the smallest of the upstairs rooms, which was a complete blackout like the ones downstairs. I checked the other three upstairs rooms, which were all the same, apart from the largest, which must have once been a bedroom. Illuminated by the torch, there, in the centre of the white room, was a small, white single mattress.

Maybe I'd been wrong and Noel had been right. Maybe this was Yates's bolt-hole. A place for entertaining. I took a closer look at the mattress. It was pristine – no stains, no wear. It looked like it had never even been slept on. There was a line in the dust surrounding it, probably where forensics had checked it over. I lifted the mattress and looked at the black floorboards underneath. Was there something there? Or was it a trick of the light?

I pushed the mattress out of the way and edged about a yard over. I shone my torch at one of the floorboards and noticed a tiny imperfection: a small, maybe two- or three-millimetre section of bare floorboard where the paint had been chipped. I pulled out my pocket knife and wedged it into the crack in the floorboards next to the chip. With a gentle push, the floorboard gave way, and I pulled it up to find a small cubbyhole underneath. Inside the hole was a shoe box. I checked the box for wires and pressure sensors; anything that might trigger a booby trap. I didn't find anything, and said a silent prayer to my maker, before removing the lid. Inside the box were six light bulbs. I picked one up and turned my attention to the empty light fitting in the centre of the room.

CHAPTER 14

The truth is always hidden in plain sight, I thought as I slipped the bulb into its fitting.

That's what Yates had said before he had thrown himself off the roof. I crossed the room and flipped the switch. The dark bulb bathed the room in ultraviolet light, illuminating occult symbols that covered every inch of every surface.

Light-sensitive ink.

I recognised some of the signs, but most were unfamiliar and I was unnerved to see so many I didn't recognise. I'd been investigating cults for ten years, and had a reputation as an expert, but standing in this room made me feel like a novice. The symbols I could decipher were all incantations that summoned great evil. Whatever Yates did here was in the service of a profound darkness. I was sickened by the thought this man even knew my daughter's name.

I collected the remaining light bulbs and put them in the empty light fittings as I retraced my steps through the house. The results were the same: every single room was covered in occult markings. The painted black floors, the blocked windows, the ceilings – everywhere glowed purple as the light-sensitive ink revealed Yates's secret. I used my phone to take photos and videos as I went, recording the evil Yates had been so careful to hide.

The truth is always hidden in plain sight.

Why had he said that? Had he hoped I would find this?

There was one bulb left. I slotted it into the fitting in the kitchen and switched on the light. Life had taught me to be prepared for anything, but even after all the years I'd spent learning that particularly hard lesson, I couldn't help but feel shaken by what I saw. Dominating the back wall was the mandala featured on the card that Gilmore had given me: three overlapping triangles, their points touching the edge of the circle that enclosed them.

The same symbol I'd found in Amber's room the day after she had been abducted.

Questions tore through my mind with such speed and ferocity I couldn't settle on any of them. I felt lightheaded and nauseous, and staggered into the afternoon sunlight, glad to leave the dark house behind.

There was a direct link between Yates and Amber's disappearance. A few minutes alone with Yates in a police interview room and I would have persuaded the man to spill his secrets. I was a fool and a failure and cursed myself for letting Yates die.

I looked up at the blue sky and thought about Amber. My giggling, bubbly beautiful girl. My legs went weak and I wanted to cry, but I suddenly realised I was feeling the familiar pang of self-pity. Feeling sorry for myself would do my girl no good, so I smothered my despair with the resolute anger that had burnt within me since Amber had been taken. I wasn't the victim. She was, and my weakness helped nobody, least of all her. I needed to continue doing what I did best: *follow the trail, find the victim.*

I pulled out my phone, dialled and got Noel's voicemail.

'Noel, it's Schaefer. Send your photographer back to Yates's house. The décor will prove you're dealing with more than an average street gang.'

I hung up and walked out of the scorched yard.

CHAPTER 15

The tenth-floor corridor was eerily quiet. I ducked under the police tape and stepped out of the emergency stairwell. I tried to imagine what it was like to be a resident in one of these buildings when a cancer like Yates moved in. How did he get control of an entire floor? Intimidation? Violence? These were local authority flats, and the people who lived in them would not have many choices. Some were hardworking people striving for a better life, others were pensioners who wanted nothing more than to see out their days in peace. And then there were the ordinary villains who would suddenly come to understand the true extremes of crime when they came up against Yates. Did they leave without a fight? I wondered about the other inhabitants of the building, and what steps Yates took to keep them in line.

I moved along the corridor, studying the intricate graffiti that covered the walls under the flickering strip lighting. Graffiti was the wrong word – these were painted occult symbols masquerading as street art. The patterns were more accessible than the ones in the house and I recognised most of the symbols: invocations of protection, commonly seen in and around dark temples. Did the acolytes, the young kids like Derek Liddle, who Yates had brainwashed into his gang, realise what these things were?

There were a handful of glyphs that were new to me. I followed them along the wall, taking photos of the strange letters – Aramaic? Sumerian? They led me down the corridor, and when I reached the fire door at the other end, I noticed an image, which I had sprinted past during my pursuit of Yates the previous night. It was etched into the plasterwork, the neat scoring creating a white stencil against the local authority grey wall. I moved closer and studied the glyph. It was a delicate representation of a man chasing a young girl in a cloak. The girl in the cloak was running, just out of reach of the man who had his arm outstretched in an attempt to get hold of her. An acidic knot tightened around my gut as I looked at the symbols beside the two figures: three bevelled stars; the insignia of a British Army captain; a crook, the symbol for a shepherd; and the Ouroboros, the mystical snake swallowing its own tail. Schaefer was originally a German surname and was derived from the word for shepherd. I suddenly felt weak; I had little doubt the man in the image was meant to be me, the girl, Amber. What was this doing here? What did Yates know about my little girl?

'*Infusco revolvo.*'

The words were like a whispered breeze.

I looked round and saw a man in a dark suit at the other end of the corridor.

'What did you say?' I demanded, closing on the man.

'I said you shouldn't be here,' the stranger responded.

'Who are you?' I demanded. 'What is this place?'

He seemed puzzled by the questions, but I was in no mood to play games. I grabbed the man by the collar and forced him against the wall.

'What is this place?' I growled.

'I don't know. Please don't hurt me,' he pleaded, reaching for his wallet. 'I'm with the council. I'm just here to survey the damage.'

I studied the man's identification – Neil Molloy, a local civil servant with the Housing Department – and deflated, like a sail suddenly robbed of wind. I let go of my shaken victim, and the adrenaline that had surged at the prospect of imminent violence dissipated. I studied the man closely, and saw the fear of an innocent in his eyes. But if he hadn't spoken the words, where had they come from?

Neil Molloy backed away and I saw the familiar efforts of a terrified man trying not to draw attention to himself – he was even trying not to breathe. I'd had that effect on people before. Civilians who'd been caught up in my world by mistake. It reminded me how abnormal my life had become.

'Sorry, I thought you were involved with this lot,' I said, offering a lame explanation for the assault.

I'm not sure my words made him feel any better, but he did visibly relax when I backed away and turned for the exit.

CHAPTER 16

As I drove across London, I tried to make a connection between Amber and Yates. Over the years, I'd pulled on thousands of threads, each followed to the ragged end, no matter how worn and tenuous. In my desperation I had followed absolutely every lead to the bitter end.

A child matching Amber's description seen in a Coventry chip shop.

An ethereal spectre seen in a psychic's dream, wafting over Exmoor.

A gangster selling young girls on the back streets of Bristol.

Just some of the trails I'd followed. They all led nowhere, but sometimes they gave me the opportunity to vent my frustration. After I'd been to see him, the gangster had never sold anything ever again. I'd put him in a wheelchair with a warning I'd be back to finish the job if he ever stepped out of line.

There was a time, around three years after the abduction, that I'd broken down entirely and, in a tornado of madness, I'd fabricated clues, created leads and spun threads that simply didn't exist. I'd tortured dozens of vile men with convictions for child abduction or abuse in the futile hope that my delusions might prove to be true. They had been guilty of something, but all were innocent of anything to do with Amber. In all the years I'd been searching for her, there had been nothing that linked her abduction to Yates, not even by the most remote degrees of separation.

I parked my beat-up BMW at a meter on Savile Row between Bentleys and Ferraris, and walked through Mayfair past the Royal Academy to the Burlington Arcade. The arcade's twinkling lights, sparking glass and polished floor always made me uneasy. This was a world I was no longer a part of. The smart young couple browsing in the windows of the bespoke jewellers. The fur-clad old lady enjoying a late stroll with her pocket-sized pedigree. The moneyed executive buying a designer pashmina for his expectant lover. Happy people living bright, promising lives that were now as alien to me as my violent, desolate, bleak existence would be to them. Truth be told, I'd never been part of this world; my life circumstances were too humble, but there was a time when I might have aspired to it.

Mathers Antiquarian Books. Embossed gold letters against gloss black paint. The sign ran above the hardwood framed window. Unlike most of the shops in the arcade, Mathers did not have a display. A red curtain hid the interior from passing eyes. A red blind delivered the same privacy at the door.

I heard the familiar ring of the old-fashioned bell as I entered. A grey-skinned customer with a pockmarked face looked up from the book he was studying. His face betrayed no emotion as he watched me shut the door, and he returned to his old book. Mathers attracted the eccentric and strange. I still wasn't sure which category I fit into.

Kelvin, the manager, always made me think of a museum curator; sombre, with more respect for the books than the people who bought them. He stood behind a counter near the window. He nodded a quiet greeting and I raised my chin in response, and pressed through the shop. The packed, floor-to-ceiling bookcases were spaced no more than eighteen inches apart, creating narrow aisles that could only accommodate one person. Every time I walked down one of these aisles, I felt oppressed by the towering proximity of all these books. They loomed over me like so many reminders of my ignorance. After twenty feet, I emerged from the aisle into a narrow passageway that ran behind the bookcases. I opened a door that was covered in embossed red leather and stepped into Mathers' private rooms.

I'd first come to see Mathers just after Amber's abduction. Ravi Gopal, a Cambridge University history professor, had recommended the strange, slight man as one of the country's foremost experts in the occult. Mathers traded the rarest of all books and had an unrivalled knowledge of the dark arts. I'd always been able to rely on him to find answers to even the most arcane questions. Ellen Ovitz, my counsellor, did not like Mathers. She said seeing him would keep me trapped in the past and prevent me from healing. She'd been quite insistent I didn't see him, so I kept my visits secret from her and everyone else for that matter.

He was well-known in certain circles and always had people waiting to see him. I looked around the waiting room and saw a scene similar to all my previous visits. Six chairs lined the undecorated walls on either side of the room, and in each chair sat peculiar men and women. I rarely used the word peculiar, but in these circumstances, nothing else would do. It covered strange and eccentric, and without me knowing them better I couldn't categorise them properly.

The woman with alabaster skin was a perfect example. Her haunted, pale face was broken by a tiny nose, blood-red lips and red-rimmed eyes that contained the most striking jewel green irises. She looked at me when I entered, and then immediately looked away, as though my gaze might break her. She seemed to be muttering something under her breath, but was trying not to be seen moving her lips. Was she a psychology student? Psychologists were all strange. Or maybe she was a patient?

The other eleven men and women in the room were built along similar lines; people who might merit a brief second glance if you passed them in the street, but who, when collected together, looked like they belonged in another world. The old man with a shaved head and eyes that were that little bit too intense. The melancholic albino youth with wavy white hair, whose eyes flitted around nervously. The middle-aged blind woman in the garish flowery dress. But I was in no position to judge. What must I look like to them? The occult does not attract the happy people one might encounter at a cocktail party.

'Good evening, Mr Schaefer,' Margot said with a smile. Mathers' clerk sat behind a small desk set against the far wall. Her striking blonde hair fell straight about her angular face.

'Looks like a busy night,' I observed.

'He always has time for you. Let me just tell him you're here.'

Margot entered Mathers' office. Her tight pencil skirt, stockings and high heels were like something out of an old movie. She moved with a graceful confidence that seemed out of place in this room full of freaks. I caught sight of

Mathers as Margot stepped into the room. The small, frail man sat at his enormous partners' desk, and was almost obscured by the piles of books that covered the area that would have been his partner's, had he had one. Margot emerged a moment later and beckoned.

'Mr Mathers will see you now, Mr Schaefer.'

CHAPTER 17

Margot pulled the door shut behind her, and left me alone with one of the world's foremost experts in the occult. Mathers finally looked up from his book. His eyes were so piercing they gave the impression they could penetrate flesh and read the soul. He never made any apology for his intensity. Mathers' life was not a light-hearted journey; it was an unrelenting quest to understand evil and how it might be beaten. He studied me for a moment, and then leant back in his leather-lined captain's chair.

'Thomas, it's been too long,' he began. 'How are you?'

I suspected he had already reached his own conclusion, but answered nonetheless, 'Keeping busy.'

'What can I do for you?'

'I found some glyphs I don't recognise,' I said, taking out my camera. I walked around the desk to share the images. The first picture was of the three-triangle mandala in the derelict kitchen in Yates's house on Chapel Street. Mathers studied the image with a look of recognition.

'Yes, yes. We have talked about this one before. It is a ceremonial mandala used in many occult rituals,' Mathers said. 'Where was this picture taken? Is that paint?'

'It's light-sensitive. These markings are concealed in normal light; they only show under ultraviolet,' I replied. 'They were in an abandoned house that was being used by the leader of the Area Boys. Have you heard of them?'

Mathers shook his head. 'Should I have?'

'It was a criminal gang run by a man called Leon Yates. He used cult techniques to indoctrinate members. It would seem from these he was dabbling in the occult.'

'More than dabbling, I'd say.' Mathers watched as I flicked through the photographs. 'This here,' he said, pointing to a section of symbols in a photo of the living room. 'This is a Sumerian Snare. It's an ancient spell of binding, designed to trap and contain a human spirit.'

'Trap and contain a human spirit?' I asked. 'Trap it in what?'

Mathers took a long, hard look at me, and managed to make me feel ashamed of my scepticism.

'When are you going to open your mind to the possibilities, Thomas?' he asked irritably. 'In all the years you have been coming to me, you still refuse to accept that there is more to life than what you can see.'

'I've been around enough cults to know that's exactly how they get you. Once you admit there's more to life, you admit that someone else might know more than you – a priest, a guru, a swami – and before you know it, they're telling you how to live. The world is what I can see and feel,' I said, patting his desk to emphasise the point. 'Anything else is just a fairy-tale.'

'Then why do you come to me?' he asked. 'I'll never be able to give you answers that are grounded in your real world.' He indicated my camera. 'This is the world of shadows. You will only ever truly understand what is happening if you accept there are things beyond rational explanation.'

'Do you know what *infusco revolvo* means?' I asked, attempting to move him along. He had spent years trying to expand my mind, and would likely never give up.

Mathers threw up his hands and sat back in his chair.

'And still you persist in asking me questions?'

'I don't have to share your beliefs, Alistair,' I countered. 'I just need your insight.'

Mathers sighed and smiled sadly. 'It's Latin. It means darkness reborn. Where did you see it?'

'It doesn't matter.'

'You didn't see it, did you?' he surmised correctly. 'You must accept that there is more to this world, Thomas. It is very important.'

'And these,' I continued, ignoring his remarks. 'I found them in a tower block used by Yates.'

I showed him pictures of the etching of the man reaching for the young girl in a cloak.

'It's you,' Mathers said without hesitation. 'The three stars are the insignia for a British Army captain; your rank when you were discharged if I'm not mistaken. The crook is the symbol of a shepherd; the German for shepherd is schäfer. And the ouroboros, the snake that eats itself, is one of many occult symbols for eternity. I can only assume that the girl is...' He left the words hanging.

'Yeah.' There was a sudden tension in my voice. 'Amber. What does it mean? Am I going to be chasing her forever?'

'I'm not a fortune teller,' he replied. 'I can only try to tell you what whoever scored this into the wall was trying to achieve, not whether they will succeed.'

'Well?'

'I'm not sure. I've never seen this combination of markings before. I'll need to look into it.'

'I'd appreciate it,' I said, turning for the door.

'Where is this Yates? Can I talk to him?' he asked.

'He's dead. Threw himself off a roof. He told me the truth is always hidden in plain sight before he made the jump,' I replied.

Mathers considered my answer for a moment. 'Did he say anything else?'

'He mentioned Amber, and he called me the Dollar Man.'

Mathers' eyes narrowed. 'Did he say Dollar Man? Or Dolor Man?'

The distinction hadn't occurred to me. 'Dolor Man,' I replied, kicking myself at not having registered the significance.

'Dolor is Latin. It means pained. The pained man,' Mathers said. 'It may have some significance.'

I was the pained man. Well Yates hadn't been far wrong.

'Thanks for your help, Alistair,' I said, reaching for the door.

'You're welcome. And, Thomas, do look after yourself,' he counselled. 'Whatever they mean, these markings are clearly intended to bring darkness.'

'I'm used to it,' I said flatly.

CHAPTER 18

The gentrification of London was a crime. The streets used to be littered and lined with dirty old buildings, but there were communities, and with each loft conversion and artisan restoration, each new roof and basement extension, the homes that had once been within reach of ordinary people became the preserve of the wealthy. The communities that had once inhabited Bethnal Green, Hackney and Mile End had been forced further east, replaced by those who were richer.

The Royal Inn on the Park was a popular pub on the perimeter of Victoria Park. The bar was clean, spacious and full of happy people enjoying their bright lives. Grimy, smoky boozers were a thing of the past, and gone were the days of walking into a pub to be greeted by a handful of wasted locals hacking up their Benson & Hedges tar, while trading stories about how well they knew the Krays.

The Royal Inn was a little too 'New London' sparkly for me, and I would normally have given the place a wide berth, but five years ago I rescued the absentee owner's brother from a cult and earned myself eternal gratitude and the run of the place in the process. I never had to pay for another drink, and the bar staff knew I was king of all I surveyed. The Royal Inn had become a home from home, and sometimes, as I watched Hackney's bright generation of young new residents laughing under the low lighting, I would try to pretend that the past ten years hadn't happened, and that I was really just enjoying a quick drink on my way home to Sarah, Oliver and Amber.

Instead, I cut a brooding figure at the bar. And I drank remorselessly. Some nights I could see the staff exchanging looks, wondering how they could refuse me. I knew I made some of the customers uneasy, but so what? There were other pubs. I'd earned my place in this one with blood and fear. Out of place and alone, I was ignored by most of the regulars. Guys gave me a couple of yards, and women gave me nothing, not even second glances. I knew they thought I was dangerous, and there was nothing I could do about that. I couldn't shake the darkness of the world I inhabited.

I downed my rum and waved the empty glass at Tilly, the bright as a button blonde who was my favourite member of staff because she never gave me 'the look'.

While she got to work on the refill, I took out my phone, dropped it, almost fell over getting off the stool to pick it up, fumbled, and eventually got it to my ear. *How many drinks had I had?*

I found the card that Gilmore had given me. I'd put off calling it all day because I didn't investigate child abductions. They were too painful. Reminded me too much of Amber. But this one was different. The mandala found at the Chapel Street house suggested the disappearances might be connected. I dialled the number, and the call went straight to voicemail.

'Mrs Blake, this is Thomas Schaefer,' I said, trying to stop myself from slurring. 'Dr Gilmore thought we should meet. Perhaps you could give me a call. My number is 07199346720.'

I hung up as Tilly pushed a brimming glass across the bar.

'Thanks,' I said.

She said nothing, but smiled sadly, and gave me 'the look'. I went right off her then and there.

Not you too, Tilly. I thought I could always rely on you.

I was used to the reaction. Even from my clients, who were often desperate for my friendship and would promise me the world when they needed me. When I'd closed a case, most of them wanted nothing more to do with me. I was a bitter reminder of a world they preferred to forget had ever touched their lives. Even Richard, the owner of The Inn, had grown distant. On the rare occasions we saw one another in the pub, he would give me a couple of minutes' stilted conversation before remembering something that required his urgent attention. I didn't bear any of them any ill will; I knew I was doomed to be an outsider. Amber's abduction had changed me. I sometimes wondered how the me of eleven years ago would have reacted to the me of today. Would old me have shuddered, given me 'the look', and moved to a safe distance as quickly as possible? Probably.

I smiled at the thought of the man I once was, but I knew it wasn't a happy smile because my vision shimmered as my eyes filled.

Cut the pity, I told myself. *That man is long dead.*

Even if I could find Amber, I would never be able to go back to the man I was. I drained my glass, and tried to confuse the warmth of the rum filling my stomach with happiness.

I held my empty glass aloft and nodded at Tilly. She was going to have a busy night.

CHAPTER 19

I woke to the dull roar of a vacuum cleaner, and my head started throbbing the moment I opened my eyes. I was lying on an old Chesterfield in a quiet corner of the pub. The cleaner, Natasha, a sour-faced prude, shook her head with obvious disapproval. She never gave me any pity, she only knew me as a drunk, who, for some inexplicable reason, was allowed to sleep off my excesses in the lounge bar when I couldn't make it upstairs to my room. My skull throbbed with the intensity of a George Clinton bassline, my eyes were gritty and stung as light assaulted them, and my swollen and fur-lined tongue oozed a disgusting film that slithered down my burning throat. As my brain struggled through its customary post-binge boot-up process, I realised I was supposed to be somewhere. I checked my watch and sat up with a start: I was late. When the pummelling head rush subsided, and I retreated from the edge of a blackout, I stood slowly, and shuffled unsteadily to the door. I didn't even have time to go upstairs for a shower and a change of clothes. I would just have to go to church as I was.

If the Burlington Arcade was a glimpse into a life I'd left behind, St Paul's Cathedral made me feel positively alien. Wren's high church loomed over me, reminding me of my insignificance. Everyone else had given up, and I was the only one left to chip away at the monumental task of finding Amber. Could Wren have built such a huge structure alone? What made me think I could accomplish my difficult task solo?

I climbed two tiers of steps and entered through the north door. A liveried attendant quietly asked to see a ticket, and I mumbled I was here for a service. I'd faced down the ugliest villains, but this quiet, slight, short man made me feel inadequate. He knew I was out of place, that someone like me who'd seen the things I'd seen and done the things I'd done, didn't belong in one of the world's most sacred sites. I must have looked a mess, but no matter how grand, this was a church and was built to receive all. No matter how dirty or dishevelled. He signalled the seating area under the dome, but I knew where I was going, and crossed the flagstones, passing the public seats. I headed for the gated portico behind the choir stalls, where another attendant waited.

'I'm here for the service,' I croaked. I could have really done with some water.

'Who are you with?' the attendant asked, looking me up and down.

'Oliver Schaefer,' I replied. 'I'm his father.'

I could feel the pity radiate from the man as he stepped aside to allow me to pass through the gate.

'You'd better hurry,' the attendant called after me. 'You're late.'

I jogged along the rear of the stalls to the small archway that cut between them, and felt queasy with every step. I walked into the aisle that ran between the north and south choir stalls, directly in front of the high altar, and stopped in my tracks. The choral procession had already started. Led by the dean and cassocked senior clergy, the men and boys of the choir, in their white and black robes, made their way down the aisle. I shrank back, trying to go unnoticed, but the choir had seen me, and my ten-year-old son, Oliver, flashed a familiar look of disappointment the moment he caught sight of me. Across the aisle, in the seats reserved for the choristers' families, I could see whispers of disapproval from the prosecco-and-cocktails crowd who sent their offspring to the cathedral school. Most of them were in suits and beautiful day dresses. I wore a dirty black leather jacket, a grey roll neck and black jeans. My stubble was a few days old, but that was in style, as was my short black tousled hair. There was nothing in my physical appearance that would cause comment on any street in London, but then this wasn't any London street. This was an oh-so-select group of parents who could see my dishevelment. They could probably smell it too. More pertinent than any of that, though; they could see my eyes. Crystal clear azure blue, windows to a soul in torment. Anguish and turmoil writ large.

Most of the parents judging me were members of North London's media set, called each other 'darling' and summered in their bijou homes in Carcassonne. And there among them sat my ex-wife, Sarah.

The look of disappointment again, but this one was tinged with a fatigue that came from years of ever-lowering expectations. With her cascading blonde hair and soft Celtic features, gentleness of spirit and movement, I still found Sarah beautiful, but her eyes betrayed her sadness. They were brimming pools of sorrow, and whenever she saw me I felt as though they might overflow. I was the tumour, the blight of the past on her present life. I was her reminder that we had failed, and she was mine. But unlike me she'd been strong, and for the sake of Oliver she'd made pretence of moving on from the past. But I knew the truth; Sarah's life was an act. A performance designed to give their son some semblance of a normal upbringing.

At her core she was just as broken as me.

When the choir had passed and were shuffling to their places in the stalls, I crossed the aisle and took one of the few available seats. The high-backed, hardwood stalls were uncomfortable and oppressive, but the music made all the disapproval, the discomfort and the shame worthwhile. For a moment I forgot my struggle and swelled with pride when I heard the beautiful music Oliver made with the cathedral choir. The light, crystal clear voices filled the transept, and for a brief time, hearing such talent, I could almost bring myself to believe there was a God. But as magical and glorious as they seemed, harmonious voices uplifted in spiritual adulation were, I knew, only proof of the evolutionary advantage of strong vocal cords. God had proved he didn't exist with the misery he'd inflicted on me, the suffering I'd seen, and the violence I'd inflicted on others. The pantheon of gods conjured by humans was just a cleverly contrived fairy-tale designed to prevent people from simply crumbling under the crushing weight of all the darkness in the world. False hope is better than no hope at all, and the promise of a paradise to come is a balm for a present Hell.

I hoped I'd feel happy again one day, but for now I had to pretend, so I sat back and forced myself to smile at my son. Oliver looked at me, then quickly looked away. I was doomed to my torment and would find no succour.
Not even there.

CHAPTER 20

When the singing was over, I zoned out. The dean's sermon was 'Keeping Faith Through Struggle' and I wasn't interested in what he had to say. The occasional word pierced my drone filter; 'courage', 'fortitude' and 'faith', but I spent most of the time trying to catch Sarah's eye. She wouldn't look at me, and neither would Oliver. Eventually I gave up. They'd made it clear I was invisible to them, but I felt very much seen by the other parents, who whispered and muttered as they cast me disapproving looks. Was I really that much of a reprobate? I certainly felt it, sitting there in the clothes I'd worn the night before, belching acidic bile.

When the dean finally finished, a priest led a prayer asking God to help those in need of strength. If only it was that simple. I'd spent hours on my knees in St Mark's, our local church, pleading with God for Amber's safe return. I was living proof prayer was a futile waste of breath, but if it gave the weak their false hope, perhaps it did some good. The strong knew force of will and strength of flesh were of more value than prayer, and it made me feel ashamed to think about how much time I'd wasted on my knees, asking for intercession.

I could tell these people a thing or two, open their eyes to truth. If you want to overcome adversity, I'd say, you need fire in your soul. For some that fire will come from ambition, and the rest of you will be driven by fear. I was a rare and evenly balanced mix of ambition and fear. The ambition to find Amber, the fear I would fail, and the two fought each other to keep me in a near-constant state of rage. Unquenchable anger that flamed within, born out of fear, ambition and an almost unimaginable hatred for the person who stole my daughter. Rage gave me the strength to endure things that would have killed other men.

When the service was finally over, I caught up with Sarah in the south transept. She was walking with Ted and Nancy, parents from the school. Their faces curled as though I was a bad smell, which, in all honesty, was a possibility.

'I'll catch up with you,' Sarah told them.

They continued towards the exit, acknowledging Sarah's burden with sympathetic looks and disapproving nods.

Sarah and I stood face-to-face in front of Nelson's Monument, and the stone lion that lay at Nelson's feet peered into the air between us.

'I'm sorry,' I tried.

'Don't worry about it,' Sarah said, her forgiveness practised and polite. She expected no better of me.

'I shouldn't have been late.'

'You turned up.'

'Sarah, I…' I hesitated. There was so much I wanted to say to her – that I wished I could be like her and have held on to our old life together, that I longed to be free of my curse, that I couldn't give up the search for our daughter, that I thought she was amazing, that I still loved her – but the words simply wouldn't come.

'What do you want, Thomas?' she asked, her voice laden with sadness. 'There's nothing more to be said.'

She turned and walked away, and I couldn't think of a single thing to say as I watched her go. I followed her out, but she skipped across the flagstone courtyard to get away from me. We moved in tandem, but separated by a growing gulf, and walked round the back of the cathedral to the school.

St Paul's Cathedral School filled a series of squat buildings dating from the tail end of the twentieth century. Surrounded by the gleaming towers of lawyers, accountants and bankers, it seemed very much a throwback to an old London, when families had lived within walking distance of the cathedral. Sarah, ever diligent, had discovered that a distant uncle had attended the school. It was a tenuous link, but it was all she had needed. The school offered scholarships to the disadvantaged and if a boy sang in the cathedral choir, then the dean and chapter would pay some, if not all, of his tuition fees. Throw into the mix the City of London livery companies, which sponsored a handful of students each year, and a canny parent could ensure that their lack of funds would not stand in the way of a top-flight education. I had to hand it to Sarah; she knew how to work the system to overcome the financial pinch caused by my failure to contribute meaningful child support.

The tiny car park in front of the school was packed with new Mercs, BMWs and Audis. I picked my way past the haphazardly parked vehicles, and pulled open the light oak door that was the school's unassuming main entrance. The supercilious deputy head, Mr Norman, stood beside a sign that read *Parent-Student Luncheon*. Two older students stood with him, satellites of fawning admiration to his giant orb of self-adoration.

'Good to see you, Mr Schaefer,' Norman said with a counterfeit smile. 'It's been a while.'

The manner in which Norman looked me over suggested he considered my prolonged absences from the school a good thing.

'Carter, give Mr Schaefer a newsletter,' he instructed.

The taller boy handed me a photocopy covered in small print.

'We're downstairs in the cafeteria,' Norman said, gesturing towards the staircase that led to the basement.

I started down. The walls were covered in honour rolls that detailed the names of head boys, cricket captains, rugby captains and other school luminaries through the ages. This rich, long heritage was now Oliver's. It was so alien to me, and made me feel uncomfortable because these wall-hangings made it clear we inhabited different worlds.

As I neared the bottom of the steps, I heard the rising hubbub of parents, students and teachers. Ahead of me, at the end of a long corridor lined with colourful student paintings, were the slatted double doors that opened onto the cafeteria. As I moved towards them, a child ran past me.

'Sorry,' the small, brown-haired boy said with a backward glance.

His expression changed when he caught sight of me. There was a look of fear tinged with disgust that reminded me I wasn't like the people through those doors. I carried the darkness of the world with me. Even this small child could see my suffering, and it made him recoil.

The boy ran on, and didn't even make pretence of holding the door open as he ducked inside the cafeteria. I pulled open the door, and scanned the room, ignoring quizzical looks from a few parents who had not been warned of the freak that walked among them. Finally, I caught sight of Sarah, standing with the headmaster, a small group of eager parents hovering around them, each eager for their opportunity to dazzle the head and win favour. Oliver was playing with a gang of boys his own age. I recognised most of them, but couldn't recall their names. They all looked happy without me, so I decided to leave their world undisturbed, and backed out of the cafeteria.

It took me half an hour to reach the Royal Inn. Tilly said nothing as I sat down at the bar.

'I'm a sucker for punishment,' I said with a sad smile. It had been a day to forget.

Tilly got to work on my drink. Goslings Black Seal with ice. She pushed the full glass across the bar.

'Here you go.'

'Thanks.'

I considered the rich, dark rum.

Strong enough to take down an ox.

Strong enough to keep me going.

CHAPTER 21

A nightmare of hideous things I can't remember the moment I open my eyes. A sudden rush of sensation. My head is on a plump, down pillow, but that can't be. This life is dead. Sarah is next to me, but doesn't stir. I could weep with relief. I dreamt a horrible solitary existence robbed of my family. Amber is crying from the next room. She must have had a nightmare too. I get to my feet and stumble over the trousers I'd enthusiastically discarded in my eagerness to get Sarah into bed. She is pregnant. Again? Hadn't we just had Oliver? Something feels wrong.

I cross the landing, and hurry into Amber's room. Unlike my own room as a child, Amber's is neat and tidy. Her toys are in a large wicker basket, her books ranked in order of size on her bookshelves, her soft toys properly arranged on her chest of drawers, and her music boxes lined up on her windowsill. Everything is basked in the faint yellow-green glow of the nightlight by the bed. Amber is hunched over, half-awake, sobbing about monsters. I draw her close to me and squeeze tightly.

'It's okay, Ammy,' I soothe. 'There's nothing to be afraid of. Daddy will always look after you.'

My stomach lurched as I woke up and realised I had been dreaming. Sleep was the only time I got to spend with Amber, and my dreams of her were rarely pleasant. I was often swept into nightmares of all the terrible things that might have happened to her over the past ten years, and these fears mingled with the memories of the evil people and twisted world I'd inhabited since she'd been taken. I drank to numb the pain and dull my mind, but every so often a dream would slip through the homespun anaesthesia. I took a moment to compose myself. Her tiny body had felt so real, her hair so sweet, but as the seconds ticked away from the dream, it dissipated like smoke on the wind and I was left with the memory of a memory.

My phone rang and I sat up to get it out of my pocket. I'd fallen asleep in the saloon bar, on the Persian rug in front of the fire. Faint early morning sunlight filtered through the blinds.

'Yeah,' I croaked as I answered the call.

'It's me,' said Mathers. 'I've found something. Meet me in the park.'

I showered and put on fresh clothes before heading for Piccadilly, which was packed with tourists enjoying the last wisps of summer. I walked through the crowd clustered around Green Park Station, and made my way into the relative calm of the park. There were a few damp orange leaves on the path, and a bite to the air that made autumn feel all too close. I saw Mathers sitting on our usual bench halfway along the path. The thin man wore a tailored woollen coat, and held a large box folder.

He looked me up and down as he got to his feet to shake my hand.

'You look like you could use some fresh air.'

'You said you found something.'

'I think you may have stumbled upon something quite sinister, Thomas. Have you ever heard of the Totus?'

I shook my head.

'Not many people have. The word is Latin for combined, but it can mean the total or sum of all things,' Mathers continued. 'It's a society that started in Central

Europe ten centuries ago. I'd come across whispers about it, but had always thought it more legend than reality. It seems I may have been wrong.'

He stopped and produced a photograph from the folder. The image showed a stone carving of people being devoured by a demon. The carving was encircled by an inscription.

'Not very pretty,' Mathers said. 'The text is Latin. It means Totus, strength in the one, strength in all. Look at the symbol at the end of the inscription.'

I saw a tiny marking on the page; the mandala containing three overlapping triangles punctuated the text.

Mathers stared at me with a degree of concern I'd never seen from him before.

'These people are dark, Thomas. They worship some kind of demon. It has many names: Astranger, Trauco, Papa Boya.'

'Papa Boya?' I interrupted. 'The kid I found, Derek Liddle, mentioned him.'

'You don't want this, Thomas. It's very dark. Let it go.'

'What is Papa Boya?' I asked.

If this lead had anything to do with Amber, I had to follow it.

'I don't know. As I said, until you showed me the photographs, I thought the Totus was stuff of myth and legend.'

I hesitated, trying to make sense of what happened.

'Leon Yates said Amber's name just before he jumped to his death. This stuff was found in places he'd been. I think he might have known what happened to her. This group might have something to do with her abduction.'

Mathers placed a sympathetic hand on my shoulder.

'I understand. Let me see what I can find out.' He handed me the folder. 'Take this. I have copies of everything. Two sets of eyes will find more than one.'

'Thanks,' I said. 'I appreciate it.'

CHAPTER 22

The tube to London Bridge had been too crowded and frustrated my efforts to examine the contents of the box. Our early morning meeting had left me with plenty of time to reach Norwood Junction, so I bought a ticket for the slow train, and picked the quietest carriage. A mother with a toddler asleep in a pram, and an old lady were my only company, and I sat as far away from them as possible. I opened the box to find photographs of a number of European monuments, news clippings and photocopies of books written in a dozen different languages. I selected a few items and spread them out on the seat. A well-thumbed sheaf of photocopied pages caught my eye. They were stapled and there was a handwritten note on the cover: *Extracted pages of The Book of Clareno – Written in 1330. Translated in 1880. A good place to start. M.*

I turned the page and started reading the closely typed, gothic script.

In the name of God, Father, Son and Holy Spirit, and by the authority of Sanctissimus Dominus Noster, His Holiness Pope Leo XIII, I, Johannes von Kuhn, faithful servant of the Lord, offer my translation of the stored journals of Angelo de Clareno, whose Order was united with the Observantists by His Holiness Pope Pius V. These journals, commonly accorded the name The Book of Clareno, *give an account of the daily life of the Clareni and their ministry. In keeping with the literature of the time, Father Angelo's writings contain references to dealings with the Infernal One, matters of possession, and widespread spiritual unrest, as the embrace of the Church was tested by ignorance and obstinacy. This translation is bound under the laws of Bibliotheca Apostolica Vaticana that it may only be read by members of the Congregation of The Holy Office of the Inquisition and such other individuals as His Holiness permits.*

6 September 1330, 8ᵗʰ Day Before Ides
Our happy colony is in turmoil at the arrival of the man Brother Roberto calls Castoro. The name seemed appropriate since Brother Roberto found him floating in the lake. He has caused much consternation among the brethren with his feverish fits and cries. Brother Ersted and some others who share his outlook believe Castoro is possessed, and ask that we send for assistance. Brother Roberto, who has established a bond with his foundling, argues that Castoro exhibits symptoms of his fever, and that, with time, his madness shall ease.

11 September 1330, 3ʳᵈ Day Before Ides
It seems Brother Ersted was correct in his concerns. Castoro's fever has broken, and the man is even more violent and delusional than before. We have removed him from Brother Roberto's cell, and placed him in one of the Monastery's empty grain stores by the outer wall. Brother Ersted mixes Root of Valerian into Castoro's meals in the hope of subduing his distemper. We sent for help and I have received word Cardinal Fournier will meet with our strange guest. I have not spoken to the others of this development, but find myself troubled. His Eminence was Bishop of Pamiers during the years of heresy, and I have heard tell he pursued his hunt against the heretics with an uncommon enthusiasm.

25 September 1330, 7ᵗʰ Day Before Kalends

My fears are as yet unfounded. Cardinal Fournier arrived two days ago with a small retinue and has embraced with warm civility the simple life we lead. He does not insist on special favour at meals, nor has he asked for preference during our services. His contact with Castoro has been tentative. He has seen the wild man twice, and both times simply watched as Castoro sprang about his room. Both times, Cardinal Fournier insisted on my presence, and separately he has asked me to recount the story of Castoro's discovery on at least four occasions.

2 October 1330, 6th Day Before Nones
His Eminence has a mind that works in ways I cannot fathom. I myself have experienced the inner workings of the Inquisition, and have encountered men of the Church who were prepared to undertake extraordinary tasks to unmask heresy. Had it not been for the clarity and charity of Friar Gaufredi, who saw that there was no malice in my heart, I might still be subject to the painful ministrations of such men. Cardinal Fournier is no such man. He does not make use of rack or brand. The Lord has blessed him with an insight into the minds of men.

The afternoon was spent with Castoro. Cardinal Fournier sat quietly and watched the lunatic cavort around his room. To begin with I thought it would be another study of madness. Instead, after a few minutes, His Eminence stood suddenly, and struck Castoro full in the face. When the man fell to his knees, Cardinal Fournier clasped the sides of his head and performed an Exorcism with what I can only describe as a passionate clarity. The force of His Eminence's incantation was unmistakable, but there was no emotion, just a purity of motive and thought. Castoro fell to the floor, insensible. We carried him to his cot, and His Eminence sent for frankincense. The sweet smoke revived Castoro, and even though he had a wild look in his eyes, he was lucid for the first time since he arrived.

Cardinal Fournier proceeded with the tentative steps of a lamb. His Eminence started gently with an enquiry after the health of the man. Castoro spoke in broken Italian, so the Cardinal offered to speak French. Conversing in his native tongue put Castoro more at ease, and he conveyed his apologies to His Eminence for his appearance and demeanour. Cardinal Fournier asked the man's name, but Castoro refused to give it. He said the revelation would place us all in mortal peril. Cardinal Fournier pressed Castoro, but the man was obdurate. Rather than becoming angered by this affront to his authority, His Eminence assured the man that his identity was not important. The more pressing matter was how a French nobleman came to be in Armenia in a state of derangement. Castoro could not hide his surprise and asked why the Cardinal thought him of the higher order. His Eminence replied that Castoro had made a fair endeavour with his clothes, but had neglected to address his boots, which were hand-cut in the fashionable Parisienne style. The boots went no better with Castoro's rags than wine might go with ale. So, the Cardinal surmised, Castoro either stole the boots, or they were rightfully his. His soft hands and face denied Castoro a history of hard labour. Castoro neither confirmed nor denied Cardinal Fournier's assertion, and the matter simply rested as they moved on to other things.

They stepped around one another for the next hour, engaged in discourse on diverse matters. The weather, the price of gold, and some tales from the Court of Valois. When the bell chimed five, Cardinal Fournier asked for permission to withdraw. I could scarcely believe my ears, a Cardinal asking permission of a lunatic, and could see the plain discomfort on Castoro's face. He assented nonetheless, and we withdrew.

CHAPTER 23

An automated announcement interrupted my reading and told me the next station was Norwood Junction. I wanted to read on, but didn't have time, so I put the papers back in the box and got to my feet. The road outside the station was similar to dozens of streets around London. A newsagent, a mid-sized supermarket, a bank, a hardware store, multiple pound shops, and scores of grimy takeaways. Only the mechanics immediately opposite the station marked Norwood out as unique. The small forecourt was packed with cars that had been kept alive longer than was natural, and the surrounding road was speckled with small patches of black grease.

I walked down the alleyway that ran behind the high street, past the two squat mini-tower blocks that loomed over the train tracks. The dangerously enticing smell of solvents from a nearby printworks filled my sinuses. I crossed Portland Road under the railway bridge, walked two streets up, and turned into Addison Road. I found number 116, a small terrace house with an immaculate garden, at the very end of the street.

I felt the unfamiliar tightness of nervous anticipation in my chest and the bite of acid in my stomach as I went through the gate and knocked on the front door. I hadn't handled a child abduction in years. I took the opportunity to check my reflection in the adjacent window, and straightened my jacket. I thought I looked pretty good.

The woman who opened the door obviously did not agree with my assessment. Her face fell the moment she saw me. The woman, with curly, shoulder-length black hair, a full face and a little too much weight around the middle, slipped her foot behind the bottom of the door. She clearly thought I might be dangerous, and I wondered whether I'd lost all sense of judgement and what other people saw when they looked at me.

Did the drinking show? Could they see the dark places I'd been?

'Mrs Blake?' I asked.

'No, I'm a friend.'

'I have an appointment to see Mrs Blake. My name is Thomas Schaefer.'

'The private investigator?' the woman asked, not bothering to conceal her surprise. 'You'd better come in.'

Penny Blake's house was much like her garden; well-kept and thoughtfully laid out. The whitewashed floorboards were covered with Persian rugs that gave the home an eastern feel. A wall of photos in distressed frames showed a happy mother with a young girl who looked remarkably like Amber. I did a double take when I first saw the images. At a distance I would have said the girls were twins, and it was only when I studied the photos more closely that the differences became apparent. It was unsettling to see a missing girl so like my own daughter.

'I'm Marcie,' the woman said as she led me down the hall into the living room. 'Penny's upstairs. She's not herself, obviously.'

The living room showed signs of Penny's distress. There were used tissues everywhere, and piles of papers were scattered on the coffee table by the telephone. Many of the sheets had hurried notes scrawled on them. A pair of jeans, pants and a bra had been tossed on the floor next to the plush sofa. Marcie sat in an armchair and looked me up and down.

'Exactly what kind of investigator are you?' she asked.

I could sense her scepticism. She wasn't one of the prosecco-and-cocktails mums from Oliver's school, but she was a civilian who inhabited the ordinary world, far away from the darkness I dwelt in. I was as far from the stereotypical professional private investigator as it was possible to get, and looking at myself through the cold reflection in Marcie's eyes, all I could see was a broken-down drunk who was clinging to the last vestiges of sanity. I felt a familiar burning sensation between my ears, as my anger started to build. Who was this woman to sit there and judge me? She didn't know who I was, or what had happened to me. I was about to walk out, when Penny Blake entered the room.

Slim and slight with auburn hair that reached midway down her back, and a gaunt, delicate face. Her only blemishes were two red-rimmed eyes that had sunk deep into her skull through lack of sleep. My rage immediately gave way to pity – I knew exactly what Penny Blake was going through, and felt an almost overwhelming urge to embrace her. Instead, I offered my hand.

'Mrs Blake, I'm Thomas Schaefer.'

She ignored my greeting, wiped away fresh tears, and slumped on the sofa.

'I'm sorry,' Penny sobbed. 'I can't seem to stop. She's all I have.'

'Please don't apologise,' I replied, sitting next to her.

'Dr Gilmore says you specialise in this sort of case,' Penny said.

'I don't usually take on children. I work with adults. Men and women in their twenties and thirties mainly. People who have joined cults.'

'When they saw the card, the police suggested I contact Dr Gilmore. They say he's an expert in this field.' Penny's voice broke, shifting into a higher register as the words spilt out. 'They said he could counsel me, but how can anyone get through this?'

I couldn't respond. The truth would have been too painful, and she seemed too smart to accept a lie. *There was no getting through it.*

'Have you noticed any changes in…' I hesitated.

'Katie,' Penny offered helpfully.

'In Katie's behaviour?' I continued.

'No.'

'Any unusual people hanging around? Anyone following you?'

'Nothing,' Penny said, shaking her head in frustration.

I could see her wracking her mind, desperately trying to remember something; a face, a car, a clue of some kind that would shine a sudden burst of truth on the situation and enable me to find her little girl. I recognised the look. I'd driven myself near-mad trying the very same thing.

'And her father?'

'Gone. He died five years ago.'

'When did you discover she was missing?'

'Eight days ago.' Penny struggled to get the words out, as her tears fell freely. 'It was the day after her tenth birthday.'

The revelation caught me off guard. I felt sick.

'Are you okay?' Penny asked.

Was this really happening? Or was it a setup? Had she been sent to torment me? To mess with my mind?

Never let them know they've got to you, I thought.

'What happened?' I asked as neutrally as possible.

'I went into her bedroom to wake her up for school and she wasn't there.' Penny's voice broke entirely, as her raw throat swelled shut with grief. Marcie got up and put a reassuring arm around her friend, and after a few shuddering, tearful moments, Penny was able to continue. 'I found the card on her pillow.'

The grief seems genuine, I thought, trying to suppress my nausea. *Let's see just how real this is.*

'Was her bed made?'

The domestic mundanity of the question puzzled Marcie, but Penny looked as though she'd been slapped.

'How did you know?'

'Were her pyjamas neatly folded on her pillow?'

Penny's eyes filled anew as she nodded. Marcie was shocked by the implication, and Penny turned to her and sobbed, 'I couldn't tell you. They…they…undressed her.'

'I'd like to look at the room,' I said, getting to my feet.

CHAPTER 24

I lingered in the doorway and studied the room for what seemed like an eternity. I couldn't breathe, because the room reminded me so much of Amber's. A single bed was pushed against the far wall, under the window. A personalised princess blanket, embroidered with the words 'Katherine Blake', lay neatly folded at the end of the bed. An old-fashioned wooden toy chest stood at the foot of the bed, so packed with toys, they looked as though they were fighting each other to escape. A pine closet loomed against the opposite wall, and next to it was a matching set of free-standing pine shelves covered with cuddly toys, books, a pink laptop, music boxes and other bric-a-brac. Along the wall that ran off the doorway was a small red laminate desk, and next to it, a chest of drawers that was swamped with yet more cuddly toys.

Penny said nothing, but Marcie clearly felt I was wasting their time.

'The police have already been through everything.'

'The police don't know what they're looking for,' I said. 'Did they leave everything as they found it?'

Penny nodded. 'I think so. What can you see?'

I could see something cops would be blind to: the past. This was the same scene I'd observed the day Amber went missing. The neatly made bed, the crisply folded pyjamas, and the toys. Every single pair of glassy eyes stared at the same point: Katie's desk. No normal person would even register where a disparate collection of dolls, animals and cuddly toys were looking, and it's not something a seasoned police officer would have noticed. But I had been on the trail long enough to understand the sick joke; the child's toys were witnesses to this heinous crime, and as witnesses they all longed to tell me something. It had been the same in Amber's room.

I stepped forward hesitantly, aware I had to be careful. If Penny and Marcie saw me recover something, they would almost certainly insist on it being turned over as evidence. They weren't to know they were in my world now, and I could do much more than the police.

I checked under the bed, and ran my hands along the bottom of the frame to the laminate desk. I positioned my body between the desk and the door and concealed what I was doing from the two women. There, wedged under a crack in the laminate, was a small, carefully folded piece of paper. I pinched it out with the very tips of my fingers.

'You find anything?' Marcie asked.

'No,' I replied, concealing it in my pocket as I turned. 'I guess you were right.'

Marcie shook her head and gave Penny her best 'I-told-you-so' look. Desperate to cling to even the smallest shred of hope, Penny ignored her friend's scepticism.

'Will you take the case, Mr Schaefer?'

I didn't want this case. I knew it led somewhere bad. Just standing in Katie's room disturbed me, but I could not help but be moved by the despair in Penny's eyes. I saw a reflection of my past self, from ten years ago when I still believed in the decent and proper lies we're all told in childhood. If you do the right thing, you'll get the right result. Virtue wins the day. Good will triumph over evil. In her faltering voice I heard an echo of myself from a time when I harboured the false hope that someone else could make everything better. Now, standing in the harsh, cold glare of truth, I knew there was no one else and that good most definitely does not triumph over evil. I also knew that if I didn't help her, no one else would.

'I'll need a recent photograph,' I replied.

Ten minutes later, armed with a photograph and more information about Katie, I left the little house on Addison Road. Penny held the door open for me.

'Please find her, Mr Schaefer,' Penny implored. 'Please find my little girl.'

'I'll do what I can,' I said as I walked away.

I didn't tell her she'd asked me to do for her what I hadn't been able to achieve for myself. She didn't need to know that. I had ten more years' experience and wouldn't make the stupid mistakes that had led me to so many dead ends.

Penny watched me for a few moments before shutting the door slowly. As I walked past the neat terrace houses, their inhabitants untouched by darkness, I checked to make sure that Penny no longer had eyes on me. When I was out of sight of the bay window in Penny's living room, I put my hand in my pocket and pulled out the note that had been concealed under the laminate of Katie's desk. I unfolded the tightly pressed paper and saw familiar handwriting scrawled in crayon. I'd seen it the day Amber had disappeared.

Hello, Schaefer. It's been a long time.

CHAPTER 25

I trembled and the strength drained from my legs. I leant against a car bonnet to steady myself. I'd found a note like this the day Amber was taken. It had said, *Let's play, Schaefer,* and had been followed by a hand-drawn version of the mandala I'd found in the kitchen on Chapel Street. There was little doubt Leon Yates was connected to Katie Blake's abduction, and to Amber's too. I took deep breaths and tried to get control of my emotions, but this was raw, as raw as it got. I wiped tears from my eyes and couldn't stop thinking of my little girl. Someone was tormenting me. Someone who'd taken my daughter. The same person who'd taken Katie Blake. I looked back at the Blakes' house and realised the monster who had taken Amber had stood in the front bedroom not more than eight days ago. I was closer than I'd been in ten years.

The thought provided me with some comfort and I found the strength to continue. I walked unsteadily to the station and took the first train north into central London. I found another quiet carriage and opened the folder Mathers had given me, desperate to return to the monk's diary. It was all important now, all linked. I had to figure out the puzzle. For Amber.

October 4 1330, 4th Day Before Nones
Cardinal Fournier revealed Castoro's true identity today. This encounter began much as the prior had ended, with some idle discourse of inconsequential matters. Then there was a pause, during which His

ADAM LOXWOOD

Eminence studied Castoro with careful diligence, and announced that it really had been necessary for His Grace, the Count Eudes of Burgundy, to give cause for his flight from France in such meagre circumstances. Castoro, the Count, acknowledged the truth with a slight nod of his head.

Count Eudes asked Cardinal Fournier for his good and holy word that he was a true servant of the Church. To ask such a question of a high bishop seemed impertinent, but His Eminence did not bridle and replied in a manner that seemed acceptable to the Count, for he began to recount his tale. I know not how much to believe of what follows. The Count's testimony lacked not for passion and if that be the measure of veracity, then he spoke the truth.

The Count asked if Cardinal Fournier had encountered Il Totus, a faction he accused of unholy, demonic practices. His Eminence said he had not. Count Eudes wept as he told the Cardinal the group had been responsible for the demonic possession of his wife, Joan, Countess of Burgundy. She had become inconsolable at the death of her last infant, the fifth to perish in childbirth. In despair, the Countess had turned her back on the Church and sought assistance from practitioners of the dark arts so she might bear the Count a healthy son. In so doing, Her Ladyship exposed herself to the machinations of Il Totus. The group promised her a child in exchange for a price that the Count is yet to ascertain. Within a year the Countess had borne His Grace a son. Three months after the birth, Her Ladyship vanished for a period of fourteen days, and when she returned, His Grace asserts that she was different, full of licentiousness and wicked thoughts.

Count Eudes confined the Countess to her chambers and inquired into her private affairs. Her Ladyship's ladies-in-waiting, all of whom had been given notice by the Countess, had seen some of the Countess's

93

private dealings with the members of *Il Totus*, and recounted to the Count the unholy pact that had birthed his son.

Troubled by his inquiries, the Count went to give the Countess the chance to refute the accusations levelled against her. As he entered Her Ladyship's chambers the Count heard noises from within. He approached the curtained bed, and drew back the drape to discover the Countess's intimacy with an ancient demon. The demon savaged the Count, and man and beast fought through the castle. Count Eudes, full of shame, and overawed by the evil power of the creature, fled. As he ran the demon promised to hunt him for eternity so that he might complete the dark marriage and seize the Count's rightful inheritance. The Count fled France and crossed Europe as a nameless beggar. The tribulations of his journey had robbed him of his sanity and any spiritual strength.

Cardinal Fournier gave Count Eudes gentle words of comfort, and, once His Grace regained his composure, the Cardinal asked questions that illuminated parts of the tale that were in shadow. His Eminence wanted to know the evidence the ladies-in-waiting had against the Countess, and asked the Count to tell him exactly what they had said. Finally satisfied that he understood the entirety of the dreadful affair, Cardinal Fournier begged leave to retire to his chambers to pray for guidance.

October 7 1330, The Day of Nones

I beg the Lord for forgiveness. My wickedness had caused suffering these past days. I have not received sufficient punishment for my earlier rebellion against the Church, and the Almighty is giving me valuable instruction in humility. I plead with the Lord in my prayers not to inflict suffering on those innocents around me, who had no hand in my youthful transgressions. My prayers go unanswered. I cannot expect to be *heard until I have attained spiritual purity and made true penance for my sins.*

Two nights ago Brother Roberto woke me before the morning bell. We hurried through the darkness to the Count's room and found horror. Cardinal Fournier and his retinue had produced the implements of the Inquisition and were making full use of them on Count Eudes. His screams were muffled by a scrap of fabric shoved rudely into his mouth. Cardinal Fournier made no excuses upon my arrival, and with righteous fury chastised our entire order for falling into neglect and heresy. Gripped by a holy frenzy, His Eminence made countless accusations of ways in which life in the monastery deviated from dogma. The Cardinal said that I had allowed apostasy to enter into our spiritual home, and that the ensuing darkness had forged it into a shrine for heretics. The Count was the first of many who would be drawn from across Europe unless the evil was purged. Cardinal Fournier instructed two priests to evict me and turned back to the Count. As I was dragged bodily, I heard His Eminence demand that Count Eudes recant his tale and withdraw the scandalous allegations he had made against his wife, the Countess.

Brother Roberto, whose kindness had brought strife to our peaceful home, counselled action. He said we must wake the others and save the Count from such cruelty. I said such a course was impossible; Cardinal Fournier was known throughout Europe as a pious man dedicated to the holy cause of the Church. If the Count was possessed of evil, and was spreading such improper accusations about his wife, then he was in need of the help of a man as dedicated and devoted as His Eminence. I instructed Brother Roberto to return to his cell and pray for peace.

My own efforts in this regard proved futile, and I was awake as the cock crowed. Had it not been for my disturbed state of mind, I would not be alive. I thought I heard a stifled cry through the stone wall that separated my cell from the next. I went to the door and saw the lock turn. Possessed by fear, I hid behind the door, and watched one of Cardinal Fournier's priests creep toward my bed. The priest had a bloodied sword in hand, raised to strike. I ran from my cell and saw the corridor full of Fournier's men, doing bloody work. I turned and ran for the stables, where I hid while Fournier committed bloody murder. I heard men yelling to each other as they searched the monastery for me, and knew I would not be safe. I crept from the stables to the outhouse and lowered myself into the foul mess that was the product of so many holy men. The acrid vapours made me gag and wretch, but I was safe. My hiding place had the advantage of proximity to the courtyard, and I heard Fournier order his men to give up the search. He instructed them to prepare for their journey to Dijon where Count Eudes would be reunited with his wife.

Fournier's men set fire to the monastery. They left in their carts as my home and the mortal remains of my brothers were consumed by flame. I waited as long as I could, but the heat soon became intolerable. I ran from the outhouse and it collapsed behind me. I fled the inferno, running until I collapsed near the very lake where Brother Roberto had found Count Eudes. Far ahead of me on the distant road I could see Fournier's train. Behind me a high column of black smoke marked the destruction of all that I had held dear. I slipped into dark oblivion.

I do not know how long I slept, but when I woke the monastery was no more than smouldering ruins. The sun had only recently crested the horizon. I washed in the lake, and the water cleansed my body, but the stain on my soul ran too deep. The walk to Gavar took most of the day, and when I arrived at the village, I said nothing of what had happened. I sought refuge with an old woman I had shown kindness to the previous winter. I had laid her son in the earth in Christian burial even though there were questions over the manner of his death. The old *woman and her husband took me in without question, and it is in their home that I write these words. I thank the Lord I always keep my journal with me, or else all record of these terrible days would have been lost.*

I have prayed for guidance, but thus far none has been forthcoming. I am left to my own fallible conjecture. I cannot believe a man of true faith would so coldly murder so many good monks. I have come to question Cardinal Fournier's allegiance. The manner in which he spoke of Count Eudes' return to Dijon and the reunion with the Countess gave me reason to fear he is in league with the dark forces that have so ravaged the Count's life. I cannot with good conscience do nothing in the face of such evil, but do not know how to unmask a Cardinal of the Church as a heretical deviant. My own troubled past, and the manner in which my entire order perished, would immediately raise suspicion even in the minds of the purest men. I feel the Lord has placed this before me as a test, and with His guidance and eternal love, I will find a way to right the terrible wrong that has befallen so many innocents.

My train pulled into London Bridge as I was reading the footnote to the translation, which said Angelo de Clareno died in Dijon in 1331. Testimony from a servant in the household of the Count of Burgundy said the impoverished friar had been caught trespassing in the house armed with a dagger, and was slain during a struggle to disarm him.

I put the document in the folder and stood as the train rolled to a halt. I tried to work out what I had to do with a fourteenth-century monk and how these papers would help me find Amber. I turned de Clareno's story over and over, but could see nothing of value. Mathers' papers would have to wait. Katie Blake had been kidnapped less than eight days ago. Her trail was still fresh and the past ten years had introduced me to people who might know where she was. I got off the train and started to mentally prepare myself for what lay ahead.

It was going to be a busy night.

CHAPTER 26

My knuckles were sore. The leather gloves prevented cuts and abrasions, but didn't do much to stop bruising. I opened and closed my fists to check there was no serious damage. It wouldn't really matter if there was; I still had work to do.

I heard footsteps stop outside the front door. Someone fumbled with a set of keys. I stood completely still in the darkness and waited. The stench of failure permeated the room; damp walls, decaying food, thick dust, stale cigarettes, spilt beer, mingling to form an overwhelming odour of neglect. This was the home of somebody who had given up. Someone once told me a deterioration in hygiene is one of the earliest signs of mental illness, and my experiences over the years had only served to validate that nugget of pop psychology.

My heartbeat jacked up a notch and I tensed as a key slid into the front door. Then came heavy, clumsy footsteps and the sound of the door being kicked shut. More oafish steps. A pause, as the mail, which I'd left undisturbed, was picked up. The footsteps resumed and grew louder and closer, and I prepared myself.

Porcine fingers reached around the doorway and found the filthy light switch. A single fluorescent strip stuttered into life, illuminating a greasy man covered in a light sheen of sweat. The man put two bags of shopping on the cluttered counter and turned to see me standing in his near-derelict kitchen.

'No,' he said weakly. His legs failed him as he tried to back towards the door, and he stumbled sideways into the counter.

Peter Taurn, convicted paedophile, panderer and all-round dreg. He had done to other parents what my monster had done to me. Just the sight of him enraged me.

I crossed the rotten lino, grabbed his arm and hurled him against the kitchen table, which collapsed under his weight. He fell on his back and held his arms up to protect himself as I kicked him in the gut half a dozen times. Taurn tried to scream, so I kicked him again and stole his breath. Adrenaline racing, I hardly noticed the man's weight as I hauled him to his feet. I head-butted him, and Taurn's nose popped like a water balloon, covering his face in blood. I pushed him against the rusting electric cooker and took a step back.

'Do I have your attention?' I growled.

Bewildered and bleeding, Peter Taurn was not quick enough with his response, so I kneed him in the gut.

'Do I have your attention?' I barked.

'Help!' Taurn yelled. Now that he had found his voice, he made use of it, screaming wildly. 'Help me! Help!'

I punched him. A little too hard. Taurn's eyes rolled, so I grabbed his coat collar and slapped some sense into him. His breath stank of stale cigarettes.

'Do you think your neighbours are going to help a convicted paedophile?' I asked. 'You're on your own.'

He recovered his senses. 'That was a long time ago.'

I punched him in the gut, and he doubled over and coughed up a little blood.

'The big wide world says you're a panderer. That you sell children,' I said, taking a step back to allow him to catch his breath.

'You've got the wrong man,' he wheezed.

I elbowed the top of his head, knocking him to the floor.

'I had a chance to look around while I was waiting,' I said, removing a bundle of photographs from my pocket and tossing them on the floor. 'I know what you do.'

Taurn focused on the badly lit images of children in their underwear. They'd been hidden in a waterproof bag at the bottom of the toilet cistern. Defeat washed over Taurn's face as he realised feigning innocence was no longer an option.

'What do you want?' he whimpered, raising the bloody mess that was his face.

'Do you know this girl?' I asked, showing him a photograph of Katie Blake.

Taurn looked down at his sordid photo collection. I grabbed his greasy hair, yanked his head up, and forced the photograph into his face.

'Look at her!' I growled.

He whimpered and struggled to turn away. 'Please. I haven't done anything.'

'Those photos are enough to put you back inside. The only choice you have is whether you walk out of here in cuffs, or get carried out in pieces. Look at her!'

Taurn focused on the image of Katie.

'Never seen her,' he said, his voice rasping with fresh blood.

I pulled his hair hard.

'Take a good look!'

'I've never seen her,' he cried. 'I would've remembered her. She's beautiful.'

What little restraint I'd managed vanished and I kicked and punched the man furiously.

'Please,' I heard him say between the blows. 'Please. I know. Please.'

I realised he was trying to tell me something and stepped back, breathless and angry. He looked up at me, his face covered in blood, his eyes swollen.

'I saw something online. In one of the groups,' he moaned. 'A place people say you can get younglings.'

'Where?' I asked.

'The Church of the Eternal Light,' he replied. 'Please. Please don't hurt me anymore.'

I looked down at the photographs of degraded innocents, and then at the bloody mess hunched over them. No punishment would ever be enough for this man. I kicked Taurn on the chin, knocking him unconscious.

I used a grubby tea towel to clean myself off and took out my phone as I walked towards the front door. Old eyes that had long lost their brightness watched me as I slipped out of Taurn's flat onto the common balcony that ran the length of the block. Taurn's neighbour was a gnarly old woman in a dirty dressing gown and wrinkled tights, who had opened her front door, attracted, no doubt, by the sounds of violence. She looked at me with neither approval nor disapproval, her face an emotionless mask.

As I walked away, I phoned Noel.

'Yeah?' he said.

'I've got a pick-up,' I replied. 'Peter Taurn, Livingstone Estate, Hackney. He's back to his old ways. He's going to need an ambulance.'

'For God's sake, Schaefer.'

I cut him off. 'You're welcome. And Noel, we need to meet.'

I sensed his reluctance in the pause that followed.

'Come by the station tomorrow at nine.'

CHAPTER 27

I arrived back at the Royal Inn a little after four in the morning, after another three visits to men like Taurn. I'd seen six in total, and my hands felt numb, but I didn't think I'd broken any bones. Apart from Taurn's tip, The Church of the Eternal Light, none of the other men had given me anything concrete.

I let myself in through the staff entrance and went upstairs, still charged with adrenaline. There was no way I could sleep, which was no bad thing. I was up against the clock. The first few days following a disappearance were crucial, and if I could find Katie Blake, I might have a chance of finding Amber. I wanted to read more of Mathers' papers.

I hurried across the landing and opened the door to my room. All the staff lived off-site and I was the only resident at the Royal Inn, so I'd had my pick of quarters. I'd chosen the Great Room, which had at one time been a private function room. It took up most of the first floor and, as the only part of the pub that hadn't been renovated, was a throwback to when the building had been a grand old house. I switched on an ancient chandelier that hung in the centre of the room. It was flanked by a pair of mutilated fittings where two siblings would have once added to the grandeur. The missing chandeliers had probably been taken around the same time the room had been stripped of its other valuable fittings: wood panelling, shelves, brass work and cornices. Robbed of its heritage, The Great Room clung to its grand past with solid oak floorboards, four large sash windows that overlooked the park, a large mirror propped against the far wall and an old Chesterfield that was so worn and stained not even the local charity shop wanted it.

I lay on the sofa and grabbed the box file Mathers had given me. I leafed through the papers and selected a set of stapled photocopies that Mathers had marked with his distinctive handwriting: *Patient mentions the Totus.*

The pages were an extract from a book entitled *Concerning Childhood Illnesses*, which, according to the preamble, had been privately published in 1864 by Dr Alfred Stern, a neurologist at the Birmingham and Midland Free Hospital for Sick Children. I grabbed a bottle and glass that were on the floor by the sofa leg, poured myself a generous measure and started reading.

CHAPTER 28

Concerning Childhood Illnesses by Dr Alfred Stern
PATIENT JONES
Patient Jones was admitted on March 12, 1863. Jones, a young male of approximately thirteen or fourteen, had suffered multiple contusions and lacerations to his limbs, torso and head. He had been discovered, insensible, in an alleyway in Digbeth. No explanation was provided as to the source of his injuries, nor was the person who delivered him to hospital properly identified. We have since changed our procedures to facilitate proper inquiries, should there be evidence of criminal activity.

 With no means of identifying him, the patient was assigned the Jones moniker, and given treatment for his injuries. I was first called to examine him on March 13, 1863, when he regained consciousness. The nursing staff had removed Jones to a secure room and bound him to his bed. When I entered, he was still raving. His words were an incomprehensible jumble of French, English and Latin. He strained at his bonds with such savage ferocity I feared he would do himself further injury. I sedated him by administration of morphine hypodermic, and Jones quickly became drowsy. Now that he was calmed of his violent lunacy, I could see he was a young man of average build. The curvature of his limbs was evidence of malnourishment in his formative years. His alabaster pallor suggested a lack of sunlight; perhaps he had been a mine worker. His teeth were beginning to show the signs of rot that so afflicts the lower orders, and his brown hair was wild and dry as straw. What lay before me was a young body already showing serious signs of neglect.

I asked the patient to give me his name. His reply was inaudible, and I asked him to repeat it.

'*Tenebris advenire*,' he said.

The body of the boy was not commensurate with that of a person who has received a classical education, and I was surprised to hear him reply in Latin. I surmised the words, meaning darkness approaches, were significant to the patient due to the fact that he repeated them a number of times. I tried, without success, to get the patient's true name, and within a short time, he drifted off to sleep.

The following day, March 14, Jones was awake and alert when I made my rounds. He had refused to answer the nursing staff's questions, and by all accounts had been silent since my visit of the previous day. I completed my physical examination, checking dilation, reflex response and visual acuity, and concluded the patient was unlikely to have suffered any damage to his brain as a result of his injuries. I found nothing to suggest he would further benefit from my specialist expertise, and was about to leave, when he spoke.

'I see you,' Jones said. 'I see inside you.'

I was startled to hear his voice, for he had said nothing throughout my examination.

'Do not be startled. Your secrets are but an open book before my eyes. The light of truth shines wherever I may cast my gaze. And of this moment I look upon your heart. I see great sadness, unfulfilled longing. For all your searching, you are lost. Your questions about our true purpose remain unanswered, and, as you have travelled through life, you have pushed the need for answers to the back of your mind until it is nothing more than a dimly lit memory.'

'Really?' I asked.

'You stand there doubting me. Tell me about your wife. Why did she leave you?'

I tried not to betray any emotion. How could this boy know about Maria? Had his admission to this hospital been planned? Had he overheard the nurses gossip? Had a third party, for some unknown reason, given him details of my personal life?

'Now your eyes are open. You see something you can't explain. Is the world as you thought it, Doctor? As you accustom yourself to the idea that all might not be what it seems, you will come to realise that we are the true source of power in the world.'

'We?'

'The Totus,' Jones continued. 'We shape the world according to our wish. Everything is known to us, friend.'

I found the conversation unnerving. If, as I suspected, the patient was delusional, he had unsettled me to a sufficient degree that I found myself starting to believe that he might be more than an injured child. I reminded myself of my training, and my unwavering belief in the power of logic and science.

'Fascinating,' I observed. 'But why don't we talk about you? What's your name?'

The patient smiled knowingly. It was a patronising expression I realised I had used many times when trying to explain something to a child, or mentally abnormal patient.

'My name is Jones. Isn't that what you called me?' he said. 'Take your time, Doctor. We expect resistance when we near the truth. But ask yourself this: what hand did you have in your wife's departure?'

I had not been prepared for this and recognised I had lost control of what should have been my examination.

'I think I shall continue my work another time,' I said, and withdrew.

Jones made no effort to strain against his bonds, but I could feel him watching me as I walked away.

'I look forward to our next talk, Doctor.'

I conferred with my colleague and mentor, Sir Benedict Usborne, who has extensive experience with delusional individuals. I recounted my conversation with Jones, and Sir Benedict immediately recognised the hallmarks of cold reading.

'Think about it, my dear fellow,' he said. 'Who hasn't asked themselves searching questions about the meaning of life? It's a general preamble stage magicians and clairvoyants use to set themselves above their audience. Did he say anything specific? No. He merely tapped into the innate human desire to answer the deeper metaphysical questions that trouble us all. And by so doing, he tried to make you believe that you were inferior to him, because he might have the answers which you seek.'

'What about Maria?' I asked.

'How do you know what he might have overheard the nurses saying? People treat those who are mute as though they are deaf. It is a very effective way to encourage people to talk freely. Or perhaps he simply noticed your hand.'

Sir Benedict's nod towards the fourth digit on my left hand immediately reminded me of the permanent fleshy indentation, the loving scar that was a consequence of having worn a wedding band for so many years.

'Perhaps he was sharp enough to spot that you used to wear a ring?'

I thanked Sir Benedict for his insight, and left his office wishing I'd had the presence of mind to challenge the boy and pierce his self-aggrandising façade. I borrowed a pair of books from the hospital library, and passed the evening reading about the parlour tricks used by clairvoyants and other supposed mystics.

The child would not outwit me again.

CHAPTER 29

I came round to dazzling sunlight. It caught lazy specks of dust that drifted through the air above my head. Mathers' papers were strewn around the sofa, and the empty rum bottle lay on the bare boards like a spent lover. I felt rough as I dragged myself to my feet. I promised I would lay off the drink, but even as I staggered into the corridor, I knew it was a promise I wouldn't keep. I stumbled into the bathroom, relieved myself and took a shower. It wasn't until I emerged, soaking wet, that I remembered my meeting with Noel. I grabbed the towel and ran into the Great Room to check the time. I was going to be late.

I caught sight of myself in the full-length mirror that leant against the far wall. I didn't look well. In fact, I looked positively unwell. I approached the mirror and dropped my towel. I noted the wrinkled bags under my eyes, my grey-tinged skin, yellow-hued sclerae and wondered how long I'd be able to punish my body like this. I wasn't under any illusions. I knew what drink was doing to me, but I also knew I needed it to get through the ugliness of life. There was one benefit of excessive drinking: a lean body, but my once muscular physique was now veering towards emaciated, apart from the area around my liver, which seemed to be protruding more than usual. My chest and back charted my miserable quest; the pocked scar of a bullet, three ragged cut-throat razor lines of smoothly slashed flesh, two jagged mounds of tissue healed over near-fatal knife wounds, and the burning lines across my back where I had been flailed with barbed wire.

I reached for my clothes, which I kept in the gap between the mirror and wall, and pulled on a pair of black jeans and a blue hooded top. I towel dried my hair, and took a final look in the mirror. A functioning member of society stared back at me, but I could see the true nature of the beast in my eyes. I put on my coat, left the pub and headed south.

Forty minutes later, I met Noel outside Kennington Police Station.

'You're late,' he said abruptly.

'Yeah, I got caught up,' I replied. I nodded towards the police station. 'You not going to take me inside? Offer me a tea?'

'Very funny.' Noel looked around furtively. 'Just being seen with you could get me walking a beat. You're bad news. Let's keep moving.'

We started up Kennington Road, heading north. Noel edged in to give passage to a strutting, rat-faced man who was walking an enormous, brutish Rottweiler.

'I could really use a favour,' I began.

'You're a fucker, you know that?' Noel interjected. 'You're in no position to be asking for favours.'

'Still, I could really use one,' I continued. 'Missing girl. Katie Blake. Ten years old. Police are on the case.'

'Talk to the detective in charge,' Noel replied coldly.

I stopped walking and pulled him to a halt.

'He isn't my friend.'

'We're not friends,' he said, stepping free. 'You don't have friends, Schaefer. You use people. But that's okay, so do I.'

I sighed. 'Then call this an investment. A favour for one or two in the future.'

He considered my offer.

'Three,' I said, and he finally nodded. 'I need information on any similar disappearances.'

'Anything else?' Noel asked sarcastically.

'Actually there is. I need to know if this symbol has been found at any crime scenes.' I handed Noel a photocopy of the mandala.

'This is like the one at Yates's house,' he observed. 'I sent the photographer down to the scene when I got your message. Where did you get this one?'

'It was in the missing girl's bedroom,' I replied.

'You think Yates was involved in child abduction?' he asked.

'Doesn't fit with what we know about him. There might be something bigger going on.'

'What?'

'I don't know yet,' I replied honestly.

I wished more than anything that I did.

'This wouldn't have anything to do with six paedophiles someone hospitalised last night?' Noel remarked. 'If you're going to do that kind of shit, don't tell me about it.'

'You found Taurn?'

He nodded. 'And the material. He's going to name the rest of his ring.' He hesitated. 'So you did good.'

'Worth another favour?' I didn't wait for him to reply. 'I need to know about the Church of the Eternal Light. I can't find anything about it online.'

'You're pushing your luck, Schaefer,' he said as he headed for the station. 'But I'll see what I can find.'

CHAPTER 30

Concerning Childhood Illnesses by Dr Alfred Stern
PATIENT JONES

When I returned to see Jones the following day, he continued where he had left off.

'Have you thought about your role in your wife's departure, Doctor?'

'No. Instead, I devoted my evening to considering the subject of specificity. The discipline of being specific is one that is inculcated into every notable scientific mind from the very earliest days of their training. We are taught to observe, to categorise and, most importantly, to question.'

'I see that you have decided to fall back on the old crutch of knowledge,' Jones began, but I interrupted him.

'How did my wife leave me?' I asked.

He hesitated.

'It suddenly occurred to me that you never said how she left me. If you can see that I played some role in her departure, then surely you can reveal how she came to leave me.'

For the first time since I had encountered the patient, I saw the uncertainty of a child.

'Or is it possible that you noticed I used to wear a wedding band?'

Jones composed himself, but it was too late; the power of the illusion had been broken.

'You seem determined to stay trapped in your little world, Doctor. We can help you. We can give you everything that you have ever wanted,' he said.

'And what if there is nothing I want?' I asked. 'Unhappiness stems from discontent with one's circumstances, believing that happiness comes from without, that the answers to the mysteries of life, the return of my wife, the alleviation of my persistent hip pain, will somehow engender a newfound satisfaction with existence. It may trouble you deeply to know that others do not suffer in the way you obviously do, but I am content. I am content not to know the answers to life's mysteries, I am content that my wife is no longer with me, and I am content with my hip, the pain of which has diminished to the point that I now consider it nothing more than an irritating old friend. And through my contentment with life, I have found happiness.'

'You're lying to me, and to yourself,' Jones replied. 'The Totus can give you everything you want.'

'What is this Totus? That's the second time you have offered me everything. And for the second time I decline. Instead of everything, give me one. Tell me how my wife departed.'

His eyes blazed with hostility.

'If you don't, then I will know you are nothing more than a charlatan who has learnt some clever tricks.'

'*Aqua est sordidum*,' Jones mumbled, as he went into some sort of trance. '*Aqua est valde sordida.*'

His eyes flashed open.

'I see pain. I see much pain.'

I betrayed no emotion.

'I see suffering. I see great sadness,' he continued. 'Your wife is dead.'

'Whoever has trained you should be congratulated on an excellent job. You almost convinced me, but I'm afraid my wife divorced me three years ago.'

'You're lying!' Jones suddenly raged.

'It caused quite a scandal. She left me for another man. The role I played in her departure was that of a neglectful husband with a compulsive devotion to his profession. I left a void in her life and someone else filled it. But enough of me. Let's talk about you.'

He turned his head away from me.

'I see,' I observed. 'Judging by the physical evidence, I would surmise you spent your formative years on the streets, and did whatever it took to survive. Open your mouth, please.'

Jones was still.

'If you fail to comply with my instruction, I shall summon orderlies who will force your mouth open. I'd rather avoid any unpleasantness.'

Jones did as I instructed, and I examined his teeth.

'A number of your teeth have a pronounced ridge of staining, which suggests to me your diet improved two or three years ago. I would hazard a guess that was when someone took you off the street.'

He said nothing.

'Now, on the matter of your parlour trick.'

His mouth curled into a slight snarl.

'Or your ability, if you prefer,' I continued. 'Someone has trained you to speak rudimentary Latin, a language which impresses the common man with its connection to antiquity. That same person has given you the burden of perception. Those sharp eyes are now always on the lookout for a person's vulnerability. Something you can exploit to place yourself in a position of power. Once you have power over a person, you can offer them your instruction, which really means recruiting them for whoever has trained you, doesn't it?'

He remained silent.

'Your injuries are consistent with a beating. Perhaps you failed in some aspect of your training, and were chastised. Perhaps, given your age, and the tempestuous feelings suffered by all young men of your years, you were aggrieved at your treatment and were compelled to escape. In the course of your escape, you eluded your pursuers but were injured in the process, which is how you came to be found, unconscious and helpless. Which is when you were brought here.'

His expression softened, and his lower lip trembled as though he might cry.

'I imagine your present feelings are somewhat confused, which is why you sought to revert to your training with me. It is what you know best. But you no longer have to pretend to be something you are not.'

Finally, I saw the young boy at the heart of the pretence. He broke down crying.

'Help me,' he pleaded. 'You'll keep me safe when they come. Promise me.'

I promised Jones he was safe and asked his real name.

'Duncan Olmsworth,' he replied.

'Is there someone we can contact for you? Your father? Your mother?' I asked.

'Father's dead. Died when I was a baby. Last I knew, Mum was on the street,' he revealed.

I told Duncan he had been through a difficult and tiring experience and needed rest. We would continue our conversation the following day. When I left, Duncan's face had changed. He was more relaxed and relieved. I informed the nursing staff of Duncan's true identity and asked for attempts be made to trace his family.

The following day I hurried through my rounds in order that I might spend additional time with Duncan. His promised to be a fascinating story. When I arrived at his room, his bed was empty and there was no sign of him. Sister Cole informed me that Duncan had been discharged first thing that morning.

His father had come to collect him.

I instantly regretted my decision to inform anyone of Duncan's true identity, and was almost certain that was how they found him. I made immediate and urgent inquiries with the police, but they had neither the resources nor the inclination to search for a missing urchin. Driven by my possible role in his disappearance, I scoured the streets of the city for weeks, searching for any sign of the boy, or this 'Totus'.

I found none.

In the months that followed, I began to question the source of my guilt. The boy had told me his father was dead, but it was impossible for me to verify that fact. Given his troubled past, it is more than conceivable he did not want to be associated with his father, and had long treated him as dead. A lie which he would tell any figure in authority lest his unwanted father be reintroduced into his life. I told myself the existence of an organisation that abducts children and trains them in mystical trickery would have been noted by the authorities or the local community, and that this 'Totus' was nothing more than the product of an adventurous imagination. Each day I try to convince myself I have allowed fanciful speculation to get the better of me. But then I remember Duncan's trickery. Trickery that had almost convinced me he was possessed of supernatural talents. Trickery which must have been taught over a period of months, if not years, by someone with considerable expertise in such matters.

Wherever Duncan is, I pray he is in good health.

CHAPTER 31

I put the pages down as the train rattled into the station. I'd decided not to drive to Milton House to give myself time to read, but Dr Alfred Stern's journal left me with more questions than answers. Was there a secret society that had been abducting children for decades, possibly centuries? To what end? How could a group like that evade detection?

I picked at Stern's story, pulling it apart line by line during the cab journey from the station to Gilmore's hospital, but I couldn't see what I was missing. When I arrived, Ken buzzed me in, and told me to wait in Dr Gilmore's office while he finished with his patients.

Gilmore had a large room on the second floor. It overlooked the parkland in front of the hospital and his large desk was situated between two sash windows. The office was a model of order and not a paper was out of place on the doctor's desk. The bookshelves that lined the other three walls were neatly arranged.

Cults in Our Midst; Faith, Healing, and Coercion; Combating Cult Mind Control; Surviving My Years in the Westboro Baptist Church – the books that lined the shelves ranged from modern pseudo-scientific accounts to ancient leather-bound tomes – *Of Devilish Incantations; Anima Comestores, Malum Intra Deos*. In an effort to know my enemy, I had read them all. There weren't many people familiar with *Anima Comestores*, which was over 600 years old and spoke of cults in terms of witchcraft, torture and inquisition.

I wandered over to one of the windows and saw a number of patients in the garden below. They looked peaceful enough, but I knew the storm that could rage beneath calm waters. These men and women were caught in a netherworld, cast free of the anchored certainties of cultish belief, drifting towards the choppy waters of the real world with its unfairness and uncertainty. Some shuffled around the garden slowly, and I took their movement as a positive sign, evidence of life, of forward momentum. Others sat alone on isolated benches that peppered the parkland, all wearing the same traumatised expressions I had seen on the faces of accident victims. The Traumas simply stared into space, completely bewildered at the change in their lives and their presence in a specialist mental institution. I knew within a few months, Gilmore's expertise would have the Traumas on their feet, moving slowly towards release from their misguided beliefs, shuffling to freedom.

Gilmore entered. He wore a Prince of Wales check suit, brown brogues and a startled expression. He had the nurse, Charlie, and two patients with him: the red-haired teenager, Anna, and the lustful Farah.

'What's he doing here? Is he going to fuck us?'

'Farah,' Charlie said, 'you know you're not to talk like that. Not even as a joke.'

Farah beamed and rolled her eyes like a rebellious adolescent, while secretly making lewd gestures at me with her hands. Anna didn't respond. She simply eyed me with the same intensity as last time, and all the times before that. I wished I could help her, but the frustration I felt must have been nothing compared to what Gilmore experienced.

'I didn't know you were coming, Thomas,' he said. 'We'll do our session another time, Anna, Farah. Charlie, could you take the ladies back to their rooms?'

'Of course,' she replied.

I sighed as I watched her go. Amber wouldn't have been much younger than her. Every time I saw a young woman of her age, I wondered what Amber might have done with her life, and what she might be doing now.

The three women left, and Gilmore crossed his office and clasped my hand.

'Good to see you, Thomas. You're well, I trust?' he asked.

'Surviving,' was the best I could say.

'What can I do for you?'

'I need to speak to Derek Liddle,' I said.

Gilmore was perturbed by the request.

'May I ask why?'

'That case you referred me. I found this in the girl's bedroom.' I handed him a photocopy of the mandala. 'Leon Yates's house was covered in occult insignia. That symbol was in his kitchen.'

'I see,' Gilmore said, returning the photocopy. 'Derek Liddle is a very troubled young man. I'm not sure how much use he'll be to you.'

'This symbol links the cases.' I indicated the mandala. 'I've asked the police to cross-check records of other crime scenes, but it would be stupid of me not to talk to Liddle. He knows what went on in those flats, what Yates was up to. Let me talk to him.'

'Of course, Thomas. I'm not about to refuse you anything. You can talk to him. Just don't expect too much.'

CHAPTER 32

The secure wings of Milton House were designed to be light, airy and pleasant. I followed Gilmore through a set of centrally locked doors, along a painted corridor. Metal mesh embedded in the thick glass windows threw a chequered shadow pattern on the brown rubber floor. The windows themselves were behind Perspex shielding, and every fitting in the wing was flush, covered and utterly safe. The doors to the patients' rooms were painted metal with a wood-effect inlay around a small reinforced glass portal.

I glanced into some of the rooms as I passed. The first patient, a dishevelled little man with long scraggly hair, sat on his moulded plastic bunk and stared at the wall opposite. The second patient, an earnest woman who would not have looked out of place behind the cashiers' counter of a local bank, paced up and down, talking to herself. The third patient, a distraught old man, pounded on the glass and pleaded with me to release him. I felt for them all. But with some bad luck and a little less anger driving me on, I could easily have been one of them.

'Mr Harker is having trouble adjusting,' Gilmore observed, nodding towards the agitated man on the other side of the door. Harker screamed abuse at him, and spat against the glass, but Gilmore remained serene and continued, 'He only arrived yesterday.'

Gareth, a short, surly orderly, opened another reinforced security door, and Gilmore stopped beside it.

'I'll leave you with Gareth,' he said. 'I've built up a level of trust with Derek and don't want it to be damaged by him seeing us together. His feelings about his capture are still somewhat confused.'

'You mean I'm the enemy?' I asked.

'The world is always so black and white with you, Thomas,' Gilmore replied.

I shook my head. 'It's nothing but grey. That's the problem.'

After I stepped through the doorway, Gareth swung the door shut, and the trio of internal locks latched into place.

'Follow me,' he said, and we set off down the corridor.

I glanced over my shoulder to see Gilmore walking back the way we'd come, shoulders slightly bowed, as though fatigue was getting to him.

The reinforced glass panel in the door to the interview room was a six-inch-wide, four-foot-long strip that ran from head height. Gilmore had phoned ahead, and I could see Derek Liddle inside, seated at a table with his back to the door. He wore Milton House's dark blue uniform and soft fabric shoes. Gareth tapped a code into a keypad, and the door buzzed open.

'I'll be right outside,' Gareth said.

Derek looked round as I entered and recognition flickered across his glassy, medicated eyes. Then came a faint smile, which didn't manage to make his expression look any less sour. The door clicked shut, and I could feel Gareth's eyes on my back.

'Life no good, huh?' Derek slurred. 'Time passin', clock's tickin', we all runnin', but stayin' oh so still.'

'You ever seen this?' I pulled the photocopy of the mandala from my coat pocket and pushed it in front of Derek.

'You driftin', Mister,' Derek mumbled, his eyes lost in the middle distance.

'What did you say?'

'Everythin' known to us, friend.' His voice was vague, like a soft breeze on a hot summer's day, but his words had the impact of a hurricane. I recognised them from Dr Alfred Stern's diary.

'What do you know about the Totus?' I pulled his collar, forcing him to look at me.

Gareth rapped on the door, and gave me a clear signal I should release the patient. I complied, but held Derek's gaze.

'What does this mean to you?' I pushed the image of the mandala into Derek's face.

I watched him carefully, but there was no reaction, not even the slightest hint of recognition. I produced the photograph of Katie Blake.

'What about her? You ever seen her?'

He looked at the photograph with the same blank expression. I crouched so that we were level.

'I know what medication they're giving you, so I know this junkie daze is an act. If you don't start talking, I'll have to use more direct methods.'

Derek suddenly focused and smiled.

'Hurt me if you want,' he said, his voice clear and lucid. 'I don't know anythin' 'bout that girl. Or the sign. I tole you everthin' Seigneur say.'

He was talking about Yates. Was Seigneur his rank? Or a nickname?

'What about the Totus?' I asked.

'What Totus?'

'You said, "Everything is known to us, friend."'

'Just words, man. Seigneur tell us they open a person's mind. Make 'em do whatever we want.'

'What else did Seigneur say?'

'Look, man. I don't know what you lookin' for, but you ain't gonna find it in here. Run on,' he replied, and his smile broadened.

I studied the self-assured man for a moment, before punching him so hard I knocked him off his chair. I knew I wouldn't have long, so I moved in quickly and followed up with a series of rapid, sharp kicks to his abdomen. I became aware of hands on me, rounded on Gareth and head-butted him. He fell back and I moved in with a right cross that knocked the orderly senseless.

Freed from further interference, I turned my attention to Derek Liddle, who whimpered as he crawled across the floor towards the open door. I stood over him.

'What else do you know?' I asked.

'Fuck you,' he replied and spat a gob of blood on the floor.

I was already angry, but rage consumed me. This man stood between me and my daughter. I crouched down, pushed him onto his back and punched his face and throat repeatedly until he was crying like a child. I heard footsteps echoing along the corridor. Lots of them, moving fast.

'Talk!' I yelled. 'Tell me what I want to know and I might not kill you!'

He tried to speak, but couldn't form the words, so I slapped him.

'Seigneur, he say...' He trailed off, drifting towards unconsciousness, so I slapped him hard.

'What did he say?' I demanded, as his bloodshot eyes focused.

'He say you talk to an old dragon,' Derek replied.

The words had a chilling effect on me and I staggered back as though he'd struck a blow.

'Seigneur say the dragon glistens in your tears as you cry about not being able to keep your women.'

I fell back against the wall, recoiling from the ugly words, my mind reeling. This was impossible.

'How do you know that?' I cried. 'Did she tell you? Did she?'

Derek looked at me, perplexed and afraid.

'Who you talkin' 'bout?' he asked. 'Seigneur. He tell me hisself.'

'You're lying,' I said. 'You're a liar.'

Only two people knew about the dragon, and I hadn't told anyone. Fear and bewilderment gave way to rage. This man was a liar. He was trying to exploit my misery to weaken me and had used some trick to gain knowledge he should never have had. He had to be punished. I had to punish him. I felt rage flood every pore and moved towards Derek with fierce purpose.

'Tell me how you know! Tell me! Tell me!'

The words became a vicious mantra as I kicked Derek Liddle repeatedly. He lost consciousness after the second kick, but I kept going. With rage drowning out all else, I didn't notice the people who stormed into the interview room, and barely felt the blow of the billy club when it bludgeoned my skull and sent me into oblivion.

CHAPTER 33

The sun shines through the trees. Leaves cast dappled shadows on the dry grass as branches sway in the gentle breeze. I am barefoot, and my feet crunch the brittle summer earth into dust as I move stealthily towards the big oak at the bottom of our garden.

She's hiding there.

She always hides there.

A flutter of purple flowers on pink cotton. A small, perfectly formed cheek. She can't resist peeking, but I know the rules and pretend I haven't seen her. I know her stomach will be churning with the excitement of the chase, anticipating that sudden moment of discovery.

The roar.

The run.

The hug. The rush of adrenaline giving way to the relief that it's all pretend. That she's safe, wrapped in my arms. That I'm never going to let her go.

I almost lashed out at the person who pulled me from the blissful dream where Amber and I were still together, but as my vision came into focus I recognised Gilmore just in time to restrain myself. I was lying prone on the couch in Gilmore's office and the old man was gently shaking my shoulders.

'Thomas, can you hear me?' he asked.

I nodded slowly, taking care not to aggravate the angry lump on the back of my head. The skin around the injury was becoming taut as it swelled. I reached up to touch it, and the dividend was instant and painful, setting my teeth on edge.

'This should help,' Gilmore said as he snapped an instant ice pack.

He handed it to me, and I sat up and pressed the gloriously cold plastic bag against the vindictive lump.

'I should never have let you see him,' Gilmore chastised himself. 'What were you thinking? You could have killed him.'

'He's alive?' I asked. My mouth was dry and sticky.

'If he wasn't, you'd be in police custody.'

Gilmore looked at me pointedly.

'He's in the infirmary. We'll log it as an accident,' he said with more than a hint of irritation. 'And I've persuaded Gareth not to press charges.'

'Thank you.'

'I know what you've been through, and I know how hard it is out there,' he continued, adopting a more conciliatory tone. 'But you must never bring that kind of aggression in here ever again. This is a place of healing.'

Another nod, tinged with contrition. Regret overwhelmed me as adrenaline ebbed away.

'It won't happen again,' Schaefer said.

'Of course it won't. I will never let you near another patient.'

His words only added to my shame.

'Was it worth it?' The doctor asked. 'Did he tell you anything?'

I hesitated. I had known Gilmore for many years, and was certain the doctor had nothing but honourable intentions, but one of my many hard life lessons was that no one could ever be fully trusted.

'He told me something he couldn't possibly know,' I replied. And that was all I would ever tell Gilmore about what passed between me and Derek Liddle.

CHAPTER 34

The man on the bike gave me a second glance as he cycled past with his family. He slowed his bike so he was at the back of the pack, a protective figure between his offspring and the haunted, brooding man whose eyes burnt with hatred as he walked alone through Dulwich Park. Apart from the cyclists, none of the other people around me gave a second glance. They were too involved in their own lives to notice what stalked through the park on this bright day. A mother chastised a crying toddler for misbehaviour as she struggled to push a baby in a buggy with a wobbly wheel. Grandparents with a pair of older children fed greedy birds by the duck pond. A young couple in tracksuits and trainers chatted as they jogged.

I walked the wide path across the park, past the café, crowded with parents feeding their broods. Happy, angry, sad, spoilt, gracious, jealous – whatever state these families were in, they were normal. I watched the men, women and children inside the busy café enviously, and wondered whether I would ever experience normality again. My earlier loss of control only put more distance between me and whatever passed for normal. I had fully intended to kill that man.

The incident with Derek Liddle had damaged my relationship with Gilmore, but I consoled myself with the one positive thing that had resulted from the violence: a new lead that took me down an old path. I continued through the park, past the busy playground where children squealed with delight as they spun, swung and slid. I branched off the main path to the exit that took me into Court Lane, an affluent, tree-lined suburban street.

I stopped outside a house I had not seen for years. An eight-foot-high sandstone-coloured brick wall split the double driveway. Two black wrought iron gates either side of the wall reinforced the impression the occupant was keen to keep the world at bay. I lifted the latch on the left gate, and walked up the driveway. A vintage gullwing Mercedes was parked outside the large Victorian house, which had two huge bay windows either side of a double-width door. The front garden gave a taste of the horticultural paradise that lay to the back of the building, and was crammed with trees, plants and shrubs. The house itself was covered in well-trimmed ivy, the pointing unblemished, the brickwork immaculate. It was as if time had stood still, but I knew the condition of the building reflected years of painstaking, expensive restoration by someone with a true passion for having things just so. Three storeys, nine bedrooms, five huge reception rooms. This place was the stuff of estate agents' dreams. I climbed the steps that led to the huge front door, and rang the doorbell.

Moments later the door opened and I was taken aback by the appearance of the young woman who answered. Blonde hair, striking sapphire eyes, about Sarah's height and build; she could have been Amber.

'Hello?' she said. 'Do you have an appointment?'

'No, no I don't,' I replied hesitantly. 'I'm an old client. Ellen knows me. The name's Schaefer. Thomas Schaefer.'

'Oh, Mr Schaefer,' she said, adopting a sympathetic tone I was very familiar with. 'I've heard about you. I'm sorry. Why don't you come in?'

I stepped into the porch, the walls of which were lined with the coats and jackets of countless unknowns.

'My name's Bernice, but everyone calls me Bernie,' she said as she took me further into the house. 'I'm Ellen's assistant.'

'What happened to Paula?' I asked, not taking my eyes off Bernie. She could easily have been my daughter. I'd always told myself I'd know Amber if I saw her, but would I? Ten years was a long time, and my child might have changed so much.

'She left,' Bernie replied. 'I look after Ellen now.'

The house was a throwback to a bygone era and everything in it venerated the past in some way. A seventeenth-century Thomas Tompion longcase clock held pride of place in the hallway, its simple case giving no hint of the grand timepiece's true value and importance. Next to it was an ebony occasional table, every inch of which was covered with tremendously detailed china figurines. The walls were lined with plush patterned fabric, and portraits of a long dead, distinguished family looked down at me.

'Are you from London?' I asked as casually as I could.

'No. Hamble originally, near Southampton,' Bernie replied. 'My mum and dad are sailors.'

'Oh,' I said, concealing my disappointment and the self-loathing I felt at being so desperate I'd allowed myself to believe a random stranger might be my child.

'Just wait here,' Bernie said, indicating the short bench that stood at the foot of the stairs.

She went through a doorway to the other side of the house. I didn't sit, and instead paced, examining framed family photographs that hung from the walls by the dining room door.

'Hello?' a voice said, and I put my head into the room to see a man and woman sitting on opposite sides of a huge table.

I'd been in the room a few times but it always struck me as out of place, too grand even for this house. The long, broad oak table, large oil paintings and high cabinets would have been more in keeping with a stately home.

The man was in his early thirties and looked Turkish or Syrian, and had the shifty look and flitting gaze of someone who wasn't comfortable in his own skin. The woman was early forties and exuded the calm confidence of someone who had the answers to all of life's questions.

'Are you waiting for Ellen?' she said.

I nodded.

'There's a bench in the hall,' she responded. 'That's where they like you to wait.'

I was being told to get lost in the politest possible terms.

'Mr Schaefer,' Bernie said with more than a hint of surprise. 'You shouldn't really be wandering around. I'll take you to see Ellen now if you'll follow me.'

She led me to the other side of the house, through the library, which always reminded me of a Victorian explorer's study, full of flourishing house plants, old books and curios, past a sitting room, and into a second, smaller hallway. We stopped outside a bare wood door, and Bernie knocked softly.

CHAPTER 35

'Come in,' a familiar voice said.

Bernie opened the door, and I followed her inside. Ellen Ovitz stared up at me from her tatty old armchair. She hadn't changed. Her curled, shoulder-length, light brown hair framed her chubby face, which, although normally warm and genial, was currently cold and stern. I had always guessed Ellen was in her mid-fifties, but she carried herself with a grandeur that gave the impression she was ageless. And despite her modest five and a half feet, Ellen was the most formidable woman I had ever met. I could never explain the dread she was able to conjure in me, a man who had faced down the most disturbing horrors. I felt her eyes upon me as I crossed the room and took a seat in the gnarly old sofa that matched her chair.

'Can I get you anything?' Bernie asked.

'I'm fine, darling,' Ellen replied. 'You?' she asked me in a most unfriendly tone.

'Nothing, thanks,' I replied.

Bernie withdrew and shut the door behind her.

There was an awkward moment of silence, during which Ellen studied me intensely. I shifted uncomfortably and my eyes darted around the room, looking for something to fix upon. There was the mahogany mantel, which was covered in crystals, small pyramids and protective symbols. Next to it was the large cluster of raw amethyst crystals. Beside Ellen's chair was the small fireplace, where a few lumps of coal and a couple of logs burnt gently. Above them the slate mantelpiece was cluttered with old family photos. A large gilded mirror clashed with the garish gold-flecked palm leaf wallpaper that adorned the whole room. There was a potted palm beside me and beyond it, I saw with a jolt of recognition, a small jade dragon that rested on the windowsill and stared out at the lush garden beyond.

The dragon I used to look at with tears in my eyes.

The dragon Derek Liddle could not possibly have known about.

'I was surprised to hear from you, Thomas,' Ellen began. 'We did not part on good terms.'

'Yeah,' was all I could manage.

'You told me what you thought,' Ellen went on. 'That you believe all this is nothing more than a fairy-tale and that I'm nothing more than a – what was the word you used?'

Ellen paused for dramatic effect. She had an incredible memory and I knew damned well she remembered exactly what I had said.

'Oh, yes, that's right, you called me a charlatan.'

'Maybe I was a little out of line,' I tried. I knew it wasn't going to be enough.

'There's one word I expect to hear from you, Thomas,' she said in the most matronly voice she could manage.

'Sorry?' I offered. 'I'm very sorry.'

'Good,' she said, her mood brightening instantly. 'So what brings you back to the fairy-tale?'

I felt the burden lift as Ellen's demeanour changed. Everything felt lighter, and even the air in the room, which had seemed oppressive, suddenly became fresh and revitalising. I'd said she was a charlatan because I'd been angry, but even as I'd spoken the words I'd known there was something very special about Ellen Ovitz. She had tremendous power to affect the world around her, but, like any human talent, if you chose to devalue it, to ignore or belittle it, you could eventually convince yourself that it had never existed in the first place. And that's what I'd done; chipped away at it until I didn't believe in her anymore.

'I don't know where else to go,' I replied. 'There are things happening that I can't explain.'

'What things?' Ellen asked.

'Have you ever told anyone about my visits?' I countered.

She seemed a little hurt. 'What? Of course not. I mentioned you were a client to Bernice, but have never given any details of our sessions to anyone. What happens in this room never leaves this room.'

'Not even in passing?' I pressed.

'Of course not, Thomas. You know how seriously I take my work.'

I nodded. 'I needed to be sure.'

I gave her the crayon note I had taken from Katie Blake's bedroom, along with a photograph of the missing girl.

'She looks like Amber,' Ellen observed instantly.

'A man going by the name of Leon Yates, in a completely unrelated case, knew Amber's name. He said it to me moments before he threw himself off the roof of a tower block. One of his associates said Yates told him I used to talk to a dragon and cry about how I wasn't able to keep my women.'

Ellen followed my gaze towards the dragon on the windowsill.

'You poor man,' she said. 'I warned you what would happen if you did not move on.'

'I have moved on,' I replied, a touch too defensively. This was how our last conversation had started. She'd warned me I would fail and die if I didn't let go.

'Amber is in your thoughts every day. You live in a blighted world. You haunt the shadows of other people's lives. You have not moved on, Thomas. You may not like the truth, but what use am I if I give you lies? Let me see what I can get for you.'

Ellen shut her eyes and felt Katie's photograph. I listened to the ticking of the gilded mantel clock and counted eight seconds before Ellen's response came.

'You're being played,' she said matter-of-factly.

'I know,' I countered.

'Listen,' Ellen responded with mild irritation. 'You're being played in a way you can't possibly comprehend. There's a block. Someone or something has placed a block around you. I've never experienced this. It's as though you don't have a future.'

'Am I going to die?'

She opened her eyes, which were tinged with uncertainty. It might even have been fear.

'It's not death,' she said. 'I don't know what it is.'

'Leon Yates said I face something worse than death,' I revealed.

'This Yates clearly had the gift. Let me see what I can get on him.'

She shut her eyes again, and I counted four ticking seconds, before there was a sharp intake of breath. Her face contorted as though she had encountered something disgusting.

'A heart of darkness. Very dark. But he was looking for more. Looking for a way to…' She trailed off, searching for the right words. 'You know I don't handle darkness very well, but this man was evil, and he wanted more. So much more. He wanted devilry.'

She opened her eyes and shuddered.

'I believe he was part of a group called the Totus,' I said. 'Does that name mean anything to you?'

'No. But if he was involved in it, I can only assume it is a thing of darkness. I don't like what you're doing, Thomas. The shadows are eating at your soul. You must leave all this behind. You must move on, Thomas.'

'What about the girl?' I asked. 'Her name is Katie Blake. Is she alive?'

Ellen looked at the photograph and closed her eyes. Five seconds ticked by.

'Yes, but she is not safe.'

'Any idea where she is?'

'No,' she replied.

'Will I find her?' I asked.

'You'll find the truth,' Ellen replied almost immediately.

She opened her eyes and put the photograph down on the arm of her chair.

'What's that supposed to mean?' My voice betrayed more exasperation than I'd intended.

'I don't get handed a set of instructions,' Ellen replied, somewhat defensively. 'I have to work to interpret what is gifted.'

'Sorry. I just don't want to let this little girl down. Or my own.'

'I know,' she replied. 'You poor boy. No one should have to go through what has befallen you. You're on a dark path, Thomas. You must turn away from it. You've got to listen to me, and move on. If you continue on, I foresee only pain, suffering and evil beyond that you have already experienced. Thomas, please, you must move on.'

'You lose your daughter and see how easy it is for you to move on!' I replied tartly.

Ellen's only reaction to my anger was a sad nod of her head.

'I can only ask you to do what you find possible. If what I have asked is impossible, then at least promise me one thing.'

My rage subsided.

'What?'

'A man is coming to see you with an offer. You must take it.'

'Who is he?' I asked.

'That's all I have,' Ellen replied. 'But listen to me, Thomas. When this offer comes, you must take it.'

CHAPTER 36

Ellen had seemed so convincing in the room, but as I walked away from her house, I reminded myself that no one could know everything. She told me my quest for Amber was doomed and that it would destroy me, but how could she know that for certain? And didn't I have to go down this path even if there was only a small chance of success?

I travelled by train to Hackney Wick, to a storage facility I'd rented in a huge warehouse, where I kept my journals and case files. The place was staffed twenty-four hours a day, and the four security guards who worked in rotation all knew me. Max let me into my lockup, which was located at the very back of the warehouse.

I sat on a tea chest and leafed through one of my old journals, considering the wisdom of my visit to Ellen Ovitz. Psychics worked in a similar, more benign way to cult leaders. They used sophisticated parlour tricks – cold reading, suggestion and aural hypnosis – in order to convince people of the truth of their prognostications. In reality, their words could influence the future only if one believed they could influence the future. 'You're going to meet a tall, dark stranger', would instantly make most people be on the lookout for a tall, dark stranger, and make them more receptive to an approach from someone of that description. I wondered why I had really gone back. I told myself it had been to confirm that she had not breached confidence and told anyone about our sessions. But maybe I had reached a place of such desperation I was ready to believe in the world beyond?

I looked at the yellowed page from my journal of four years ago.

Suspect gave no useful information even under stringent questioning. Stemmed the most serious blood loss and left him tied up outside the police station on Savile Row.

How long had I been doing this? The more terrifying question was how long could I continue? I'd seen action in the military, but combat was nothing compared to the sustained damage I was taking to body and mind.

Temple of Fire recruiting members in West London language schools. Will pay their head recruiter a visit.

I remembered the man had cried like a little girl, a strange high-pitched scream that had almost made me feel pity. But the Temple of Fire was a violent, subversive cult that believed in the subjugation of women. They focused on recruiting young women in their twenties to service the sexual desires of their leader, Solphan Ozwalt, born Stephen Oswald, and his cabal of priests. When the men grew bored with a woman, they sold her into the sex trade. Lindsay Miller, that was the name of the young woman I'd rescued. I still remembered the look of relief on her mother's face when the two were reunited. I'd cried then and was crying now at the memory of the jealousy, fear and grief I'd felt in case I never experienced such a moment with Amber.

Through the tears, I looked around the small storage unit and realised these boxes and books were my life now. If I died in a knife fight tomorrow this would be all I'd leave behind. My only hope was that Sarah would follow the instructions of my simple will and pass the contents of the unit on to Paul Baker. A morally reprehensible, corrupt scumbag, Baker was the best investigator I had ever worked with. If anyone could complete my work and find Amber, it would be him. My other hope was Oliver would one day forgive me for being the world's worst parent, leaving him with no memories of a loving father, nor any inheritance. Any money left in my estate would be paid to Baker to look for Amber for as long as possible.

I caught sight of my distorted reflection in one of the unit's metal dividers and felt ashamed. *Look at you, a pitiful excuse of a man, wallowing in the stinking filth of self-indulgence.* I wiped my eyes. No one else was looking for Amber. Everyone else had surrendered her to her fate. Not me. I would never leave her. I would never stop believing I could find her. I would never stop loving her.

When I felt weak, or tired, or my mind drifted to the evils that might have befallen her, when my nerves frayed and fear gripped my soul, I remembered the promise I made to always keep her safe. I would find strength in that promise.

This was just one of our games of hide and seek, and one day I would find her.

CHAPTER 37

I was dead to the world until a knock on the door roused me.

'You've got fifteen minutes,' Max said through the metal panelling.

The guards let me sleep in the lockup every now and then, but they liked me to be gone before shift change. I rubbed my face, stretched and checked my phone to see I had been sent a text message from a number I didn't recognise: *I need to see you urgently, Penny Blake.*

An hour later, I was on Penny Blake's doorstep on Addison Road. I had no idea why she wanted to see me. Did she want an update on the investigation? If so, I had nothing to share. I certainly wasn't going to mention what Ellen had told me about Katie. The moment the door opened, I realised I hadn't been summoned to give a progress report. Suspicion and hostility shone from Penny's red raw eyes. She stared at me for a moment, sizing me up as though I was vermin.

'You wanted to see me,' I said.

'You'd better come in,' Penny replied with rancour.

I followed Penny into the living room.

'Have a seat.'

I sat on the coarse brown fabric sofa next to the window and Penny took the chair opposite.

'Marcie had some concerns about you, Mr Schaefer. She did some digging.' She hesitated, and I guessed what was coming. 'Why didn't you tell me your daughter disappeared ten years ago?'

I didn't allow clients to interview me for a very good reason; they would not like what they found. I didn't want my people raking through my private life and using it to question my methods and effectiveness, so I had a policy of only working with people who were sufficiently desperate not to ask questions. I was about to leave when Penny picked up a manila folder that contained a bundle of printouts.

'The Internet lays all our secrets bare, Mr Schaefer,' Penny said as she examined the contents of the folder. 'Thomas Schaefer, ex-army. Dishonourably discharged ten years ago after being sentenced to six years for the attempted murder of Liam Cross.'

'If I'd tried to kill him, he'd be dead,' I interjected.

'Liam Cross was the leader of a cult called the Black Dawn, and it seems you blamed them for the disappearance of your daughter.'

Penny stared pointedly at me. I wasn't sure what she wanted me to say.

'I don't think I can have you working for me, Mr Schaefer. You seem troubled.'

I stood suddenly, and she flinched. Did she really think I was that unstable? That dangerous? I looked at the doorway. Walking out was the easy option, but Katie Blake had been kidnapped by the same people who had taken Amber, I was almost certain of it. I needed this case. I could look for Katie off the record, but it would rob me of valuable information Penny might share, and would put me into a very grey legal area.

I didn't work with people who interrogated my background, but I also didn't look for missing children. I'd broken one rule, perhaps it was time to break the other.

I pulled the crayon-scrawled note from my pocket and handed it to Penny. 'I found this in Katie's room the other day.'

Penny unfolded the piece of paper and sat seething for a while, her anger clearly building. She stood and slapped me hard, her eyes brimming wet.

'The police should have this!'

'The police wouldn't know what to do with it. I've been hunting the person who wrote that note for ten years,' I replied.

I sat down, slumping on the sofa heavily, and for a moment I felt defeated. I'd spent ten years looking for this person and they'd evaded my every effort. What made me think I could find them now? Penny was right; I should have given the evidence to the police.

She sat next to me, deflated and with a similar air of defeat. She sobbed for a while and finally took a series of deep breaths to calm herself.

'You think whoever took Katie also took your daughter? Cross? The Black Dawn?' she asked.

'I think it's the same person, but it's not Cross or the Black Dawn,' I replied. 'I put Cross in a wheelchair. He lives with family in Australia and needs constant care. The police put pressure on his group and it disintegrated without him. It's not them. Not after all this time.'

'How can you be so sure? Why did you suspect them in the first place?'

I hesitated. Nobody, not even Sarah, knew the whole story. I had been too ashamed to tell her. Gilmore had asked once, but had the good sense never to ask again. I looked at Penny's grief-stricken eyes and felt the eddies of desperation wash over me, corroding my tight-lipped resolve. This was the one person in the world who might be able to understand what I'd been through. She was going through it herself. Maybe I was tired of facing the world alone? Maybe it was a tacit admission my solitary and secretive methods had failed me? Maybe I wanted a connection with someone that wasn't grounded in disapproval, hatred or fear? I wasn't thinking clearly enough to understand my own reasons. All I knew is it felt right. For the first time in ten years, it felt right to tell someone the whole story.

CHAPTER 38

'It started with my sister,' I said. 'We grew up in Stoke. Our dad was a drunk who left when we were little. Mum did what she could, but we both got into trouble. Jess and I were both looking for answers. I found what I needed in the army. Eventually made it to Hereford. I tried to help Jess, but she just drifted through life going from one good time to another.

'I was in Afghanistan, picking up insurgents who were trying to cross the Pakistan border, when I got word that my sister had disappeared. I went spare, then I went AWOL, hitched a transport to Qatar, then got a ride on an oil company's private jet; a friend of mine was running security for them. I came back to London to find my sister.

'Jess and I, well, we didn't have what you would class as a traditional brother and sister relationship. She's two years younger than me, so we were always hanging around together. We'd squabble, but there were none of the hair-pulling, eye-gouging fights. We were best friends, but when I think about what finding her cost me, I just know I wouldn't do it again.

'I tracked her to this run-down shithole in Hackney. One of those four-storey Victorian terrace houses that have been left to rot. I don't know if they were there legitimately, but it looked like a squat. There were two dozen Black Dawn acolytes living in this five-bedroom house. It was a conditioning centre, where they indoctrinated new recruits before sending them down to the main compound in Sussex.

'I watched the place for three days until I'd figured out their routine and knew when Jess would be in the house. It was 4.00 am on the third night when I broke into the place. I went through the front door. They weren't particularly security conscious – just a Yale lock, which I forced with a plasterer's blade. Inside there was a guy asleep at the bottom of the stairs. I don't know whether it was because they didn't have the space, or if he was supposed to be a guard, but I smacked him hard to make sure he wouldn't wake up, and crept up the stairs. It was the first time I'd encountered a cult, and I was shocked by the squalor of it all. The one bathroom they had was barely functional and the smell of so many dirty people living in such filth was overpowering. The walls were covered with prophecies and drawings that were supposed to illustrate the coming apocalypse.

'I crossed the first landing and checked the two bedrooms on the first floor. Six sleeping women in each. Back then I couldn't understand what these beautiful young girls were doing there, but now I know that beauty is no guarantee of self-worth. These foul men preyed on damaged girls with low self-esteem and offered them belief in something bigger than themselves; a man they convinced them was a living god.

'Jess was on the second floor. I found her asleep in bed with one of the scumbags that had taken her away from us. This sweaty, fat, balding guy in his fifties was lying next to my sister. I couldn't get her out without the risk of him waking, so I tapped him gently on the shoulder until he opened his eyes. Before he could react to the sight, I throttled him. With my half-naked sister lying next to him, I was tempted to finish him off, but I'm no murderer. When he blacked out, I let go and he slumped back on the bed, breathing heavily. I put my hand over Jess's mouth and woke her. She tried to scream, but I held her. They had got to work on her mind, indoctrinating her against her family, turning her against me. I saw the hate in her eyes as she bit my hand. She drew blood, but I knew that I couldn't fight the six men who slept on the third and fourth floors, and tried to ignore the pain. When it got unbearable, I smacked her hard, and knocked her out. I slipped an old t-shirt over her, and carried her quietly through the house and out to my car. I knew it wasn't the end of it because we had to undo the damage done to Jess's mind, but I thought that was the last I'd ever see of the people in that foul place.

'The police recommended Dr Gilmore as an expert in cult deprogramming, so we took Jess to his hospital, Milton House. She screamed the whole way there, punched, kicked, scratched and bit me whenever she got the chance. I dragged her in, signed the committal papers, and handed her over to Dr Gilmore.

'From the first moment I met him, I knew he would be able to fix Jess, bring my sister back to me. I visited her every day for a week, and you could really see her getting better. At the end of my last visit she hugged me and apologised for what she'd done. I'll never forget that day. I cried like a baby. I had my little sister back.

'Amber was abducted fifteen days after I'd rescued Jess. It was the day after her tenth birthday. My wife and I were asleep in the next room. The police reckon whoever did it used gas to knock us out. We woke up that morning and she was gone. Her bed was made and her pyjamas were neatly folded under her pillow. There was a card on her pillow with exactly the same symbol as the one you found on Katie's bed. All Amber's toys were looking at her toy box. Hidden in an old crack in the lid I found a folded note that was written in exactly the same handwriting as the one I found in Katie's room.

'The note said *Schaefer, let's play*.

'I was convinced Amber's abduction was something to do with the Black Dawn, and I told the police, but they found nothing when they investigated the cult, so I went back to the house. I waited two nights, living as a derelict in an alleyway behind the house. I'd suffered worse in the service, so living in my own shit and piss for two days didn't bother me. Jess had told me Liam Cross was the leader, so I watched and waited until he paid the girls in the house a visit. The leader of Black Dawn, a living god come to get down and dirty in his East End slum.

'I didn't bother waiting for them to go to sleep. I kicked the back door in. The first two guys had knives, but I had a police baton. It was all I needed. I put them both down and ran upstairs. The next guy tried to pull an old revolver, but he didn't know what he was doing and couldn't fire it in time. I sent him down the stairs. The other three guys didn't give themselves enough space to take me on simultaneously, so I hammered them one at a time.

'The girls had been brainwashed to defend their masters, and were all over me, screaming like banshees. They could hurt me, but not badly, so I ignored them and climbed up to the third floor where I found Liam Cross with two naked girls. He'd heard the ruckus and had armed himself with a samurai sword. For a living god, the guy didn't have a clue. I disarmed him, broke his left knee so he couldn't run and bundled the girls out of the room. Cross alternated between begging me to let him go, and threatening me with wrathful vengeance if I laid my hands upon his divine person. I toppled the wardrobe so it blocked the door, and got to work.

'By the time the police smashed down the door, Liam Cross was mentally and physically broken. He would never walk again. I'd carried out enough interrogations in the field to know that a jumped-up egomaniac like Cross couldn't have resisted what I'd put him through. He'd told me the truth; he didn't know anything about Amber.

'The police took me in and I was charged with attempted murder. There were plenty of witnesses, and they'd caught me at the scene of the crime. The judge said there were mitigating factors, and gave me six years. I did three. Three years inside with my little girl slipping further and further away. I wanted to lash out. I wanted to kill the guards and escape. I wanted blood. But I knew that if I stepped out of line they'd add years to my sentence, and I needed to get out and find her. So the days went past and my life fell apart.

'The army kicked me out. Sarah couldn't handle the loss of Amber. She couldn't deal with me being stupid enough to land myself in prison when she needed me most. We divorced during the second year of my sentence. Jess killed herself in the third year. Hanged. They didn't find her body for three weeks. Her suicide note said she couldn't live with the guilt of what she'd done to me and my family.

'I almost lost my mind in prison. Can you imagine what it's like to know your little girl is out there? And to be trapped? Locked in a tiny room, unable to do anything to find her? The first year was hard, but I tried to use the second and third to learn everything I could about finding missing people.

'When I finally got out I went wild. I spent every waking hour, all the money I had, trying to find her. I hired investigators, badgered the police – I even got desperate enough to see a psychic recommended to me by one of the nurses who work at Milton House.

'When everyone else gave up, I kept working the case by myself. If you look hard enough, you'll always find something and I began to find other missing people on my travels. I started to build a reputation and soon specialised in recovering people from cults.

'Dr Gilmore helped. He talked me through the darkest days and began referring me cases – friends and families of people who needed to be rescued. He knew they would keep me occupied, and that with each investigation I had a better chance of finding a clue, link or someone who might lead me to my daughter. This world; this dark, brutal, violent, disturbing world became my life. I live and breathe to find my daughter and any other people the darkness takes.'

CHAPTER 39

Tears streamed down Penny's face. She opened her mouth a couple of times as though trying to speak, but the emotional strain of my story robbed her of words. Tears filled my own eyes. It was the first time I'd ever told anyone the whole story, and all the emotions of the past ten years swirled within me; all the anger, frustration, sorrow, hatred, self-loathing, failure flared anew as though I was living each and every horror for the first time. I wiped my eyes and tried to be strong. I had to be strong for Amber.

'I keep finding other people,' I said, aware my voice was cracking under the emotional strain, 'but all the time my little girl is fading away.'

Penny had hired me to find her daughter, to be a professional, but I couldn't control myself anymore, and wept freely.

'She was my little girl,' I cried.

Penny reached out and pulled me towards her. She squeezed me tenderly, and her kindness broke me. I was supposed to be strong for her, for her daughter, for my little girl, but I just couldn't. My world had crumbled and the last ten years had been disastrous. Penny sobbed too and buried her face in my neck. We both shook with raw emotion that was beyond words. She shifted and her face sought out mine. She kissed me, and driven by a simple need for comfort, I let her. She pulled away and looked at me with endless sorrow. Stripped of the veneer of logic and reason, made raw and laid bare by loss and longing, we were just animals seeking comfort in each other's arms. I leant forward to kiss her and she pulled me closer.

Neither of us spoke as she took me to her bedroom. We stripped each other's clothes, and the sex was tender but primal. Grief made us vulnerable and we were gentle with each other, but no words were spoken, and I think we both wanted this to be a healing experience. I relished the sight of Penny's smooth, unblemished body, and if she was perturbed by my scars, she gave no sign. I couldn't remember the last time I'd touched skin so soft, smelt a body so fragrant, or tasted lips so sweet. An expression of uninhibited pleasure swept Penny's face as she climaxed, and I was so pleased to take her out of her misery, but the moment I came inside her, I felt the weight of the world hit me. We'd lost ourselves in pure lustful pleasure, but it was transient and now we would have to return to the cold horror of our lives. I could see Penny felt it too and, as she rolled off me and pulled the covers around us, a sadness came over her. She turned on her side and faced the window, and I stroked a lock of her hair absently.

Feathered sunlight framed the edges of the heavy drapes, and as we lay there I listened to the sounds of distant traffic and a world carrying on regardless. I stroked her hair, trying to soothe her pain, until Penny's breathing got progressively heavier and she fell asleep. A few minutes later, I joined her.

CHAPTER 40

It had been years since I'd slept in a proper bed. I'd had the
sofa in the Royal Inn, the floor in my lockup and the
occasional night on the street. Penny's mattress was so soft I
thought it was going to consume me, and the blankets and
quilt comforted me with their cosy warmth. It took me back
to Sunday mornings as a child, when I'd lie in my bed,
listening to the birds outside my window, knowing I wouldn't
have to worry about my dad for a while because he'd be
sleeping off his Saturday night. I would wish time would slow
so I could stay in my little bed beneath my bedroom window
forever.

Penny was still asleep and her rhythmic breathing
soothed me. Her body was soft and warm and I tried to think
of the last time I'd been this close to a woman.

I resented my phone the moment it started ringing.
Penny stirred.

'Schaefer.'

'It's Noel. We need to meet.'

'Where?' I asked.

'Baker Street tube station. Northbound Metropolitan
line. Ten-thirty.'

I checked the time on my phone. I had an hour.

'I'll be there,' I said, before hanging up.

Penny turned to look at me. There was uncertainty in
her eyes. Did she regret what we had done? It had felt so
right, but now I wasn't sure. She was a vulnerable client and

our situation was already difficult without this added complication.

'I have to go,' I said, getting out of bed and pulling on my underwear and jeans.

Penny tugged the quilt over herself awkwardly, and watched me finish getting dressed. She was silent and I didn't know whether I should say something. I couldn't help feeling there was an atmosphere in the room, that she felt we'd made a mistake, maybe even that I'd taken advantage of her vulnerability. I hurriedly put my boots on, and stood awkwardly for a moment.

'I'll let you know if I find anything.'

I felt that kissing Penny would send the wrong signal, so I leant across the bed and took her hand and held it for a moment. I realised it was an odd thing to do, the instant I'd done it, but I was committed and tried to ignore her look of puzzlement.

'Thanks,' she said awkwardly.

I let go, left the bedroom and hurried out of her house without looking back.

CHAPTER 41

Baker Street Station was quiet. The homeward rush hour was long over, and the late-night revellers were yet to spill out of London's pubs and bars. The platform was peppered with a few white-collar types unlucky enough to have had to work late, a group of youths talking excitedly about a party that awaited them in Wembley, and a handful of tired manual workers who had spent fourteen hours toiling for minimum wage to keep the city's cogs clean and turning. I saw Noel standing halfway along the platform, and could tell by the way that the policeman deliberately avoided my gaze that something had made him very nervous.

He grabbed me when I was within reach, and pulled me close.

'What have you got me into?' he asked abruptly, not letting his voice rise above a whisper. 'I asked a few people about that symbol and the Church of the Eternal Light. A couple of hours ago I got a call back asking me about my interest. Do you know who it was from?'

I shrugged.

'MI5. The Security Service. The fucking heavy dudes. They wanted to know why I was asking questions about it, so I told them, and they wanted to meet you.'

'Here?' I asked.

'They said 10.30 p.m.'

I looked at the platform clock, which read *22.29*.

'I don't know what you've got yourself into, Schaefer, but you keep me out of it,' he said tersely.

The PA system came to life with the platform guard's voice. 'Ladies and gentlemen, the next train to arrive at this platform is out of service. The next in-service Uxbridge train is due in two minutes. Please stand away from the edge of the platform.'

We watched empty carriages roll into the station, until midway along the train we saw three suited men on opposing bench seats. As the train stopped, one of the suited men stood, scanned the platform and approached the set of doors nearest us. The doors opened and the man stepped out.

'Thomas Schaefer?' he asked.

I hesitated.

'Come on. Don't piss about.'

I looked at Noel, who shrugged. He was many things, but he wasn't crooked. Why would MI5 be interested in the Church of the Eternal Light or the symbol I'd found at the abductions? Why would they want to talk to me? I needed to know the answer to these questions and there was only one way to find out.

I eyed the man at the door and my instincts told me he was dangerous, but what choice did I have but to step further along the path? I followed the man into the carriage, and the doors closed behind us. Noel started to walk away before the train even started moving. He couldn't wait to be shot of me and my troubles.

I moved along the carriage and took a seat opposite the two men who had remained on the train. The man who brought me on board sat next to me and adjusted his suit in the manner of a nightclub bouncer who wanted to make a punter aware of his size. He was big, but I wasn't intimidated.

As the train pulled out of the station, I felt like an animal caught in a trap, but if they tried anything these men would find out that only made me dangerous.

The train gathered speed, and I studied my three companions. The one directly opposite, in the window seat, looked as though he could handle himself. The narrow line that ran down the man's cheek was a razorblade scar. His nails were cut short and his hands and fingers were rough and callused. A pronounced break in his nose, and a mashed-up ear that was hidden under mid-length brown curly hair, suggested someone who had been in his fair share of fights. The tall, athletic black man next to him was looking at me carefully. No obvious signs of danger, other than his eyes, which were cold and dead, like a shark's. Everything else about him suggested calm civility. His navy herringbone suit was lined with light purple silk. It was the kind of embellishment added by expensive tailors to make their conservative clients feel like adventurous trend-setters. Unlike his neighbour's shoes, Shark Eyes' were highly polished and the cut of the expensive leather suggested they might even be bespoke. Semi-precious cufflinks and a Patek Philippe completed the man's moneyed appearance. The shaven-headed Caucasian who had walked me onto the train had no neck. Rolls of flesh simply smoothed out from his shoulders to form the bald pate of his skull. His thick arms and barrelled torso were shrink-wrapped by his tight suit, and he watched me aggressively, almost goading me to try something.

The three men said nothing as the train sped through London. I knew they were testing me. A weaker man would have tried to make conversation, tried to ease the tension, but I knew better than that. Silence suited me. If they were expecting someone who would do the expected and follow their playbook, they would soon discover their mistake. I made it clear I wasn't the slightest bit bothered by them and turned my attention to the world rushing by. As I looked out of the window, I saw the blurred faces of travellers waiting on the platform at Finchley Road Station.

At Harrow-on-the-Hill, the train branched north, and after Chalfont & Latimer branched north again until it reached Chesham, the tiny station at the end of the line. Of the three, Shark Eyes stood up last, adding weight to my belief he was their leader. I followed them off the train, and caught a glimpse of a spectacled, liveried London Underground driver, who couldn't resist sneaking a glance at his passengers from the shadows of his cab at the front of the train.

As we walked through the station, there were no signs of life. The only things watching us were the ever-present closed-circuit television cameras. Waiting outside the station in the otherwise deserted taxi rank was a black Mercedes M-Class. A squat, heavy-set man, who could have been No Neck's twin, leant against the driver's door and smoked a cigarette. He was holding something in his left hand. As we approached, the smoker tossed his cigarette and revealed a black canvas hood.

'Put this on,' Smoker said.

'No chance,' I scoffed.

'Put it on, Mr Schaefer,' Shark Eyes said. 'And we will help you find your daughter.'

I realised why they hadn't bothered talking to me. They knew everything they needed to know. My one overriding purpose gave them all the power over me they could ever wish for.

I took the hood and pulled it over my head.

CHAPTER 42

The hood was very effective, and I couldn't see anything in the total darkness. Rough hands patted me down, presumably searching for a wire.

'You'll get these back,' one of them said, as my wallet and phone were taken.

I felt hands on my shoulders.

'In you get,' someone said, as I was guided onto the back seat of the Mercedes.

I was pushed into the middle and I felt people get in either side of me. Doors slammed and moments later there was the quiet rumble of the engine, and the car pulled away.

The driver took us on a twisting and turning journey, changing direction, speed and doubling back every so often in what I'm sure was an attempt to disorientate me. He was probably unaware the army had trained me for this eventuality. The palm of my left hand was divided into imaginary quadrants, each corresponding to a compass position. The car had been parked facing due east, and as it changed direction, I placed my middle finger in the corresponding quadrant. The system was imprecise, but it was better than nothing. My right hand measured time travelled in each direction. Each of my right fingers was assigned a compass heading: north, south, east and west. By counting seconds, I was able to build a rough estimate of time spent travelling in each direction.

By the time the car slowed, and I felt a breeze as the driver's window was rolled down, I calculated we had been driving for fifty minutes, but the net effect of all the direction changes was thirty minutes travelling north.

The four men had been silent throughout, and the first voice I heard came from someone outside the car.

'Passes, please.' Whoever it was didn't sound in the slightest bit perturbed by the sight of a hooded man on the rear seat. There was a pause, then, 'Thank you, sir, please go ahead.'

The car drove for two minutes and sixteen seconds, before coming to a halt. I heard the doors open, and felt the two men on either side of me get out. I was eased off the back seat into a standing position, walked across a hard road surface, up a kerb, across another hard surface, and then up eight six-inch steps. I was held back for a second and heard the beep of a swipe card and the dull click of an electric lock. Nudged forward, I felt the change in temperature and ambient sound as we stepped inside a building. Sharp heels crossed a hard floor.

'Good evening, sir,' another voice said.

We had been walking for a minute and forty seconds since leaving the car. I heard the sound of another security door opening, and we moved from an expansive space to a small one, probably a corridor. The floor was carpeted. I counted thirty paces before a hand on my shoulder pulled me to a stop.

The hood was removed, and I squinted into the sudden burst of light. The figures around me came into focus; Shark Eyes directly ahead, No Neck to his left, Smoker behind his left shoulder, and Scarface behind his right. The corridor was instantly forgettable. White walls, blue carpet, guards in suits at either end. I guessed the black double doors to our right led to our final destination.

'What you see next never leaves this building,' Shark Eyes said plainly. 'Do you understand?'

I nodded.

He pushed the doors open and took me into a large situation room. Half a dozen men and women worked at computer terminals dotted around the place. Large flat screens on the side walls displayed images of the aftermath of terrible accidents and terrorist attacks. The far wall was covered with dark brown hessian and pinned to the fabric were hundreds of photographs of similarly troubling incidents: violent crimes, murder, arson, bombings, interspersed with posters of missing people, news clippings and crime scene photographs. I drifted closer in astonishment as I realised that there was something pinned to each item: *a mandala card.*

CHAPTER 43

'This is our case,' Shark Eyes began. 'Hundreds of crimes with a single connection. Three days after they occur, a photograph from the crime scene and one of these cards are mailed to the local police station. Murders made to look like accidents. Mass murder disguised as catastrophe.'

'Someone is behind all this?' I asked in disbelief.

'We think there are multiple individuals involved,' Shark Eyes replied. 'But they answer to one individual. The police got nowhere, so the government tasked my team with bringing the perpetrators to justice.'

'How long have you been working on this?'

'Five years.'

'You people and your damned secrets,' I said, my eyes dotting from one missing person poster to another. I'd often felt there was something bigger happening, that I was caught in a web whose edges I couldn't see. 'If I'd have known sooner, I might have been—'

'You know now,' Shark Eyes cut me off. 'Follow me.'

Shark Eyes led me to a whiteboard covered with photographs. It was the organisation chart of a criminal enterprise, with a number of gnarly-faced men and women populating the lower levels. The ranks grew thinner up the levels, until, at the very top, isolated and alone, was the photograph of one man. Caucasian, about sixty or seventy years old, grey hair, thin face, tight lips and sad, unyielding eyes.

'This is Edward Lomas,' Shark Eyes said. 'He leads a cult known as the Totus.'

I felt a rush of excitement. This was it, the key I'd been searching for. The way in. This man. This Edward Lomas would lead me to Amber.

'We believe he has masterminded all these crimes, including the kidnappings. He knows what happened to your daughter, Mr Schaefer. We've tried everything we can to find him, expended all our resources, but he's elusive. We think your experiences might give you a different take on things. You might be able to see things we've missed. Help us find him and we will get your daughter back.'

'What's his story?' I asked, looking at the photograph of the man I now hated more than anyone else on Earth.

Let's play, Schaefer.

Hello, Schaefer. It's been a long time.

Had Edward Lomas written the notes to me? Or had they been written by an underling on his instruction?

'He used to earn a living as a psychic. Hard to believe people get fooled by such things,' Shark Eyes said.

I was too angry to feel any embarrassment about my relationship with Ellen Ovitz.

'He disappeared eight years ago. Just vanished,' Shark Eyes revealed. 'We think that's when he became leader of the Totus.'

'Someone should've told me,' I said. 'Someone…I might have…'

'We couldn't, Mr Schaefer. Very few people know about this. It's too sensitive,' Shark Eyes said. 'You have an impressive talent for finding people. This is a chance for you to do some real good. Find him. Put an end to this. And bring your daughter home.'

CHAPTER 44

I sat hooded and alone in the back of the Mercedes and considered what I had just been shown. If Noel hadn't vouched for these people I might have thought they were paranoid nuts, but they were MI5 and had presented me with evidence of a conspiracy so extensive it was beyond my wildest imaginings. It would involve tremendous planning and effort to inflict such evil upon the world, but the one thing Shark Eyes had not been able to tell me was why he thought anyone would go to such lengths. How did these people benefit from perpetrating such horror? Was this the deal Ellen Ovitz had spoken of? I hated myself for resorting to the occult, but had she known I would meet these men? Was this what she'd meant? That I would find Amber if I took on the job of locating Edward Lomas?

My return journey to Chesham Station was similar to the one out, only this time I didn't measure direction or distance. Instead I clasped the thick folder Shark Eyes had given me, which contained all the information he and his team had on Edward Lomas.

When the car stopped, my driver, Smoker, removed the hood, and returned my wallet and phone.

'There's a new number on it,' he said. 'It's listed under Esme. Call when you need to reach us.'

I got out of the car and watched it drive away. I had no intention of calling anyone when I found Edward Lomas, not until the old man had told me exactly where to find Amber.

When the car was out of sight, I crossed the road towards a lone taxi waiting in a rank on the other side.

'Hackney,' I said, as I climbed into the back seat.

'That's a stretch,' replied the bearded driver.

'Fare plus a tenner in it for you.'

He nodded, and as the cab pulled away, I pointed at the driver's mobile phone, which was charging in a holster on the dash.

'Any chance I could borrow your phone?' I asked. 'One of my mates dropped mine and I need to call someone.'

I was almost certain that in addition to a contact number, the nameless spies would have added a bug to my phone. I'd have to pick up a replacement in the morning, but in the meantime, paranoia would serve me well.

'Go ahead, mate,' the driver said, handing me his phone.

I dialled a number I'd committed to memory and the call went through to the manufacturer's generic voicemail. Paul Baker was not known for answering calls from numbers he didn't recognise, so I dialled again. On the third attempt, I heard a familiar gravelly, slurring voice answer. He sounded like such a degenerate.

'Hello,' Baker said.

'It's Schaefer.'

'Do you have any fucking idea what time it is?' he demanded.

'I'll be at your office in an hour.'

'Fuck that,' he scoffed. 'Whatever it is can wait until morning. I'm entertaining.'

I shuddered. Baker's idea of entertainment was procuring the services of at least two young prostitutes for the night. Twenty, maybe twenty-one; as Baker put it, old enough to be legal, young enough to feel fresh.

'I can always make a home visit,' I replied.

There was a pause, as he considered the implications of disappointing me. He knew I wasn't a forgiving man.

'Okay, okay, I'll see you there,' he relented.

I hung up and returned the phone to the driver.

'Thanks,' I said.

'No problem, mate,' the driver replied as he steered the car towards the city.

CHAPTER 45

It was gone 2.00 am by the time we reached Whitechapel Road. No amount of new money could wash away the ingrained filth. New buildings went up and within a few years they had absorbed the rotten aura that permeated the area. Windows covered with grime, doorways soaked in urine, graffiti, garbage…Maybe Whitechapel was proof London's underbelly could never be bulldozed out of existence.

The taxi pulled up outside The Rocket, a rough nightclub that attracted a grim mix of city workers seeking adventure, clueless students, minor criminals, dealers, hustlers and underage local girls looking to take advantage of the club's lax door policy. As I paid the driver, four girls spilt out of the club. One of them was sick in the gutter behind the cab, while her friends, barely able to fend for themselves, tried to comfort her. Short skirts, heels, skin mottled and goose-bumped in the cool night air; these girls were probably even too young for Baker to consider.

'This one's free,' I said, indicating the taxi. 'You be alright taking these ladies home?' I asked the driver, and he nodded.

One of the girls focused on me, smiled and rallied her friends into the car as I headed for Baker's office.

The Whitechapel Kebabish was packed with drunks eager for something to soak up their worst excesses. The pavement outside was covered with detritus: mashed chips, grease stains, discarded packaging, wilted salad and congealed meat. Two drunks leant against the takeaway window and wolfed down their food. I stopped by the reinforced metal door next to the kebab shop, and the drunks didn't even give me a second glance as I pretended to take a leak. In reality, I was using a set of pocket tools to work the locks to Baker's office.

A minute later, I was inside the derelict hallway, and shut the steel door behind me. The paisley carpet was a stained hangover from the eighties and ranged from old and dirty by the door, to almost non-existent and threadbare as it ran up the uneven stairs. I climbed them and passed a large brass sign that listed the names of dozens of companies that paid Baker for the use of his address. I crossed a small waiting area that consisted of two plastic chairs, a tiny round table covered with a grey lace doily and some old magazines, and a tired old fish in a tiny tank.

I opened a door with a sign that read *Baker & Baker Collections Agency, Debt Recovery and Asset Foreclosure*. The office Paul Baker shared with his younger brother probably did more to put off prospective clients than any of the Whitechapel filth and ne'er-do-wells outside their door. An old desk was buried beneath mountains of ageing paper. There was a bin full of discarded fast food containers, and there were filing cabinets and shelves overflowing with documents. Almost every spare inch of floor space was covered with stacks of folders and papers. Fire hazard? Hoarder's dream? There were many ways to describe this office. The home of one of London's best investigators was not one of them. Reprehensible in his morals, disgusting in his personal habits, Paul Baker was nonetheless the person I had entrusted with finding my girl if anything happened to me. The short, chubby man was the most tenacious investigator I'd ever known, and had an uncanny knack for out-of-the-box thinking. If I was a hunter, he was a tracker. We met when I'd been hired to find the son of Ronald Nash, a notorious East End gangster. Nash insisted Baker, who had done what he euphemistically termed 'debt-recovery work' for him, was part of the investigation. Initially resistant, I'd been impressed by the man's doggedness and results, and we'd collaborated on a handful of cases since.

I picked my way through the clutter and took position by one of the two large sash windows that overlooked the street. After a minute or so, I saw a figure roll out of Vallance Road and head towards the building. Roll was the best way to describe how Baker moved. Five-foot six, he accentuated his rotund look by hunching his shoulders and pushing his hands deep into the pockets of his tatty old hoodie. The hunched shoulders and downturned head were his attempt to get through life without being noticed or bothered, but it did make him look like a ball on a pair of fast-moving pins. Baker always walked quickly, as though being outside made him feel exposed. I got the impression he only really felt safe when seated, either behind his desk, in his favourite chair at home or in his car. Baker's curly, greasy shoulder-length hair was showing touches of grey, and his ragged stubble made him look older than his forty-three years. He wouldn't score highly for stealth; when he entered the building and started up the staircase, he tripped and let out a loud curse. I heard him pick himself up and lumber to the top, where he engaged the fish in conversation.

'You alright, Buzzy Boy?' Baker asked, his normally deep, gruff voice taking on a playful tone. 'Been keeping an eye on the place?'

The door opened and Baker started as he turned on the light and caught sight of me. He put his hand to his chest.

'Fuck, Schaefer!' Baker exclaimed. 'Are you trying to kill me?'

'You need a better guard fish,' I said dryly.

'Let's get this over with. I've got two girls on the clock.'

I shuddered, but his pleasure wasn't my business. I handed him a photograph of Edward Lomas from the folder Shark Eyes had given me.

'His name is Edward Lomas,' I said.

'And this couldn't wait until morning?' he asked condescendingly.

I marched through the office, knocking stacks of paper and files this way and that as I closed on the little man.

'You're going to look for this man like your life depends on it.'

He clocked how serious I was and dropped any pretence of being my equal.

'Sure. Whatever you say, Schaefer. I'll get on it right away.'

'I'll be getting a new phone number tomorrow morning. I'll call to give it to you. I'll expect your first progress report.'

'Okay. No problem.'

'I knew you'd do the right thing,' I said, putting Shark Eye's folder on Baker's desk. 'Make a copy.'

'Of course.'

'Good man,' I said as I left the office.

When I shut the door, I heard Baker say a quiet, 'Motherfucker!'

I started down the stairs but stopped halfway to listen to Baker on the phone.

'Billy,' Baker said to his brother. 'Yeah, I know what fucking time it is. I'll explain when you get here. Get out of bed, you lazy fuck! Yeah I'm serious. On your way over, drop by my place. There's a couple of girls there. Pay them and kick them out. Yes, now. It's Schaefer. Yes, that Schaefer. We've got to get to work.'

CHAPTER 46

Sarah is pregnant. She stands at the edge of the lake with my gorgeous little girl. Amber's smile warms my heart when she turns and waves me over. The day is so perfect, but a troubling thought nags at me as I walk towards them; there's something wrong.

The feeling is palpable and I scan the park for danger, but everything looks perfectly fine. This isn't Afghanistan. There's no danger here. It's a bright summer's day and the Dulwich families are out in force. Ice creams are being eaten, balls are being kicked and ducks are being fed.

Don't look.

The words echo around my head, but no lips have spoken them. I'm unsettled, but feel compelled not to say anything. I don't want to scare my family.

'That one is cheeky,' Amber says, pointing to a fat drake with a twinkle in his eye.

She throws a generous crust of bread at the duck, and he gobbles it greedily.

'He looks almost as cheeky as you,' I say with a strange sense of inevitability.

I'm like a train running on its tracks, unable to change direction.

Don't look.

The voice of a woman. I don't recognise it, but I do remember it. We haven't met yet, but we will. It's the voice of someone I will come to know well.

Something's wrong, *I think as I look at Amber and Sarah, lost in the simple happiness of feeding ducks. The bright sunlight catches the crests of the tiny waves on the lake, sparkling and shimmering. Perfection, or as close to it as I'll ever get.*

Don't look.

The voice is more urgent. More insistent. I feel the sudden urge to look at everything. There's nothing to fear. Everything that means anything to me is right by my side.

'That one doesn't look well,' Amber says.

'Which one, sweetie?' I hear myself ask.

'Down there,' Amber says, pointing towards the lip of the pavement that runs around the lake.

Don't look.

The voice is insistent, matronly.

'I can't see anything,' I say, stepping closer to the edge.

'Yes you can, Daddy,' Amber says. 'You can see him.'

She's right. I see something.

Something terrible.

A man's face, grey with death, staring up from beneath the perfectly calm water. The left side of the man's skull is broken and his hair is matted with blood. I know this should terrify me, but I look at Amber and am reassured to see she is calm.

It's a perfectly fine day. The dead man in the water is nothing to worry about.

'He's trying to get out,' Amber says.

I turn back to the corpse.

Edward Lomas.

The name comes to me suddenly, but it doesn't mean anything. The grey face ripples with movement, and Edward Lomas's eyes open. They are completely white.

'Infusco revolvo.' The dead man's voice fills my head.

I turn to ask Amber what the words mean, but she is gone. In her place stands Ellen Ovitz.

'Don't look,' she says, and now I recognise her voice. She is my guide.

The world loses any semblance of reality and there is an instant when I recognise this is a dream built of memory. A beautiful day in Dulwich Park with Amber and Sarah. One of our last together. I want to stay there, in that moment, but I'm pulled away by an incessant sound.

I experience a sudden rush of consciousness, the profound and disorienting transition from dreaming to waking.

CHAPTER 47

My phone was ringing. I was splayed on the old Chesterfield in the Great Room at the Royal Inn on the Park. Papers from Mather's box folder were spread all over the place, along with a selection of journals and files I'd brought back from the storage locker at 4.00 am. A half-empty bottle of rum lay at the end of the sofa, an accomplice in crimes perpetrated against my pounding head. I touched it gingerly as I answered the phone.

'Schaefer.'

'Where are you?' It was Sarah, and the sound of her angry voice sparked a memory: it was Sunday. The third Sunday of the month. I checked the time and realised I was late. It was almost 11.00 am.

'I'll be there,' I replied.

'He can't take much more of this,' Sarah began, but I cut her off.

'I said I'll be there.'

I got to my feet, put on my jacket and left the room as fast as I could.

It took me twenty-five frantic minutes to get to London Bridge and my train south was ten minutes late departing. By the time it got moving I wasn't sure whether my churning stomach was the result of the previous night's drinking or the nervous guilt at letting my son down.

There was nothing I could do to fix things on the train, so I tried to unpick what I'd read the previous night after I'd returned from the lockup. The trawl through my journals proved fruitless. I'd never encountered anything about an Edward Lomas or the Totus. My reading just reminded me how little progress I'd made. Leads that went nowhere, suspects who knew nothing, prospects withering on the vine. My written account of the past few years gave me the feeling that I was moving in ever-decreasing circles. Shark Eyes had given me the only truly promising lead in recent memory, and I had no intention of letting Edward Lomas slip through my fingers.

Mather's box file had yielded little in the early hours. After scouring my journals, I read translated pages from *Excommunicare*, an arcane manuscript created by the Sacred Congregation of The Holy Office of the Inquisition in 1588. The text was aimed at inquisitors and had been written with the purpose of codifying the process of identifying and outing heretics. Much of it dealt with the processes that could be used to extract confessions from wayward individuals. The text also dealt with the punishments that would appropriately chastise the heretic and show the Church's resolve in dealing with devilry. I was shocked to read about such torture and murder carried out in the name of what was supposed to be an omnipotent God. Why did an all-powerful being need the protection of violent men?

Among the sanctified violence, I had found a passage on *Il Totus*. It commanded any inquisitor who discovered a member of *Il Totus* to refer the case to a higher authority and send the accused heretic to Rome for judgement. I wondered why this organisation had been singled out for special treatment. Were its crimes so much worse than anyone else's? Or did the Totus's reach extend to the Church of St Peter?

To Rome itself? Would the Totus heretics be given sanctuary and allowed to slip quietly out of the Vatican unmolested? I needed to talk to Mathers, find out what the bookseller had discovered. I also needed to keep the pressure on Baker to make sure he didn't slack in his hunt for Edward Lomas.

I opened the carrier bag between my feet, and pulled out the phone I'd bought from a shop in the station. I assembled it and switched it on. The battery would soon die, but there was enough power for me to send texts to everyone who mattered, informing them of my new number. If Shark Eyes and his people had bugged my old phone, they were going to be disappointed. It was still back at the pub.

I disembarked at Norwood Junction and walked the three miles to Sarah's place, a small terraced house in West Norwood she bought after we sold our family home. She must have been watching from one of the front windows, because she opened the door as soon as I came through the garden gate.

'You're two hours late!' Sarah fumed.

I stumbled over the front step and caught the porch wall to steady myself. It wasn't the sort of arrival that would impress.

'Look at you,' Sarah seethed.

'Please. Keep your voice down,' I tried.

'If you don't want your son to be ashamed of you, stop doing shameful things.'

'I'm sorry. I'm here now,' I said quietly. 'I'm really sorry.'

'You're not taking him like this,' she countered loudly.

'Like what?' I asked. 'I was working late.'

She leant in to smell my breath, and quickly backed away.

'Bloody hell. Are you still pissed?' she asked.

'No, I'm not,' I protested, but in truth I wasn't sure. 'I just haven't had much sleep.'

'Sort yourself out,' she said. 'You know where the bathroom is.'

She stood aside and allowed me to pass. I flushed with shame and humiliation, and knew I was beaten, so I hurried straight upstairs and locked myself in the bathroom.

CHAPTER 48

Sarah and Oliver sat in silence. I caught sight of them as I came down the stairs quietly, and what hurt me more than Sarah's disapproval was the miserable look on my son's face. He didn't want to spend the day with me, well, what was left of it. I couldn't blame him. I was a terrible father and knew it, but like an addict chasing an elusive high, I couldn't let go. Amber meant too much to me, and I kept telling myself if only I could get her back I could patch things up with Oliver, but he was getting old, and there would come a point at which I wouldn't be able to undo the damage.

I walked into the shabby chic living room, decorated with hand-me-downs and mismatched reclaimed furniture. Sarah was careful with money and earned just about enough from part-time nursing to provide for her and Oliver. A handful of photos of her and Oliver dotted the room and there was one of the three of us together as a family on top of the old upright piano in the corner. None of Amber, but I knew better than to ever point that out again. I'd mentioned it once before, and Sarah had exploded, accusing me of self-righteousness. She'd pointed out I was in fact a reckless drunk who refused to let himself believe his daughter was dead. That had been one of our worst fights, and unlike the physical wounds I'd suffered, the injuries inflicted by Sarah's words never healed. I wondered if she had any idea how much I still loved her and Oliver and how much anguish I suffered not being with them.

She stood up awkwardly as I entered. My quick shower had taken the edge off her resentment.

'There's a fair in the park,' Sarah said. 'Oliver's wanted to go all week, but I thought it was the sort of thing you two might enjoy doing together.'

'Sure. Sounds good,' I said enthusiastically. 'You up for some fun, boy?'

Oliver looked at his mother, who smiled encouragingly. He turned to me and nodded uncertainly.

'Well, let's get going then,' I said, ushering him towards the door.

'Have fun,' Sarah said as she watched us leave.

We walked along Linton Grove in silence, heading for Norwood Park. Grey clouds obscured the sun, but it was just about warm enough for an afternoon at the fair. I struggled to think of something to talk to him about, and my search made me realise how little I knew about my son. What was his favourite music? Film? Food? I had no idea. I reached for something, anything to break the silence.

'Mum's still got you wearing that coat.' I nodded towards the faded blue parka that was a size too small.

'Yeah,' Oliver replied. 'She says I can have a new one for my birthday.'

'Very sensible, your mum,' I noted, and we continued on in silence, me feeling more of a failure with each wordless step.

Someone had torched the public toilets and the charred remains greeted us when we entered the park. Oliver didn't even ask why someone would do such a thing.

'It shouldn't be like that,' I said suddenly. I didn't want my boy to think this was normal. 'The world, this place, it should be better. You shouldn't go through life expecting this sort of thing.'

Oliver looked pleased, if somewhat bemused by my sudden burst of paternal advice.

'Okay,' he replied uncertainly.

The fair had been erected on the large playing field near the ice cream kiosk. It was the typical collection of thirty-year-old rusty rides that looked more likely to result in death than pleasure, but Oliver's face lit up as he surveyed the garish signs, gaudy decorations and bright lights.

'Can we go on the wheel?' he asked excitedly. 'And the dodgems?'

'Whatever you want,' I said with a smile. I was just relieved to see him happy.

'A ghost train!' Oliver exclaimed, pointing at one of the least terrifying structures I'd ever seen. A huge, peeling balsa wood Grim Reaper loomed over a cartoon crowd of terrified people who were trying to avoid his sweeping scythe.

'Zero G!' Oliver yelled, pointing at an old-fashioned round-up. 'I wanna go on that one first!'

'Well, let's go then,' I said with a smile.

I bought a book of ride tokens from the grimy old man who sat in a booth at the centre of the fair. With one arm and one leg missing, the old man wasn't a particularly good advert for the safety of the rides, but as he ferreted for my change he explained he'd lost them to diabetes. Oliver was fascinated by the old amputee, and I had to nudge him a couple of times to get him to stop staring at the man's limbs.

'Come on,' I said. 'I thought you wanted to go on the Zero G.'

We walked over to the ride. Riders stood against the inside of a wheel, which spun so fast it forced them back against a metal mesh rim. The loudest screams came when the floor dropped away and riders were held in position by centrifugal force. I handed three tokens to the teenage attendant.

'You not having a go, Dad?' Oliver asked.

'Not my thing,' I said, noting his disappointment. 'We'll go on something else together.'

Oliver brightened and joined the short queue. I leant over the barrier and watched the ride come to a halt. A crowd of queasy, unsteady people left through the exit, and the next batch of victims was allowed in. The attendant spread them out evenly so that the wheel would be balanced. Oliver had a space either side of him, which was good – less chance of him catching a blast of someone else's vomit. The attendant ran through his brief safety checks and stepped into the operator's cab. Moments later the round-up started spinning. Oliver smiled and cried out with delight as the ride spun faster and faster. His face became an intermittent marker of each accelerating revolution and then, as the round-up reached full velocity, he was gone. There was just a mash of faces that morphed into a single fleshy mass. When the floor fell away the screams were impossible to distinguish.

'Schaefer.'

The voice seemed clear and real, but I could not identify the speaker. I looked around and saw nothing in the passing fairground crowd. Unsettled, I looked back at the

Zero G. Where was Oliver? I scanned the spinning machine but could not pick out his face. Panic welled in me. Was this a dream like the one I'd had about Amber feeding the ducks? I started to feel flushed with anxiety, but then I saw Oliver's face as the ride slowed. He looked a little off-colour, but was smiling broadly. The sight of his beaming face was such a relief.

'That was awesome,' Oliver said as he staggered over. 'I think I need something to eat.'

I bought a couple of sweaty hot dogs. Oliver smothered them in watery ketchup and luminous yellow mustard, and we stood by the old snack van to eat.

'Schaefer!'

The same voice, clearer this time. I was overjoyed to see Oliver had heard it too. I wasn't losing my mind. I scanned the crowd and picked out a familiar face. Captain John Coombes, an eager Labrador of a man. His brown hair was now flecked with grey, but he still wore the ever-present smile of an enthusiast on his lean, unblemished face. Coombes had a horsey blonde woman and two young children in tow. The last thing I needed was a ghost from the past, but here it was, heading straight for me.

CHAPTER 49

'Thomas Schaefer,' Coombes said as he approached. 'I thought it was you. I tried to grab you at that oversized record player, but Todd needed the toilet, and you know how it is; when they've got to go, they've got to go.'

'Hello, John,' I replied.

'Gosh, that sounds strange.' Coombes laughed. 'I've got the terrible urge to call you sir.'

Coombes turned to the woman with him. 'Tom was my superior – Squadron Sergeant Major Schaefer until they bumped him up to 2ic – Captain, second in command.'

Coombes snapped to attention, and earned a half-hearted laugh from the woman. The two children rolled their eyes in practised embarrassment.

'I haven't seen you in what – must be twelve years. This is my wife, Willa,' Coombes said, indicating the woman. He patted the two children on their heads. 'And these monsters are Sophie and Todd. Short for Toddney.'

'Dad!' Todd exclaimed.

'Alright, not really,' Coombes conceded. 'It's Sir Toddious of Stinksville.'

'That's just lame, Dad!' the boy fired back.

Coombes tousled his son's hair, but grew uneasy at the ensuing silence. I didn't know what to say. I was so far from this man now. I looked at him and his family with a mix of shame and envy.

'Who's this fine lad?' Coombes asked.

'This is Oliver,' I said.

'You look just like your dad,' Coombes observed. And then, with the awareness of a lolloping dog bounding towards a ball, 'Is your mum around?'

Oliver shook his head, and my expression hardened.

'Of course,' Coombes said. 'I was so sorry to hear about your little girl. Froggie – Major Froggart – told me what happened. Must have been terrible.'

Oliver's head sagged, and all the joy the fair had instilled evaporated. I wanted to punch Coombes, but his happy, dopey expression was devoid of malice. He was just thoughtless, and I wasn't about to smack the man in front of his wife and kids.

'So, what are you doing with yourself now?' Coombes asked.

'It's been good seeing you again, John,' I replied. 'Enjoy the fair.'

I put my arm around Oliver and steered him away.

I glanced over my shoulder to see Coombes watching us in utter bemusement and heard his wife say, 'How rude. Come on kids, let's go on the Waltzer.'

I had no doubt word would get back to the lads that I'd lost it, but I didn't care. Most of them already knew I was a mess. A few years back, some of them had staged an intervention and tried to talk me into therapy, but I told them in no uncertain terms where to stick their psychobabble, so Coombes would only confirm their expectations of me.

I made sure we didn't bump into Coombes and his family for the rest of the afternoon. Oliver soon brightened up when we hopped in a couple of dodgems and started haphazardly chasing each other around the crowded rink.

'You're too slow, Dad!' Oliver yelled over the surrounding bedlam. He turned away with a backward glance that challenged his father to give chase.

I spun my steering wheel and went after him, and we spent a happy few minutes bashing into each other and enjoying the mayhem.

After the dodgems, we went on the Ferris wheel, the vertical drop, and then played some of the rigged games at the hook-a-duck and shooting stalls. Oliver pleaded for some candy floss, and as we watched a young goth girl wind the sweet, pink strands around a stick, I checked my watch: 5.15 pm.

'Time for us to go, champ,' I remarked.

'One more ride, Dad,' Oliver implored.

According to the custody agreement, I had until 5.30 pm, and it was my loss if I was late. I was pretty sure Sarah wouldn't go running to the lawyers if we were a few minutes late. She always said she wanted us to develop a normal relationship, and there were few things more normal than spoiling a child.

'One more,' I replied. 'What do you want to go on?'

'The Ghost Train,' Oliver said excitedly.

He started pulling me towards it. I handed six tokens to a grey-haired woman who wore a gaudy old floral dress. Her bony fingers and the corners of her thin-lipped mouth were stained yellow with nicotine.

'Take the front cart,' she said, pointing at an old rust bucket that had the flaked painting of a bandaged mummy on its side. 'Keep your hands inside the ride at all times.'

Oliver skipped ahead, and clambered into the lead cart. I followed him and when I'd pulled down the guard bar and locked it into position above our laps, the operator stepped into her booth and got the old train running. The rickety cart clattered and shook its way to what the bloody painted text said was the *Portal to Fear*, but was in reality a pair of warped plywood doors covered with a cartoonish painting of the Grim Reaper. The cart pushed the doors apart and trundled inside. I could make out a coffin, gallows and a small graveyard, before the whole place was plunged into darkness when the doors swung shut.

Oliver clasped my hand as the cart clattered forward. We were surrounded by the sounds of screaming, tortured souls. Suddenly Oliver was illuminated by a green glow, as a luminous body dropped from the gallows. A piercing scream and the crack of a neck bone echoed around us. Oliver beamed with excitement and even I had to smile at the absurdity of the green zombie hanging from the end of the rope. We passed through another set of doors and were enveloped by darkness. A gruesome witch dropped directly ahead of us, and Oliver screamed. The cart turned abruptly to avoid the hideous cut-out, and three skeletons popped from the wings, startling the boy even more. A coffin opened suddenly, revealing a red-hued vampire who roared and lurched forward with all the violence his aged mechanism could muster. Oliver jumped, and his thighs jolted the guard bar.

'You okay?' I asked above the sounds of terror.

'This is stupid,' he replied with an overdose of bravado.

The cart rumbled through another set of doors into darkness. This time there was no instant shock to greet us, and the cart rattled along the track for a while, before stopping. Everything fell silent. As my eyes grew accustomed to the pitch black, they started to play tricks. I thought I could see movement, wraith-like figures rushing around at the edge of my vision. My pulse quickened; something was wrong.

'Oliver?' I said.

There was no response, and when I put out my hand to touch my son, there was nothing there.

CHAPTER 50

'Oliver!' I yelled.

There was a flash of light and a figure appeared in front of me. Once I'd overcome my shock, I realised it was Edward Lomas. The side of his head was bloody and caved, his hair was matted and his eyes were milky white. I recoiled in terror, as Lomas opened his mouth.

'*Tenebris renascentis*,' he said.

His voice was inhuman and terrifying, and I was gripped by a fear that surpassed anything I'd ever felt.

And then the figure was gone, replaced by a set of double doors that opened onto grey daylight. Panicking, I looked round and saw Oliver laughing. The operator smoked a cigarette and stared at us as the cart clattered to a halt. I was bewildered and disorientated and the fear must have shown on my face because Oliver's laughter died suddenly.

'Dad, are you okay?' he asked.

I couldn't answer. My body trembled at the memory of the words, the hideous voice and the face of the man I was hunting. But that hadn't been a dream. What was it? Was I losing my mind?

'Dad?' Oliver asked with a touch more concern in his voice.

'Ride's over.' The operator exhaled a plume of smoke as she came over and lifted the guard rail.

'I'm okay,' I said, getting to my feet.

'You sure?' Oliver pressed.

'I'm fine. Just got a lot on my mind,' I replied with the best smile I could muster.

We picked our way through the crowded fair, and headed for the exit. The families who were leaving were being replaced by an early evening clientele that was a mix of teenage gangs, couples on dates and loners looking for something to do.

I scanned the eyes of the people we passed, wondering if any of them were like me. I couldn't bring myself to look at Oliver. What would have happened if I'd lashed out at my hallucination? I could have hurt Oliver or done something worse.

If Oliver sensed anything was wrong, he didn't show it, and started chatting enthusiastically. The horror of my hallucination faded as he spoke and I reminded myself this afternoon was supposed to be about my son.

'What was your favourite ride?' he asked. 'Mine was the Zero G. You should have come on it, Dad. It made me feel so dizzy. The world was going so fast you couldn't see it. I thought I was going to be sick. I bet you thought I was going to be sick. I think the dodgems were my next favourite. Or maybe the ghost train.'

'I didn't like the ghost train,' I replied. 'My favourite was the Ferris wheel.'

'The Ferris wheel? It's pretty boring,' he scoffed.

'What can I say? I like heights,' I replied with a playful nudge. 'Come on. Let's get you home to your mother.'

The sun had broken through the clouds by the time I got Oliver home, and it was turning into one of those perfect, warm September evenings. Sarah was watching from the living room window, a look of mild concern on her face. She opened the door as we started up the path.

'It was amazing, Mum,' Oliver said before Sarah had the chance to speak. 'We went on everything. And I had a hot dog. And candy floss.'

'I hope you've got room for dinner. It's on the table,' she replied.

'What is it?' Oliver asked as he attempted to push past.

'Hey!' she exclaimed. 'Where's my hug?'

With an air of mock petulance, Oliver gave his mother a hug.

'It's sausages, chips and beans,' Sarah said, releasing him.

'Ace,' he said, heading for the kitchen.

'Say goodbye to your father.'

Oliver turned on his heels and ran to give me a hug.

'Bye, Dad,' he said quickly. 'Thanks for a brilliant day.'

'You're welcome,' I replied. It felt amazing to see my son so happy, and for a moment I forgot my hallucination and felt like a normal father.

Oliver turned and ran for the kitchen.

'Brilliant?' Sarah observed.

'I know,' I replied.

'This is what he needs, Tom. He needs his father.'

'I know. But I just can't...' I trailed off.

'Can't what?' Sarah asked. 'Can't what? Give up on her? Abandon her like the rest of us?'

'No, no. It's not like that. I just don't know how you do it,' I countered.

'Do what?' Sarah challenged.

'I don't know how you stop yourself thinking about her.'

Sarah's shoulders sagged, and she was silent for a moment.

'I think about her every day, Tom,' she said with so much sadness in her voice I could have cried. 'I see her face every time I close my eyes. I catch myself talking to her.' She had tears in her eyes now. 'I dream about her, and when I do, I don't want to wake up. But I won't let it destroy me. We have a son, and he needs us.'

I hesitated. This was raw ground and the last time we'd had this conversation it had ended badly.

'You always were the stronger one,' I said at last.

'Is this it for you?' she asked sadly. 'Oliver's stopped asking what's wrong with you. He's stopped asking why you never talk to him about anything. Why you're always sick. Why you never smile. He's stopped hoping you'll ever get better.'

Her words stung, but I knew she was telling the truth, and I didn't blame my boy. In trying to be a good father to Amber, I'd been a terrible father to him.

'Your son has stopped hoping you'll ever get better,' Sarah repeated. 'Doesn't that scare you?'

I struggled to find the words. I didn't want this life. I wanted something much better; the life of the buffoon we'd met at the fair, a bright happy family taking joy at life's simple pleasures, but I could never have that as long as Amber was out there. And there was no way to explain that to Sarah without making her feel guilty about the fact she had moved on.

'Is this your life, Tom?' Sarah asked.

'Until I find her,' I replied.

She shook her head.

'I'm worried about you, Tom. The life you lead – it's – difficult,' she hesitated. 'I think you should see someone.'

'What good would it do?' I asked. If she knew the truth about the life I lived, she'd know I was beyond saving.

She was about to respond, when I cut her off.

'I'll see you in a fortnight,' I said.

'Tom,' she tried, as I walked away.

'Thanks for the advice, Sarah,' I replied without looking back. 'I'll see you soon.'

CHAPTER 51

Kelvin greeted me with a smile. Mathers' was the kind of shop that never really closed, not even on a Sunday night. The grey-skinned customer with a pockmarked face was back, leafing through one of the old books. He nodded in recognition as I headed for the back room. The peculiar folk who sought Mathers' advice waited patiently and many of them were familiar from my previous visit.

'Mr Schaefer,' Margot said brightly. 'Let me just see if he can fit you in.'

She disappeared through the door to Mathers' office, and I caught sight of the bookseller, hunched over an old manuscript. Moments later, Margot emerged.

'You can go right in,' she said. 'Can I get you a drink?'

I shook my head. 'No thanks.'

I entered Mathers' office and found him in poor spirits. He seemed troubled.

'Did you read through the papers?' Mathers asked without his customary preamble.

'Most of them,' I replied, and my response seemed to irritate the old man.

'This is very serious, Thomas. You must take every opportunity to protect yourself. In this situation, knowledge is most definitely power,' he said urgently. 'I studied the images in the house. Look here.'

He led me to an easel covered by a red drape, and drew it aside to reveal enlarged copies of the photographs I had taken of the luminous inscriptions in Yates's house.

'Here, in this picture, next to the Vitruvian Man, is this tiny inscription.' Mathers indicated some indistinct Latin text. 'I think it says *Libri Ex Baezeal – The Book of Baezael*. It is an extremely rare text. The librarian at the Bodleian is an old friend. We trade books every so often. He was kind enough to lend me a copy.'

He took me to the corner of his office where a lectern supported a huge book with a hard gilt cover. It took a moment for me to pick out the contours of the gilt relief, but when I did, I realised the engraving on the front cover was a depiction of a hideous demon surrounded by tortured souls. Mathers put on a pair of pristine archive gloves and opened the book to a specific page near the middle. The pages were thick and brittle with age, but the text looked fresh, and the illuminated illustrations seemed to have lost none of their vibrancy. The page Mathers selected featured a magnificent illumination of a demon standing on a bed of skulls. The beast's jaws were locked open in a fearsome roar and I could see, inside the creature's throat, the faint illustration of children who were screaming in terror as they slid into oblivion.

'*The Book of Baezael* was a condemned text. Legend has it that the book was commissioned by Lothair when he was Duke of Saxony. Baezael was a heretical priest who claimed to have discovered the secret to taming the forces of Hell and using them to acquire worldly power. Lothair was an ambitious man, and had Baezael's rantings transcribed and twelve copies of this book made. It is said that when they were finished Lothair put Baezael to death, along with the twelve scribes who made the books. They were burnt as heretics. Lothair was said to have given copies of the books to the most corrupt men of his time in an effort to unlock Baezael's magic. It is not known whether he succeeded, but his worldly ambitions were certainly achieved. Lothair went on to become King of Germany, and then, in 1133 A.D., became Holy Roman Emperor – the most powerful man in the known world. That year Pope Innocent II issued an edict requiring the destruction of a number of books condemned as heretical. Listed among them was *The Book of Baezael*. This is believed to be the only surviving copy. Look here.' Mathers gestured towards a specific passage in the book.

'*Trauco est anima comedentis. Fons ultimum potentia. Immensas opes ex omnibus terrae adorabunt possidebit,*' he said in unfaltering Latin. '*Il Totus pascet eum. Il Totus honorabit eum.*'

'Trauco the soul eater. The source of ultimate power. The riches of the Earth shall come to all who worship him. The Totus shall feed him. The Totus shall honour him,' I said quietly. I had taught myself Latin to better understand books like this. 'You don't believe this stuff, do you?'

'It doesn't matter what I believe,' Mathers replied. 'What matters is there are people out there who think it is true. The people you are dealing with, they worship this thing. The soul eater is evil, Thomas, and the Totus believe they gain power in our world by feeding it.'

'Are you telling me they kidnapped my daughter to feed a demon?' I asked incredulously. This was darker than anything I'd ever encountered and I was struggling to take it in. I could tell Mathers was also finding it difficult.

'I don't know,' Mathers replied slowly.

'Do you know how crazy this sounds?' I asked. I couldn't accept this. Not for my little girl. 'None of this is real. There are no demons. The only evil in this world is what we inflict on each other. There is nothing beyond what we can see. There's nothing beyond...'

But I trailed off when I was suddenly taken back to my vision of Edward Lomas at the fair.

'What is it?' Mathers asked.

I was not about to share my experience with the old man. It might frighten him into believing this stuff and stop him from helping.

'Nothing. What else have you learnt?' I asked.

'Not much. Traces of the Totus dotted throughout history.'

'I read the monk's journal, and the doctor's account of the boy he treated, which suggests they target children,' I said.

'So it would seem,' Mathers acknowledged sadly.

'See what else you can find out,' I said. 'Find out what they do with their victims.'

'I will,' Mathers replied. 'Thomas, whatever the people in this group believe, they seem capable of great evil. Please be careful.'

I nodded. 'You know me. I'm a survivor. I've had to get a new phone. I'll leave the number with Margot.'

I left Mathers with his books, gave Margot my new number and left the shop, struggling to come up with a rational explanation for what I'd just heard.

CHAPTER 52

Tilly didn't smile when she handed me my first drink.

I'll just have a couple, I told myself, *then I'll get back upstairs and get stuck into Mathers' file and my journals.*

I knew I was lying to myself. After the vision at the fair and what I'd learnt from Mathers, I needed to get well and truly obliterated.

I have vague memories of that Sunday night. I got pally with a couple of the regulars, almost started a fight, and at one point I think I was singing, but most of it is a blank, lost to the rum I was drinking neat.

The next morning, I woke to an unfamiliar sound. I rolled off the sofa onto the Great Room's hard floor and scrabbled to get my new phone. I hadn't changed the ring tone, so it was blaring out an irritatingly catchy tune.

'Hello,' I croaked into the phone.

'You sound healthy,' Baker chirped. 'Meet me by the river in an hour.'

'What time is it?' I asked, looking out of the window. Night was tinged with the first light of dawn.

'Five-thirty,' Baker replied brightly. 'While you've been doing – whatever, me and Billy have been burning the midnight oil for you, Schaefer. Get yourself up and at 'em.'

I took my time in the shower. It wouldn't hurt Baker to wait. I struggled to get dressed. I was exhausted and was probably still drunk, but the cold early morning fresh air puffed away the worst of my hangover. I took a minicab from the office down the road from the pub and was at the

Southbank a little before six-thirty. London was only just starting to wake as I hurried past the drab concrete of the Southbank Centre and headed for the Festival Pier. A handful of enthusiastic runners pounded the pavement, but otherwise the promenade was quiet. I saw Baker on a bench opposite the pier and walked over to join him.

'Fuck!' Baker exclaimed, as I slumped next to him. 'You look like shit.'

'What have you got for me?' I asked.

'Fine. Just an old friend trying to show concern,' Baker replied, feigning hurt.

'We're not friends,' I said. 'We just share similar interests. Now are you going to tell me what you've found? Or are you going to sit there and pretend you love me?'

He picked up a cardboard folder that was on the bench next to him and handed it to me.

'Your man's a nut,' Baker said matter-of-factly.

I leafed through the folder, which contained photographs of Edward Lomas along with articles taken from the pages of publications such as *Fortean Times* and *Psychic News*.

'He thinks he's a psychic,' Baker continued.

'You're not a believer?' I asked with a wry smile.

'Fuck that. What you see is what you get. We're meat.'

'My thoughts exactly,' I said. Only I wasn't so sure now.

I scanned the articles, which all seemed to be of the opinion that Edward Lomas was a powerful and, more importantly, genuine psychic.

'He disappeared a few years ago. Just vanished,' Baker said with his variation on a magician's gesture. 'No sign. No trace. No hope of ever finding him.'

He paused theatrically, but I didn't lean into the drama. I knew Baker hadn't summoned me to read through old magazine articles. This was all part of our relationship. I never praised Baker for his skills, so he felt compelled to play up his achievements.

'Unless you happen to know a fucking genius,' Baker concluded with a smile.

'Then I guess I'm out of luck,' I said dryly.

'Fuck you!' Baker laughed.

He handed me a photograph and a couple of pieces of paper. The photo was of an auburn-haired, ethereal woman in her late twenties. Printed on one of the pieces of paper was an address. On the other was a satellite photograph of a house in the country.

'That's his niece, Mary. Lives off the grid. No credit card. No bank account. I tracked her down through an old mobile number. Not that you give a shit of course.'

'I'm very impressed,' I replied mockingly.

'Her place is in the middle of fucking nowhere. The Wye Valley. Way out west.'

I studied the satellite image. The remote, isolated house had good visibility on all sides. It was the perfect place for someone who wanted to see what was coming.

'I'm going to need you to come with me,' I said.

'I don't do country,' Baker replied. 'I prefer my grass in bags.'

'I need you to come with me,' I repeated flatly.

'Shit.' Baker shook his head in defeat. 'You're a fucking bastard, Schaefer, you know that?'

I knew it all too well.

CHAPTER 53

The Royal Inn on the Park had a twenty-five-year-old green Land Rover Defender that was used for wholesale runs, driving drunk regulars home and other odd jobs. I could take it whenever I needed it, which was rarely. London had become actively hostile to big cars. I didn't want to take my BMW to the Wye Valley in case Lomas and his followers knew what car I drove, so I asked Tilly for the keys to the four-by-four, which was affectionately nicknamed Smokey. Heavy, sluggish and unforgiving, it was nonetheless the vehicle that I wanted in the event of Armageddon. When all other cars turned to ash, this two-tonne beast would be chugging through fire and flame, running on aftershave, rum or mouthwash.

I followed Baker's brand new Mercedes E-Class along the inside lane of the M4. I could tell by the way Baker was driving he was annoyed at having to go so slowly, but Smokey topped out at sixty-eight. Baker's slick black E-Class was designed to impress his clients, fill his friends with envy and sweep away the inhibitions of accessible young women. It was not meant to be in the slow lane. I lifted the stiff, plastic indicator column when I saw Baker's left tail light start blinking yellow. He pulled onto the services slip road, and I followed.

'What d'you want to find this guy for?' Baker asked, before forcing a handful of chips into his mouth.

He and I sat at a small plastic table in Burger King, where I was getting a salutary reminder why I never liked to

eat with Baker. I had a black coffee while my companion
gorged himself on three Whoppers with cheese, three
portions of fries, a milkshake and some kind of chicken in a
bun.

'I got given his name,' I replied.

'Who gave it to you?' Baker took another bite of burger
and wiped the grease from his lips.

I grimaced, but he was too engrossed in his meal to
notice.

'Come on, Schaefer. This is me,' he protested, giving
me a good view of the churned matter inside his mouth. He
took a gulp of his vanilla shake.

'Security Service,' I replied.

'What the fuck?' Baker laughed. His laughter quickly
evaporated when he realised I was deadly serious. 'You're
kidding me?'

I shook my head.

'Why did they come to you?' he asked.

'Lomas heads a cult called the Totus. You ever come
across it?'

Baker put down his burger. 'The Totus?'

'Yeah.'

'Fuck,' he said quietly. 'I never expected to hear that
name again. It was about twelve, maybe thirteen years ago. I
was hired to find this missing kid. Scotty Costa. I went to
school with his mum, Leanne. She met this Spanish DJ,
Eduardo, and brought him back to the East End. He got big
in clubland and then fucked off to Ibiza, leaving her with
their kid. Sent money and all, but never really spent much
time with the boy, so Scotty fell in with a rough lot. He

regularly spent days away from home without telling his mum where he was. But when he went missing for two weeks, Leanne came and begged me to find him. I wish to fuck she'd gone to someone else.'

Baker shook his head at the memory. I'd rarely seen this bravado-filled man troubled by anything that a smutty joke and a knowing wink couldn't solve.

'It took weeks to piece together his last movements, but I tracked Scotty down to this old fuck, Morris McCarthy. McCarthy had picked the kid up at Waterloo Station. I have no idea what Scotty was doing there, but the security cameras snapped him going off with McCarthy. I didn't know who the old git was, but then I got really lucky. McCarthy had made an illegal right turn on The Cut, and got snapped by a traffic camera. Scotty was sat right next to him in the passenger seat. We had the two of them together, and we had McCarthy's number plate. When the cops raided McCarthy's shithole in West Ruislip, they found the remains of five kids buried in the garden; all teenage boys. McCarthy claimed he had to kill them to save the world. He said they were all being groomed for great evil by this thing called the Totus. He copped an insanity plea, and somehow managed to hang himself. In Broadmoor. You got any idea how hard it is to kill yourself in that place?'

'You ever look into the Totus?' I asked.

'What for? I thought it was a figment of a nutter's imagination,' Baker said in genuine disbelief. 'It's real. Fuck. What is it?'

'Some kind of cult. Seems to have been around for hundreds of years. I read a fourteenth-century journal that mentions it.'

'What do the spies want with it?' Baker asked.

I hesitated, recalling Shark Eye's instructions outside the situation room. 'I can't say.'

'I see,' he said flatly. 'This is heavy, even for you, Schaefer. And this guy Lomas runs it?'

I nodded.

'And you think the Totus has got something to do with Amber's abduction?' he asked.

I nodded again.

'I wouldn't want to be in his shoes when we find him,' he observed.

I simply stared at Baker with hard, unforgiving eyes.

CHAPTER 54

The Wye Valley was ancient, the kind of place where the roots of trees ran deep. I didn't spend much time in the country and noticed the absence of glass and steel. Life in London was so far removed from the natural world, it was easy to forget how much we'd changed it. Freed of man-made interference, the world greeted me with a craggy landscape and rock formations that were millions of years old. But it wasn't just the land; I felt something more profound. Try as I might, I couldn't shake the sense that an ancient consciousness permeated the region. It was as though the world around me was alive and aware and it made me feel very uncomfortable.

I turned off the dual carriageway that cut through the hills, onto a narrow road that ran towards Symonds Yat, alongside the River Wye at the base of the valley. Rocks carved by the forces of ice and water loomed above me and I had the sudden sense the world was closing in.

'*Inretus vir.*'

I heard the voice before I saw the dog. It was the largest Rottweiler I had ever seen, and it stood proudly in the middle of the road. I stepped on the brake and the tyres squealed. The heavy car came to a halt a couple of feet away from the impassive beast.

'Watch where you're going, you fool!' exclaimed a grizzled old man, as he emerged from the bushes beside the road.

He grabbed the dog's collar and pulled it out of the way, and I put the Land Rover into gear and drove further into the valley. I checked my rear view mirror and saw Baker give the cantankerous old man a leisurely view of his middle finger as he drove past. The man yelled something at Baker, who simply smiled back.

I turned off the narrow road onto an even smaller one that wound up into the hills. The Land Rover clipped the lush foliage that overhung the road as it climbed out of the valley. The landscape changed as I crested the hill. Bushes and ferns gave way to trees, and soon I was driving through farmed forest; the pine trees evenly spaced to make for easy harvesting. About four miles out of the valley, I caught sight of my destination through the trees.

Mary Lomas's house was a large white Victorian building, with gothic arched windows and a grey slate tile roof. The window frames had been painted black, which made the house look like a poorly designed chessboard. I scanned the area for Baker, and couldn't see his car anywhere.

I turned off the forest road onto the private drive that led up to the house. The rough dirt track was sufficiently potholed to test the Land Rover's suspension. There wasn't a garden as such; the land around the house just seemed to blend into the surrounding forest. A brand new blue Toyota Hilux was parked out front. The only dilapidated element of the property was the badly potholed drive, and I wondered if it had been left in that state deliberately. It would discourage accidental tourists from confusing it with a public road, and force any vehicles approaching the house to slow to a crawl. I had a feeling I was being watched and the moment I parked beside the Hilux and stepped out of the car, the front door opened.

'Who are you?' Mary Lomas asked aggressively. She was on the painted white porch, and held the collar of a huge German Shepherd. She wore a white linen blouse and dark blue jeans, and her lustrous red hair fell around her alabaster face, which was stern and unwelcoming.

'My name's Thomas Schaefer.'

The dog barked suddenly as I took a step forward. I had been mauled by a German Shepherd once before and decided not to test my luck.

'Are you Mary Lomas?' I asked, staying very still.

There was no response, but I didn't need one. This was the woman from the photograph Baker had shown me.

'I'm looking for your uncle Edward,' I continued. 'There are some things I need to talk to him about.'

'I haven't seen him for years,' Mary replied.

'It's very important that I find him,' I countered.

'I can't help you,' Mary said angrily. 'I don't know where he is. Nobody does. He could be dead.'

'If I could just talk to you,' I said, taking a step forward. The dog snarled.

'There's nothing more to say,' Mary responded. 'I'd like you to leave.'

I looked at the big dog, which was now straining to be unleashed, decided not to push things any further and stepped back towards the Land Rover.

'Sorry to have troubled you,' I said.

Glad to have the car door between me and Mary's guard dog, I started the engine and drove slowly up the bumpy drive towards the road. I looked in the wing mirror and saw Mary Lomas watching me from her porch.

At the end of the drive, I turned right, and headed further into the forest. I looked through the trees and could see Mary was still watching me. Ahead, concealed behind a long stretch of large rhododendron bushes, was Baker. When I was out of sight of the house, I stamped on the brakes and came to a rapid halt beside Baker's E-Class. He was already out of his car.

'Billy's got the phone covered,' Baker said as I climbed out of the Land Rover. 'If she calls anyone, we'll know.'

I could picture Baker's greasy, thin brother in some tiny windowless room in London, sat in front of whatever monitoring equipment enabled him to illegally wiretap people's phones.

'How long are you going to wait?' Baker asked as he clambered into the Land Rover.

'I'll give it a couple of hours,' I replied. 'If we don't get anything, I'll have to go back and try the direct approach.'

Baker shook his head.

'Don't fuck up my baby,' he said, indicating the pristine E-Class that abutted the bushes.

'I'll look after it,' I said. 'Now get lost.'

Baker slammed the Land Rover door shut, and sped away.

CHAPTER 55

I moved carefully, taking care not to be seen, and crept to a point where the branches of two rhododendra intertwined. I crouched down and was able to find a small gap in the foliage that offered a view of the house. Mary Lomas watched the Land Rover as it carried on along the forest road. She waited until it was gone from sight and then pulled the large dog inside and shut the door.

My plan was to shake the niece with my visit. If Edward Lomas was in the house, I'd find out soon enough. If he was elsewhere, Mary would try to warn him somehow. With her phones being monitored by Billy Baker, and me watching the house, anything she did would be found out.

I didn't have to wait long. A few minutes later, Mary came jogging out of the house, jumped in the Hilux and drove hurriedly over the potholed drive. It bumped and bounced around until it reached the road, where Mary turned left and headed down the valley. I broke cover, jumped in Baker's E-Class, pulled a U-turn and followed.

Mary took the winding road back down towards Symonds Yat. She turned left when she reached the junction, and headed further along the valley, towards the source of the river. I kept my distance. Baker's windows were tinted and if Mary caught sight of the car, hopefully she'd assume I was a flashy estate agent or second-home city-boy.

She drove for another six miles, until we were well away from civilisation. The regularly spaced holiday homes had given way to countryside interrupted by the occasional house. As we progressed, there were fewer and fewer reasons for a stranger to be out in this neck of the woods, and I had to be careful not to be noticed. I dropped back even further, allowing Mary's truck to move out of sight on the curves. The road followed the bend in the river and swung right. When it straightened up, Mary was gone. A few moments later, I saw the Hilux parked in front of a two-storey wood-panelled red boathouse. The boathouse stood on the south bank of the River Wye. It was the last house before the end of the valley. Beyond it, the road swept in to run alongside the river, before an abrupt turn that forced vehicles over a single-track bridge that stretched over the water to the north bank.

I pulled into a lay-by and moved the car behind some bushes so it would be hidden. I opened the door quietly and crept towards the boathouse, as Mary made her way up the red wood stairs. She hurried along the balcony that ran around the first floor. When she was out of sight, I moved towards the house quickly. I climbed the stairs silently, and, as I made my way along the balcony, I heard voices through an open window.

'A troubled man came to see me today,' Mary said. 'He was looking for you.'

'I know, Mary,' a man's voice replied. 'He followed you here. He's outside.'

CHAPTER 56

I had no idea how the man knew I was there. Maybe he had a sensor system or cameras? There was no time to lose. I rushed at the door, put my full weight behind it, and the lock splintered from the frame. The door swung open wildly to reveal Mary standing in a cluttered hallway with Edward Lomas.

She turned round in shock, but Lomas did not look the slightest bit surprised. I charged at the old man and grabbed him by the throat.

'Where's my daughter?' I demanded, hurling him against a bookshelf.

He crashed into it and collapsed, and as books fell on him and I moved forward for more, Mary tried to pull me away. When that didn't work, she hit and punched and pinched me, but with Lomas within reach, I hardly registered the blows.

'Leave him alone!' Mary yelled. 'Leave him alone!'

'You've made a terrible mistake,' Lomas said as I lifted him by the collar. 'The man you work for knows more about your daughter than I do. You've been followed.'

I hesitated, my grip suddenly less certain.

'Mary, we fought the inevitable for as long as we could,' he said to her sadly. 'Our preparations have been for nothing.'

This wasn't how it was supposed to go down. I had imagined beating him to a pulp and forcing him to reveal Amber's location.

'Shut up,' I said. 'Where's my daughter?'

'Ask the man with the Shark Eyes,' he replied, and I released him and staggered back.

How could he know that? I hadn't told anyone I'd named my MI5 contact Shark Eyes. It couldn't be a coincidence, could it?

'Look outside and you'll see for yourself,' Lomas said, catching his breath.

I ran to the window, and had a horrible sick feeling when I saw a grey Lexus pull up next to Mary's pickup truck. There were two suited men in it. With growing dismay, I realised it was Smoker and Scarface, Shark Eyes' henchmen. What were they doing here? How had they tracked me? I was trained in counter-surveillance and would have noticed a tail. The only weak link was Baker, and he knew better than to betray me.

I turned to Lomas, wondering how he knew these men had arrived.

'How did you—' I began.

'You know how, Mr Schaefer. You just don't believe it yet,' he said. 'We must leave.'

I didn't want this. I wanted it to be over. I wanted Lomas to be the final piece in the puzzle, to lead me to Amber, to give me what I needed to bring her home.

'Follow me,' Lomas said.

He led Mary and me into a study that was overflowing with books and papers, moved the battered old captain's chair that languished behind his messy desk, and lifted a metal hoop in the floor. A trap door opened, revealing a simple wooden staircase below. As we descended, I heard the heavy footsteps of the two men clambering up the exterior steps. Lomas hurried down the stairs, and went straight to a small vessel that bobbed in the berth that occupied most of the boathouse. Mary and I followed him onto the motorboat as he got the engine started. The noise drowned out the sound of the heavy footsteps above us, and I lost all sense of our pursuers' positions in the house. The boat roared out into daylight, and Lomas steered a course towards the other side of the river.

'Mary! Take the wheel,' Lomas called. 'I must talk to him.'

Mary glared at me as she took the helm. Lomas joined me on one of the low bench seats near the stern.

'We don't have much time, Mr Schaefer,' Lomas began. 'You must listen carefully. The man who gave you my name is evil. The word is used so frequently that it has lost its meaning. I use it in the precise sense.'

'Why did he use me?' I asked with the growing realisation I'd been played for a fool.

'Mary has the gift,' Lomas replied. 'If they had sent an assassin, she would have seen murder in his heart. They used you because they know the power of the loss that drives you. You would do anything for your daughter. They knew you would find me. They used you to lead them to me. I pose a threat to them. I can see the truth. The dark alliance of the Totus is responsible for so much suffering.'

I looked back at the boathouse; no sign of the men. The boat was far enough away to be safe. I turned to face Lomas.

'I came so close. I have spent so many years hunting Trauco, their leader. He is a blight on the Earth. A great evil,' he said. 'I have almost uncovered his identity. I might have killed him.'

'Who is he?'

'I don't know. I only know he attends a church. The Church of the Eternal Light,' Lomas replied. He grabbed me by the arms, taken by a sudden sense of urgency. 'You must listen to me. The path is very narrow now and there is grave danger on both sides, but with good fortune and faith, there is hope. There is one who can guide you to the light. You must listen to her.'

Her? I wondered. *Who?*

Lomas's eyes were almost aglow with the intense fervour of conviction.

'You must listen. The messenger will speak only the truth. You are important to him. Trauco must have you.'

'Why?' I asked.

He smiled as though indulging a child. 'Because you have the gift, Mr Schaefer. Just like your daughter, Amber. You are powerful, Mr Schaefer. Like me.'

He hesitated.

'When all seems lost, keep your eyes open. Look for the count.'

Lomas released his hold on me, and put his hands in his lap. He looked away and his face took on a dreamy expression, as though straining to hear a distant voice.

'I wonder, will it hurt?' he asked softly.

I heard a crack and the whistle of something speeding through air, and watched in disbelief as a high-velocity round struck Lomas's skull, tearing it wide open.

CHAPTER 57

The bullet left a bloody mess of devastation in its wake, and as Lomas fell to the deck, I realised I'd seen him like this before, in my dream, when Amber had been telling me not to look. His eyes were glassy, one side of his skull had been caved in, and the back of his head was soaked with blood. Mary started screaming until a second bullet ripped into her torso, piercing her heart. She looked at me with growing horror, as blood spread over her white blouse. She clawed at her breast, as though trying to pull away the terrible wound, but it was no good. She fell face-forwards and died in a pool of her uncle's blood.

I ducked, expecting the assault to continue, but when I looked over the side of the boat, I saw the two suited men packing up. Smoker opened a gun case, while Scarface dismantled a tripod and a high-powered rifle. For some reason the men had no interest in killing me. That gave me a tiny advantage. I took the helm, and turned the boat back the way we'd come. I glanced down at Lomas, whose eyes were empty, and couldn't shake the fact I'd seen this before it happened. This was the face from my dream.

Vision, I found myself thinking, but part of me recoiled at the word.

I felt terrible guilt at my lethal mistake. My blind pursuit of Amber had caused this. My loss had been used against me and now two innocents lay dead at his feet. I would make these men pay for what they'd done.

I realised I wasn't going to make it back to the boathouse in time. Scarface and Smoker had packed the gun away. Smoker carried the case as they headed back to their car. I memorised the number plate, but as they pulled away, I realised I might not need it. Instead of heading out of the valley, Scarface, who was driving, steered the car up the little lane towards the bridge.

I turned the boat around and pushed the throttle as far as it would go. The engine kicked in with a satisfying jolt. About half a mile away, the road came to a dead end and cars were forced to dogleg right across the narrow humpback bridge. I noticed a tractor parked in a lay-by beside it. This was going to be tight, but I had the advantage.

The river curved south, giving me a shorter distance to travel. I watched the Lexus wend its way towards the bridge. Smoker and Scarface obviously didn't see me as enough of a threat to kill, so they weren't in any particular hurry to get away from me. I moved to the bow of the boat, and jumped as it hit the bank. I rolled to my feet and raced towards the tractor, a bright yellow JCB. I grabbed a large stone and used it to smash the locked cab, forced open the door and pulled down the dash panel to reveal the electrical wiring. I'd hotwired a number of cars, but never a tractor. The principle was the same, and once I'd identified the ignition system, I got to work.

Smoker and Scarface were almost at the bridge. As they reached it, I got the first turn of the engine. When they crested the humpback, the tractor roared into life, and as they came down the other side of the bridge, I slipped the heavy machine into gear, turned it onto the road, and drove the tractor directly at the oncoming car.

Scarface tried to swerve but there wasn't the time or space, and the tractor smashed into the Lexus and sent the car crashing against the bridge wall. The tractor barely registered the collision, but the Lexus was a mangled wreck. I was out of the cab before the vehicles had stopped moving. Surrounded by smoke, dust and deflating airbags, Smoker was unconscious, but Scarface, who was badly injured and bleeding from a head wound, watched as I clambered across the buckled bonnet and approached the driver's door. As I reached out and grabbed Scarface, the bloodied man produced a Heckler & Koch P30 and held it against my chin. We stared at each other for what felt like an age.

This was the end of the road.

'You'll never know,' Scarface said with a wicked smile.

I expected death, but instead Scarface turned and shot Smoker in the head. As the dead man's body fell limp next to him, Scarface put the barrel in his mouth and pulled the trigger. I stepped back as the bullet ripped through the man's skull.

Reeling, I checked the road and saw nothing in either direction. What had started as a plan to find the man who'd taken my daughter had ended with the deaths of four people; two innocents and two evil men who died rather than give up their secrets. Trembling and struggling to understand what had happened, I found my army training was kicking in, and the part of my brain that always looked for tactical advantage realised I only had one hope of recovering anything from the situation.

I took out my Leatherman, selected the sharp knife and moved towards the wrecked car.

CHAPTER 58

My mind was racing and for the first time in ages, I was genuinely afraid. How had I been so blind? How had I allowed myself to be used? And how had I seen the way Lomas would die before it happened?

Until I knew how they had tracked me, I couldn't trust anyone or anything. I ran back to Lomas's boathouse along the deserted country lane, and collected Baker's car. I drove the E-Class into Ross-on-Wye and parked it on a side road that ran off the high street. I went into a menswear shop and selected an entire new wardrobe: black jeans, dark blue shirt and a black leather jacket. New boots, new socks, new underwear and a new wallet, which I picked up at the checkout. I emptied my wallet and left it and my clothes in the shop's changing room and stepped onto the high street a new man.

What might have seemed like paranoia to others was simply caution. I couldn't take the chance they'd concealed tracking devices in my clothes. The only other potential weak spots were my new phone and my tainted Leatherman. If Baker had given them my new telephone number...I took out the SIM card, tossed the phone in the nearest bin, and ground the SIM against the pavement with the heel of my new boots.

I bought a new phone and car charger from a shop on the high street and returned to the quiet side road, but instead of going back to the E-Class, I selected an old Ford Focus. Using a wire hanger I'd uncoiled and slipped into my pocket in the clothes shop, I broke into the car and circumvented the alarm in moments. I hotwired the engine in under a minute, but before I drove away, I slipped out of the car and dropped my bloody Leatherman through the grimy slats of a nearby drain. Other than myself, my only physical link to the events at the boathouse were the contents of the crumpled carrier bag in my pocket, and there was no danger that they contained a tracking device. I returned to the car and drove out of Ross-on-Wye, considering my next move.

I started with Baker and weighed the possibility he'd betrayed me. Baker didn't know who had given me Lomas's name, and even I didn't know Shark Eyes' real identity. There was no way Baker could have been able to make the connection without more information, unless he had some existing relationship with MI5. Assuming Shark Eyes and his people were MI5. I never saw any identification and had taken Noel at his word. I couldn't rule out the possibility Baker had betrayed me. Baker had said he would wait at the service station just outside town for three hours in case we got separated or something went wrong and I needed him. When I got there, two hours after we had parted, Baker was gone. Not a good sign of the man's loyalty. Perhaps he already knew I wouldn't be needing his help because he was expecting me to have been killed.

The Focus chewed up the motorway between the West Country and London, and my raw fury with Baker grew with each devoured mile. By the time I reached Marble Arch, and dumped the stolen Ford Focus in Seymour Street, I had convinced myself of Baker's betrayal. Whoever these people were, Security Service, Totus; even if they had managed to bug me, they wouldn't have relied on electronic tracking alone. They would have found a human element to compromise, and that element had to be Baker, or his brother.

I took the tube from Marble Arch and, forty minutes later, crossed Whitechapel Road towards Baker's office. The lights were on and, through the slatted blinds, I could see Baker's familiar shadow cast against the discoloured wall. I pressed the buzzer and looked directly into the video camera beside the door, alert for any sign of an abnormal response. But there was none, and after a short pause, the door buzzed open and I was allowed inside.

As I climbed the stairs, I could hear Baker joking with his younger brother.

'So he's sitting there in this tiny plane, on this chemical toilet, with a curtain held up to his neck, apologising to all the other passengers, and shits out the most disgusting sounds and smells ever,' Baker said, laughing loudly.

Billy chuckled with the lack of enthusiasm of someone who's heard a joke many times before.

'And this happened to a mate of yours?' he asked.

'Yeah, Pike-O, from down the way,' Baker replied confidently.

'Only it sounds a lot like a story I read on the Internet a couple of years back,' Billy countered.

Baker was saved from further humiliation by my entrance. I pushed the door open and stood in the doorway, studying the two men. Billy, with his dark, greasy hair, sallow skin and acne-ridden complexion, leant against the desk, while Baker kicked back in his old chair. I watched their body language for the slightest hint of betrayal. The two brothers looked at me for a moment, before Baker finally broke the silence.

'So?'

I didn't answer immediately and scoured the men for signs of anything other than the mild discomfort they were starting to show as a result of my scrutiny.

'Schaefer?' Baker asked. 'Are you okay?'

'How long have you been working with the Totus?' I asked.

Might as well get straight to it.

'What?' Baker countered. 'What the fuck?'

The brothers exchanged a look that might have been complicity, or it could have been bewilderment at the accusation. I wasn't certain but I couldn't afford to give them the benefit of the doubt.

'How long have you been working with the Totus?' I asked again, this time more forcefully.

Billy tried to step away from the desk, but I moved forward and pushed him back.

'Stay where you are,' I commanded. 'You both know how this works. Guilty until proven innocent.'

'Fuck, Schaefer,' Baker said nervously, 'I have no idea what you're talking about. I told you everything I know about the Totus. What happened out there?'

Baker's reaction seemed genuine, but I knew the kind of training MI5 gave their people. Throw in the prospect that Baker was involved in a cult, and the truth would be very hard to get to. Hard, but not impossible.

'How long have you been working with the Totus?' This time I punctuated the question with a fierce punch to Billy's left ribs. I felt the familiar crack of bone, and Baker's little brother doubled over, wheezing in pain.

'Let him go!' Baker said, producing a pistol from one of his desk drawers. 'Let him go, or I'll shoot you right in the face.'

CHAPTER 59

'What are you doing?' I asked calmly. 'You're only going to make it worse for yourselves.'

'I've had enough of your shit, Schaefer! Get out!' Baker exclaimed. 'I've put up with this for years because I felt sorry for you. You and your fucking hard luck story. But you're just another nutter. So. Get. The. Fuck. Out!'

Baker had miscalculated. He was no expert with firearms, and had overplayed his hand against someone who was. Flashy gangsters and the calibre illiterate didn't realise that the shiny stainless steel favoured by so many gun fetishists made it very easy to see the black plastic safety lever above the hand grip. The manual safety on the Walther PPK/S had to be horizontal in order for the gun to fire. Baker's was still down.

I leapt across the desk and was surprised that Baker actually tried to take the shot, but nothing happened and I grabbed the gun. I pushed him to the floor, and smacked him with the heavy pistol. Billy, who had recovered, rushed over, wheezing loudly, but I wheeled round and cold-clocked him with the butt of the gun. He fell hard, and cracked his head against the desk. Running on automatic, but as senseless as a punch-drunk boxer, Billy tried to get up, but his legs gave way and he passed out on the dusty carpet. Baker came to his senses and saw his unconscious brother had a trickle of blood running from his nose.

'What the fuck have you done?' Baker exclaimed, his voice high-pitched and cracking. 'We helped you.'

I looked down at Baker, who was bleeding from a deep cut on his cheek. As degenerate as he was, this man was one of the few people who had shown me kindness in recent years. But *they* would use human emotion against me.

Trust. Love. Faith. Loyalty.

These priceless human connections had been subverted by cults countless times. How could I not proceed? How could I not test Baker's honesty? My resolve wavered as I stood over the injured man who was probably the closest thing I had to a friend. What had I done? Could I trust myself? I was seeing things. Things before they happened. Or maybe I'd just tricked myself into thinking that. Could I still trust my judgement?

'Please, Schaefer,' Baker begged, now terrified. 'Please let me get him help. Please don't do this.'

I felt tears running down my face. Is that what had scared Baker? Could he see me losing control? I leant against the desk and wondered why I was crying. I'd interrogated people before and hadn't felt a thing.

It's because you're losing your mind, came a voice from within. *Look at what you've done.*

Baker's fear was writ large and he was crying too. His eyes darted nervously towards the pistol, which was pointed at his head, safety off.

Was I really prepared to kill this man? This frightened man who'd shown me kindness? I started shaking. Sarah was right; I needed help.

Trembling violently, I flipped the safety and dropped the gun.

Baker immediately rushed to check on his brother, who stirred at his touch.

'What the fuck has happened to you, Schaefer?' Baker yelled. 'You used to be one of the good guys.'

I fought for composure. Amber needed me to be strong. I held on to a vision of her running in our garden. My sweet little girl. Come back to me. I wanted to cry and cry and cry, but I knew if I did, I might never stop, and the gun stared up at me, talking to me, telling me it was the way out.

That's when I knew I had to fight whatever was happening. I couldn't leave this world. Not without seeing my little girl again. I sucked down the tears in big gulping breaths and brought myself back from the brink.

'Two men followed me,' I said when I was finally able to speak. 'They ambushed us at Lomas's house.'

'And you think I had something to do with that?' Baker countered, as he helped Billy into his chair. 'You okay, Bill?'

Baker clicked his fingers in front of his brother's eyes, and Billy focused.

'Follow my finger,' Baker said as he moved it laterally in front of Billy's face, and his younger brother's eyes tracked the moving digit. 'Well, at least you've not got any brain damage.'

'Not any more than usual,' Billy countered. He looked up and caught sight of me. 'What the fuck is he doing here?'

Billy tried to stand, but Baker restrained him.

'You'd better go,' Baker told me.

'I...I don't,' I started, but I wasn't sure how to go on.

'Get the fuck out!' Billy shouted.

'They killed Lomas and his niece,' I blurted out. 'Two of the MI5 agents. They shot them with a sniper's rifle. But they let me live.'

'Just get the fuck out!' Baker yelled. 'Psychics! Cults! MI5! You sound like a fucking nutjob! Get out!'

'I need to know who they are,' I said, standing firm as Baker came toe-to-toe.

'You're kidding, right?' Baker asked. 'After what you've just done?'

'I need to know who they were,' I said, taking the crumpled, plastic bag I'd found inside the tractor out of my pocket. I'd used it to store the index fingers I'd cut off Smoker's and Scarface's hands and I unwrapped the bag to reveal them now.

'Are those…' Baker trailed off, dismayed. 'What did you do?'

'Nothing,' I replied. 'I caught them. One of them killed the other, and then turned the gun on himself.'

'You didn't kill them?' Baker pressed.

'They're no use to me dead, Paul,' I protested. 'These men had something to do with Amber's disappearance. I know it.'

Baker looked at his brother, who shook his head slowly.

'This is it, Schaefer,' he said. 'I do this, and we're through. I don't need this shit in my life.'

I nodded.

Another door closed.

The circle of my life becoming ever smaller. My attempts to stay afloat becoming ever more desperate.

'I've got a new number,' I said. I grabbed a pen and wrote the number of the phone I'd bought in Ross-on-Wye on a notepad, then placed the rumpled carrier bag on Baker's desk, and backed out of the room.

Baker went to check his brother's head.

'I'm sorry,' I said quietly.

Baker looked at me coldly.

There was nothing more to be said, so I left. As I walked down the stairs I heard Billy observe to his older brother, 'Fucking nutjob!'

'Tell me about it,' Baker replied. 'Does this hurt?'

Whatever Baker was doing must have been painful, because Billy howled and then exclaimed, 'Fuck, Paul! I don't need you mashing my skull as well!'

Well and truly alone, I opened the front door and stepped into the Whitechapel night.

CHAPTER 60

I woke with a start. My cheek was firmly pressed against the cold glass of the night bus window. I'd been dreaming of a different time, another life that felt as though it was mine, but which I could never reach. What was happening to me? Was I losing my mind? I placed my palm against my forehead and pressed hard. Frustration. Anger. Sorrow. They were all present but swamped by fear, which coursed through me. How had I foreseen Lomas's death? How could I trust myself? I felt as though I was coming apart, and no matter how hard I tried to hold it together it was like something inside me had broken.

'Fucking mentalist.'

The whispered words caught me by surprise. I looked around the crowded upper deck for their source. Night workers travelling home, drunk students and clubbers. And then there was me; an investigator.

Drunk.

A father hunting for his missing girl.

Lunatic.

A military man.

Fucking mentalist.

'You don't know me!' I yelled at my fellow passengers. 'You just don't!'

A couple of people rolled their eyes. Two men near the front of the bus whispered to one another and broke into jeering smiles. Everyone else was well trained in the London art of avoiding eye contact with strangers and shrinking back.

Expert in the art of pretending nothing had happened. I wondered why I couldn't pretend nothing had happened. Be like Sarah and the rest of the world, and move on.

'I didn't ask for this,' I said.

What was I doing? Why was I talking to strangers? I needed to get a grip.

I looked out of the window and tried to centre myself by taking in my surroundings.

'I didn't ask for this,' I repeated to myself.

I realised I was near my destination, so I got to my feet and pressed the button that alerted the driver I wanted to get off. I sensed relief from the other passengers; the unhinged one was leaving.

The rain felt good.

Cleansing.

I staggered away from the bus, shaking and unsteady. I had ridden three night buses, drifting in and out of consciousness, wondering what was happening to me, how I would ever get better, how it felt as though I was further from Amber than I'd ever been. And Katie Blake. Poor Katie Blake. Her mother had made the mistake of hiring a drunk who was losing his mind. I recalled the look on the face of Penny's friend, Marcie. She'd known what I was: a loser.

When I'd looked at Baker's gun, I'd realised how low I'd sunk. Even in my darkest moments in prison, I'd never considered taking my own life, but now...I was losing hope, and that was dangerous. The hope I'd find Amber was the only thing that had kept me alive and if I was thinking such dark thoughts, did it mean somewhere inside I'd given up?

At some point on my night bus odyssey, I'd realised that there was only one person who could help me, and took a fourth bus south.

I checked my watch: 4.45 am. I was early, but she would have to forgive me. I stepped through fast-forming puddles and walked towards the large double-fronted Victorian house that had always somehow managed to make me feel better.

I pounded on the front door for some time before a window opened above me.

'Who's there?' Ovitz asked.

I stepped back and looked up.

'Thomas? Do you have any idea what time it is?'

'I didn't know where else to go,' I replied. 'I need help.'

CHAPTER 61

The tea smelt good. Lady Grey with a slice of lemon. I could smell it from the large dining room that adjoined the galley kitchen. I sat alone at the long oak table. A relic of a time when the house had been alive with people. Ellen had often talked of her life before her husband, Michael, had passed away. The two of them had been active socialites, with self-admittedly tenuous connections to the lower echelons of minor royalty. Ellen's social connections were strongest in the arts. She said there was something about creative people that drew them to psychics, and she counselled many artists, filmmakers and musicians. Long ago, her huge house had buzzed with lively parties populated by London's boldest and brightest. Now, there was just work; Ellen's desire to celebrate had passed away with her husband. I looked at the oil painting of the distinguished man that watched me from the far wall. A member of England's landed gentry, Michael had scandalised his family by marrying a divorced psychic. Ellen never talked about her first husband, but I had always sensed a dark secret.

I was surrounded by the legacy of Ellen's marriage into an old English family. A huge oak sideboard that dominated the room, an antique mahogany armoire, and chairs that looked like they dated back to the Norman Conquest. Every surface was covered with small antiques and bric-a-brac that had some financial or sentimental value. The only surface that was relatively free of clutter was the expansive table. A pair of laden fruit bowls resided at the far end, nearest Michael's portrait. In the centre was a large glass vase that was crowded with fragrant, oriental lilies.

Hanging on the wall, between the two French doors that opened onto Ellen's lush garden, was an unusual sixteenth-century ceramic clock, formed into the shape of a shooting star. I found its loud ticking soothing; there was something reassuring about the definite way it marked the passing of each moment. The whole place made me feel rooted, calmer, tied to a reality. Maybe not my reality, but someone's, and that soothed away the shakes and dark storm churning inside me.

'Things always look better over a cup of tea,' Ellen said as she shuffled to the table.

She handed me a large fine bone china mug, and placed her own on a silver coaster, as she took her place at the head of the table. She managed to look regal in spite of the midnight hair and shabby pink dressing gown.

'What can I do for you, Thomas?' she asked.

I told her what had happened; the assassinations of Edward Lomas and his niece and the murder-suicide of the men who'd killed them. I told her about what I'd done to the Bakers, and how I thought I was losing my mind. I told her about the vision of Edward Lomas in the park. I told her everything.

'I knew Edward Lomas by reputation,' Ellen said when I was done. 'He was said to be a very powerful man. His passing is a great loss to the world.'

'He said you could help me.'

'I tried,' Ellen countered softly. 'I tried. You didn't believe in me. You said terrible things to me, Thomas. Do you remember?'

I nodded. 'I'm sorry. This is so alien to me. I'm a practical man. Lomas said this was happening to me because I'm gifted. And Amber was the same. What does he mean?'

'You do have the gift,' Ellen replied. 'But you're not ready to believe it, which is why I haven't spoken of it. You and your daughter are very powerful. In a way you've always known that. Your hunches are good; you can sense danger, anticipate what your enemies will do.'

'I…that's just instinct,' I replied.

She smiled. 'You see. You're not ready. Are you religious, Thomas?'

'Not anymore.'

'Some people believe the Bible is just a fairy-tale,' she explained. 'I believe it is an accurate history of the times. Throughout the Bible, God speaks to man. Think about that for a moment. If God spoke in the past, why do we not expect him to speak now? Do you think God has stopped talking? Or have we stopped listening?'

She paused and took a sip of her tea. She winced, and put the cup down.

'Still too hot,' she observed. 'What you call alien was regarded as normal for thousands of years. People tried to connect with something better than themselves to nourish their spirits. The few of us who still seek such nourishment can develop sight beyond sight. We can see the truth. Beyond fear, beyond distortion, beyond anger. We can see the truth in all its simple beauty.'

'Lomas said the man who sent me to find him was evil,' I said.

'There is another path,' she replied quietly. 'Some say that it is easier, but it is not one I could face.'

She pushed back her chair, stood up to reach across the table, took one of the long-stemmed lilies from the vase and placed it in front of her.

'This flower here is me,' Ellen said, pointing to one of the blooms on the stem. 'And this one is you. We are connected. In my world I seek to use this connection to better understand you. To nurture you. To help you. If a person has enough connections to the world around them, they can see things that will be. They can use their gift to heal. They can be a positive force. But for those on the other path…'

Ellen stared at the stem and her eyes took on an intensity I had never seen, and I followed her gaze to the lilies. The change was almost imperceptible at first, but it quickly became apparent the flowers on the stem were wilting at an unnatural pace. The stem itself was withering away.

'How are you doing that?' I asked.

'There are those who do not use their gift for good,' she replied, her concentration never wavering. 'By turning to darkness, they corrupt themselves. But there is freedom in that corruption; they can spread it and use it to gain power. Darkness begets darkness.'

The tips of the desiccated petals were now turning black, but still Ellen continued to inflict ugly transformation on the flower.

'They thrive on hatred, fear, pain, and the more they inflict, the greater their power. That is evil.'

Ellen relaxed, and sat back down in her chair. The flower in front of her was blackened and dead.

'How did you do that?' I asked.

'The gift, Thomas. Or rather a savage distortion of it,' Ellen said.

She suddenly shook with the force of a nasty, hacking cough that came from deep within her.

'Are you okay?' I asked.

She took a sip of her tea and her coughing fit receded. 'I'm fine, thank you. Just this old body giving up. Takes a lot out of a person, going to the darkness. There's a price to be paid.'

'You told me to take the deal,' I remarked. 'Why? I got people killed.'

'Perhaps that was not the deal,' she said. 'Perhaps there is one to come.'

'That's the problem, isn't it?' I responded tersely. 'If something works out, you take the credit, but if it goes wrong, the message was unclear or might have applied to something else.'

'Didn't you see what I just did?' she scoffed. 'Do you still think I'm a charlatan?'

I grew angry. 'The flower might have been a prop. Or there might be a heater in the table. Or you might have a strong alkaline on your fingers,' I countered. 'There are plenty of ways to explain what just happened.'

'My goodness you're a stubborn man. Listen to me, don't listen to me. It doesn't matter to me, but if you want peace, what I said before stands true; you must forget about your daughter and choose a different path. Only by doing so can you save yourself.'

'I'll never let her go!' I shouted. 'Never. I need answers, not sermons and mumbo jumbo.'

I stood up and stepped away from the table.

'This isn't like ordering ice cream, Thomas,' she said with more than a hint of resentment. 'You're asking me to see the unseeable. It is difficult and it does not always come in a form we would like. I can only tell you what I know. If you are ever to achieve peace, you must give up.'

I recoiled at the suggestion. The search for Amber defined me. What kind of man would I be if I let my daughter slip away? I didn't care if it drove me mad or took me to my death.

'The violence you experienced yesterday. The bloodshed? The murder? These are just a taste of the evil that will befall you if you continue on your path,' Ellen warned.

'You're asking me to give up!' I railed against the idea.

'I'm asking you to take a leap of faith,' she countered softly.

I cracked a wry smile. This woman didn't understand me. She didn't understand what I was going through. No one could.

'I lost my faith a long time ago,' I said. 'I'm sorry to have disturbed you. Thanks for the tea. You've helped me see things more clearly.'

I marched towards the door.

'Thomas,' she said. 'If you must do this, find the church.'

I stopped and turned to face her.

'Find the church,' she said. 'The answers lie there.'

I nodded.

'How do I reach you if anything else comes to me?'

I gave her my new phone number and she scribbled it down on a scrap of paper. She was a good woman, better than I deserved. She was still trying to help me even though she disagreed.

'Thank you,' I said.

'I'm sorry I couldn't do more for you,' she replied sadly, as I left.

The front door closed behind me with a satisfying finality. The rain had stopped and the soft glow in the sky hinted at the oncoming dawn and the promise of a new day. I walked away from Ellen's house more determined than ever. The self-pitying, confused mess of a man who had entered her house died inside it. I'd emerged with a clear sense of purpose, strong enough to take on the world and win. I would find my daughter at all costs.

CHAPTER 62

The first trains were running by the time I reached East Dulwich station, but the carriage was sparsely populated; a few well-to-do lawyers and stockbrokers trying to conceal their wealth under heavy, plain coats. Some of them kept giving me uncomfortable glances, but I stared back with hard indignation. I had just as much right to be on this train as them. Just because I lived in the shadows didn't mean I wasn't allowed into the light. One of the men got up and moved to another carriage, a second sidled along his bench seat, until he was out of my sight.

Masters of the universe? Cowards to a man.

As the train bounced and rocked its way into London, I caught myself nodding off, waking with a start every minute or so, my head snapping back from a wild loll. Eventually, fatigue took hold and carried me away.

To a dream.

A dark castle. Stone underfoot. Worn. Ancient.

Flicker of light ahead. A corridor lined with statues of the long dead. A sense of darkness ahead, but an irresistible compulsion to approach. Something hard and cold in the hand. A knife? No. Heavier.

Look down.

The long blade catches the light. A broadsword. Razor-sharp. Intricately carved with runes that carry unexplained magic and meaning.

A liveried tunic. A mail shirt. A warrior. A quest.

Vengeance.

Closer to the light now. An archway. A throne room. Tapestries. Paintings. Treasures of a rich kingdom. The throne glorious gold and red. But empty. No king. Step forward.

Dread.

Clasp the sword firmly. Step forward. A flicker in the corner. Movement behind the throne. Shadows coalesce.

Terror.

Hold strong. Shadows and darkness form around the throne. Swirling death. Step forward. Darkness congeals into a shape. A figure. A Spectre. Tall. Long muscular arms. Talons. Pure, faceless evil. Step forward.

A black sword materialises. The Spectre strikes out.

Fight.

My blade rises. The sound of clashing swords rings out. The Spectre attacks. Fast. Furious. The swords dance.

Too slow.

You're human, nothing more.

Too slow.

My blade is too late to a parry, and is knocked from my hand.

Skid.

Clatter.

The Spectre strikes out with an ethereal fist and I feel the chill force of the blow.

Flying. Fast.

The smash of bone against stone. Hard. Head wet with blood. Darkness closing in. Hold strong.

Fight.

Reach for my blade. Clasp the hilt. Hold strong. Spin. Toss the sword to the strong hand.

Fight.

Furious battle. An opening. A thrust.

The searing pain of a blade plunged into the heart of evil. An inhuman scream.

Darkness destroyed. Victory. Vengeance.

Hold strong.

CHAPTER 63

I woke to find the carriage empty and the train at a standstill in London Bridge station. I had no idea how long I'd been there. I rubbed my face and got to my feet. Flashes from my dream came to me, but I ignored them.

Dreams.

Messages.

Voices.

This was the world Ellen wanted me to enter. A world of mysticism and signs. Reading meaning where there was none. Guessing at the future and claiming credit for accuracy only with the benefit of hindsight.

What about the flower? And the vision of Edward Lomas?

A trick and a coincidence, I told myself.

The only thing that mattered was reason and the action of flesh. I warned myself never to look for meaning in the dreams of a mind that can be deceived. I'd been played for a fool and used to lead killers to Lomas. I would never allow myself to be played for a fool again. Not even by myself. I left the train and headed for Kennington.

Fifteen minutes later, I walked into Kennington Police Station and asked the uniformed officer at reception if I could see Noel. The lobby was busy with the usual mix of people reporting crimes mingling with those who might have perpetrated them. I shuffled about impatiently, having been told my enquiry was being dealt with.

The security door opened and a young plainclothes officer emerged. His colleague behind the desk singled me out for him and I stepped forward.

'Mr Schaefer,' Plainclothes began. 'I've asked around. Nobody's seen Detective Noel for a couple of days. He phoned in sick.'

'I need to find someone he introduced me to,' I responded. 'Someone from the Security Service. It's urgent.'

'Are you a friend of his?' was all he asked.

'We worked together,' I replied.

'If you give me your name, I can try to get a message to him,' Plainclothes offered.

I shook my head slowly. I wanted a name or number, something I could use to get to Shark Eyes, and I wanted to see if Noel had managed to find anything on the Church of the Eternal Light. I didn't believe Ellen had magical insight; it was just the next logical step.

'No. Thanks. It's better if I talk to him directly.'

'Can I at least take your name?' Plainclothes persisted.

I could tell from his tone he was no longer interested in helping me. He was worried I was some sort of threat.

'You're alright,' I said, backing away. 'I'll catch up with him myself.'

CHAPTER 64

Twenty minutes later, I was on Bethnal Green Road at the entrance to Noel's apartment block. I'd run background on him a few years ago, when we'd worked our first case together. I'd wanted to know if I could trust him and had been in the habit of running my own checks on everyone I worked with to ensure they weren't connected to any of the people I was investigating.

Noel's block was a huge, sprawling building that dominated the north side of Bethnal Green Road, near the tube station. Cityview House. Despite it being in the city, there wasn't much of a view for most of the flats. It was encircled by old warehouses that had been converted into pokey flats for young professionals brimming with dreams of making their mark on London.

I had tried Noel's buzzer, but there was no answer. I waited near the front door until a young woman in a sports kit and headphones left for a jog. I timed my move perfectly, caught the door just before it closed behind her, and slipped inside the building without the jogger even noticing.

Hundreds of wooden mailboxes stacked in rows like cheap little coffins, worn carpet and stained walls; this was exactly the type of place I'd expect police to live. Anonymous and ordinary. I checked the directions for apartment 618, and headed for the west wing of the building.

The lift stank of stale beer, urine, disinfectant and damp. The control panel was covered in graffiti. Among the modern-day satyrs parading their enormous members and notices of who would suck who for a pound was a message scrawled in black marker: *Life may suck, but it's better than the alternative.*

I wasn't so sure, but wouldn't be going to that dark place again if I could help it. I stepped out of the lift into a bright, airy corridor. The sixth floor was higher than any of the surrounding buildings, and the reinforced windows that ran down one side of the corridor offered great views of East London. The carpet was clean and the walls were a freshly painted pure white. There were four apartments off the corridor, all in a row down the western side. Noel's flat, 618, was the second one along. I knocked and waited. I knocked again, but there was no response. I hadn't replaced my Leatherman or lock picking tools, so I checked the corridor was clear, and forced the door open with my shoulder. I let the splintering wood settle and waited to see if there was any reaction from the neighbouring flats. There was none, and apart from the sounds of the city there wasn't even the slightest noise, so I pushed the door wide and went into the flat.

The smell hit me the moment I entered. That familiar mix of putrid sweetness and acrid decay. Death was here. I checked the master bathroom, which was by the front door: empty. I crept along the hallway and pushed open the next door, to what turned out to be a second bedroom. Noel had converted it into a home gym, where he sweated to prolong his lonely life. The next door along was ajar and I put my head round to see the master bedroom; curtains drawn, bed unmade. The en suite light was on and the extractor fan was whirring furiously.

I backed out and carried on down the hallway, which dog-legged round into an expansive living room and diner. A large leather sofa faced the panoramic windows that offered an enviable view of central London. Seated with its back to me, was Noel's still and lifeless body, the man's head listing to one side. I crossed the room and took in the gruesome scene. A curved, long-handled knife was embedded in Noel's chest. Blood had caked over his sweatshirt and pooled and dried in his lap. His staring, gelatinous eyes accused me with their unflinching gaze. More troubling than the dead policeman was the symbol daubed in blood on the wall behind him: the mandala that linked Amber's abduction with Katie Blake's kidnapping and Leon Yates's gang.

The sign of the Totus.

I turned back to Noel and noticed something in the dead man's hands. I leant forward and prized it from fingers that yielded more easily than I'd expected. The absence of rigor mortis suggested that Noel had been dead for over twenty-four hours. I studied the small, bloodstained card and immediately recognised it.

Thomas Schaefer, Private Investigator.

Planted in an attempt to put me in the frame. I wasn't moving in ever-decreasing circles. I was caught in a rip tide, flailing desperately in a wild effort to stave off drowning. These people were trying to push me under, and they'd come close to succeeding.

I pocketed the card, and closed Noel's eyes. For a split second, I envied the freedom and peace the dead man had. But as my eyes caught the curved blade, I reminded myself that I had work to do. This was another body at the feet of whoever led the Totus, and it was up to me to ensure they paid for what they'd done.

I scanned the room and saw Noel's coat hanging on the back of one of the dining chairs. I ferreted around and found what I was after, Noel's wallet, his identification and his warrant card. I pocketed them and slipped out of the flat. Taking great care to avoid being seen, I went down the fire stairs, and emerged onto the narrow side street beside Cityview House.

I leant against the rough, redbrick wall, legs wavering, mind spinning, body shaking. Another innocent life lost because of me. One more ally gone. One less friend. His death finally hit me and I vomited violently. Passers-by would only see a degenerate drunk hurling his life away. Only I knew my sickness was fear.

If these people would do that to police, what would they do to a child?

CHAPTER 65

The image was crystal clear. The days of fuzzy blurs indistinguishable from a vaguely grey background were long gone. I could clearly make out Shark Eyes as he stood by the open passenger door of the M-Class. Smoker, Scarface, No Neck and the Mercedes' number plate had been visible in other frames.

'Can you print that one, too?' I asked.

'No problem, Detective Noel,' the manager of Chesham station said eagerly.

I'd used Noel's warrant card to get into the control room and had talked the bored station manager into letting me review footage from the station's security cameras. Images from the night of my visit to Chesham filled the half-dozen screens that dominated one wall of the tiny control room.

'Were you undercover?' the station manager asked, indicating my presence in one of the pictures.

'Yeah.'

'What'd they do?' he probed. This was probably the most exciting thing to have happened to him all year.

'I'm not at liberty to discuss it, sir,' I replied solemnly, doing my best by-the-book cop impression.

'They look like nasty pieces of work,' he concluded. 'It's got to be something pretty bad.'

I collected the photo of Shark Eyes from the printer, and added it to the others I was already holding.

'Thanks,' I said. 'You've been a real help. I'll be sure to mention you in my report.'

The station manager beamed with pride as I left the control room. I knew that within a few minutes, the eager man would be on the phone to his friends and family, sensationalising my visit, but I didn't care; I had what I needed.

I leafed through the glossy images of the four men, and settled on a shot of the Mercedes as it drove away from the station. There, clearly visible at the bottom of the image, was the car's number plate.

CHAPTER 66

Noel's key card still worked. I used it to get into Kennington Police Station through the staff entrance at the rear of the building. I moved with confidence, nodding at the police officers I passed. They would be used to seeing dishevelled, unfamiliar faces. In my experience, undercover cops often looked rougher than real criminals.

I found my way to the central information office, which gave officers access to a variety of local and national law enforcement databases. I had chosen lunchtime for my incursion in an effort to minimise traffic in the room, but I had misjudged.

A group of young officers clustered around one of the terminals, and were arguing loudly over who could find the ugliest mugshot of any woman booked for soliciting in the area. I stopped in my tracks – this was too risky, but my window to escape closed suddenly when the data manager, a young woman with a sharply cut bob, caught sight of me.

'Try and ignore them,' she said. 'You new here?'

'I'm on assignment,' I said. 'I need to run a plate.'

'I'm Cassandra, but everyone calls me Cassie.'

'Tom,' I said.

'You got the digits?' Cassie asked.

I produced the photo from my jacket pocket and handed her the image of the Mercedes.

'Nice car,' Cassie observed.

I nodded, and followed her to a computer terminal on the far side of the room. I was careful to position myself with my back to the group of rowdy young officers and leant over Cassie as she fired up the machine.

'I've told them if the guvnor catches them they'll get suspended, but they don't care,' she told me.

'No, we don't,' one of the cops laughed. 'It's just a bit of harmless fun.'

'But it's not harmless,' I said to Cassie quietly, and she shook her head.

'Here we go,' she said a few moments later. She indicated the vehicle ownership details on the screen. My heart sank; the Mercedes was registered at an address I recognised: Thirty-Four Chapel Street – Leon Yates's house. The owner was a limited company – Area Boy Limited.

'Do you want a printout?' Cassie asked.

I shook my head.

'It's okay. I know the place,' I replied honestly. 'Thanks for being so quick.'

I turned for the door, as Plainclothes, the officer who'd come out to talk to me about Noel, entered.

'What have you freaks got for me today?' he yelled at his colleagues in the corner.

I hurried forward, hoping that the rowdy jeers would distract Plainclothes, but the young policeman spotted me and did a double take. I didn't hang around, and pushed past Plainclothes. I sprinted into the corridor and Plainclothes gave chase.

'Stop that man!' he yelled.

A klaxon sounded, and a uniformed officer came out of nowhere and tried to hit me with a baton, but I ducked the blow and kept running.

I burst out of the staff entrance into the path of two startled motorbike cops. One dropped his helmet, which I grabbed. I wheeled round and used the helmet to smash both officers in the face, knocking them cold.

I jumped the car park barrier and raced onto Mead Row. Four or five officers were coming down the street, and Plainclothes was leading a charge of half a dozen through the car park. I banked left and sprinted across the street towards the low rise council flats opposite. I could hear heavy footsteps closing and the yelled threats of violence as I scrambled up a six-foot wall. I pulled myself clear of danger just as Taser contacts spat into the bricks below.

I leapt into the communal rubbish enclosure, and pushed past the huge bins to emerge in a small grassed courtyard that was encircled by the low rise flats. A nervous young mother with two small children hurried into her ground floor home, as I raced across the yard. I knew I had another two or three minutes at most before a chopper arrived. The air felt like acid as my chest heaved with effort. More footsteps and shouts from behind. I looked over my shoulder to see the first officers spill out from behind the bins. I raced across a concrete path and ran up a narrow gap between two buildings.

I burst onto St George's Road and was relieved to see the police hadn't got ahead of me. I sprinted into the middle of the road and forced an oncoming driver to make a choice: kill me or stop.

The driver chose the latter, and I rewarded the shaken young woman by yanking her from her car, and stealing it. I accelerated and forked left along Westminster Bridge Road.

Distant sirens.

And the dreaded thrumming above me.

I craned my neck to look up through the windshield, and saw the underbelly markings of a police helicopter tracking the car. Ground support hadn't yet arrived, so I still had a chance – albeit a slim one.

I pushed the tiny Fiat 500 to its limits as I sped through traffic. I pulled in front of oncoming cars in order to pass a ponderous lorry, but there was no space for me to get back onto my side of the road. Amid the screech of tyres and a cacophony of horns, I mounted the pavement on the wrong side of the street, and headed for St George's Circus, trying not to hit any pedestrians, who were diving out of my way. I checked the rear view: still no cars, just the chopper to worry about.

The Fiat bounced as it flew off the high kerb onto the roundabout. I didn't attempt to take it the right way round, but wove through oncoming traffic and turned violently onto Borough Road, and sanctuary. Borough Road was one of the few streets in London that had extensive tree cover. I pulled the car to a sudden halt, jumped out, ran across the street and hailed a black cab as it came round the corner.

'Croydon,' I said breathlessly, as I clambered into the back of the taxi.

The driver nodded and hit the meter. I was pumping with adrenaline and had to fight the urge to scream at him to get going. After what seemed like an age, the cab started moving. A couple of passers-by, who had seen me ditch the Fiat, watched with suspicion, but this was London, and nobody was going to do anything to endanger themselves.

As the cab reached the roundabout, I looked up Westminster Bridge Road, to see four police cars approaching. The cabbie waited until they roared past, sirens blaring, lights flashing. I looked at the passing cars, their drivers and passengers so focused on their target that they didn't even give the cab the slightest glance. Once they were gone, the taxi driver moved on at a steady pace.

'I'm not going back that way,' the driver observed. 'Looks like something's kicked off. We'll cut east if that's alright with you.'

That was more than alright with me.

'You're the expert,' I said.

I knew I'd have to ditch the cab before Croydon, just in case one of the passers-by had taken down its number. But I'd let the driver enjoy the prospect of a big fare for a little longer.

The police would soon find out I'd used Noel's card to get into the station. That would lead them to the horror in Bethnal Green. I knew it wouldn't be long before I became a suspect in a murder inquiry. Whatever I was going to do would need to be done fast – I was about to run out of time.

CHAPTER 67

Her soft shoes were soundless. I watched her feet move in graceful silence as I followed her down the corridor. Young, full of promise, surrounded by madness. Charlie Simmons was too vulnerable to be working in a place like Milton House. Her blonde hair and blue eyes reminded me of Amber — *could it be her? They would have been about the same age —* and she seemed to have the same gentle spirit as my daughter. She shone with the same innocence and empathy.

Would I know her? Would I recognise my daughter if I passed her in the street? Had it already happened? I felt sick at the prospect.

Stop doing this to yourself, man, I thought.

'Dr Gilmore is normally quite strict about his therapy sessions,' Charlie warned me.

'This is urgent,' I insisted.

I'd changed cabs near Peckham and had spent much of the journey south worrying about whether I'd even be allowed into the hospital. Gilmore might have banned me following my attack on Derek Liddle, but when I arrived, Charlie, who'd been the duty nurse when I'd brought Liddle in, had greeted me as though nothing had happened.

She nodded, now, and led me through a security door, down another corridor until we came to a door marked *'Group Therapy Room'*.

Charlie knocked and opened the door. The room was a depressing, featureless space lit by bright sunshine that came through high windows, but instead of flooding the place with light, the height of the windows created a strip of gold against one wall, many feet above the heads of the occupants. Gilmore sat in a circle with eight patients, their chairs drawn into the centre of the room. There were three women, the rebellious Haley, the quiet Jane and the deeply troubled Anna, and five men, all staring at a large clock held by Gilmore. One of the men was the person I'd really come to see: Derek Liddle, carrying the evidence of the injuries I'd inflicted.

'With each passing tick, we become aware of our own mortality.' Gilmore spoke in a modulated, soothing tone. 'Another tock, and, if we do not have answers, we can seek to fill the void with false prophets and empty promises.'

Charlie cleared her throat and Gilmore looked up and caught sight of us.

'What's he doing here?' Derek asked. He groaned as he got up and backed towards the wall. 'Keep him away from me.'

'Nurse,' Gilmore said. 'Get the orderlies.'

'I'm sorry, Doctor,' she said. 'I didn't think.'

'Get the orderlies,' Gilmore repeated, and Charlie ran from the room.

'I'm not here to hurt him,' I said, closing on Derek.

'Stay away from me,' he warned.

'Thomas!' Gilmore yelled. 'Don't you dare.'

I felt hands grip my arm and looked down to see Anna trying to pull me away from Derek.

'Anna, don't get involved. You'll get hurt,' Gilmore said. 'Anna!'

I shook her free and walked on.

'I need to show him a photograph,' I said, producing the image from my pocket.

'This is wholly inappropriate,' Gilmore protested.

'Don't get in my way,' I replied.

'Would you turn on an old friend?' Gilmore asked.

I didn't answer, but stepped forward to confront Derek with the photograph.

'Do you know him?' I asked, thrusting the image of Shark Eyes into Derek's face.

Derek looked past the photo, directly into my eyes. His face was disfigured and swollen from our last encounter.

'What can come of evil, but evil?' he asked.

'Thomas, please don't do this,' Gilmore pleaded as he stepped forward to intervene. 'He's at a delicate stage of his treatment.'

I placed my hand on Gilmore's chest to keep him at bay. The old man was not about to prevent me following up my only lead on Shark Eyes.

'His car was registered to Leon Yates's home address,' I told Gilmore. 'He and Leon Yates knew each other. That means there's a good chance Derek here knows him.' I turned to Derek. 'Do you know him?'

'He is the background of all our lives,' he replied.

'Who is he?' I demanded.

'Who are you?' Derek responded.

I felt rage start to build. This was going to have to turn ugly.

'Go to Hell,' Derek said with a goading smile.

'Get everyone else out,' I told Gilmore, but he didn't move.

Instead, the door burst open and four orderlies steamed in and dragged me from the room.

CHAPTER 68

I struggled against the men, but there were too many of them. Gilmore followed us out, furious.

'You're never to come here again!' His face was red and contorted with anger. 'You've become a monster, Thomas. Living in this world has changed you! I don't want to see you again.'

He stopped when we were halfway along the corridor.

'Throw him out,' Gilmore shouted at the orderlies. 'And make sure no one ever lets him back in.'

'You brought me into this world,' I said, as I was dragged away. 'You made me! You did this!'

'You did this to yourself, Thomas.' He looked at me sadly before returning to the therapy room.

I raged and fought against my captors, but it was no use. Within minutes they'd thrown me out of the hospital, hurling me bodily onto the drive before running inside and locking the front door.

I picked myself up, fuming, and walked away, already planning how I was going to break into the place and get some time with Derek Liddle.

My phone rang as I stalked along the driveway. When I pulled it out of my pocket, I saw I had three missed calls.

'Hello?'

'Mr Schaefer, thank God you answered,' came a woman's voice.

'Who is this?' I asked.

'It's Bernie. Ellen Ovitz's assistant.' Another young woman I'd desperately thought might be Amber. 'I've been trying to reach you.'

'I was busy.'

'Ellen needs to see you, Mr Schaefer. It's important.'

'I'll be there in about an hour,' I replied, before hanging up.

CHAPTER 69

The jade dragon watched me from the windowsill. I sat opposite Ellen Ovitz and waited. Bernie had shown me into the room and backed out to leave the two of us eyeing each other. I'd been close to a breakdown, or maybe I'd broken, and had said some cruel things the last time we met. She'd only been kind in return, and I had left her house feeling so much better than when I'd arrived.

'I'm sorry,' I said, breaking the silence. 'I didn't mean...'

'I understand, Thomas. You're under a great deal of pressure. I'm glad Bernice found you,' Ellen said. 'I have something important to tell you. Before we continue, I need to know exactly what Edward Lomas said to you.'

'He said the man from MI5 was evil,' I replied. 'He told me to look for the count when all was lost.'

'The count?' Ellen asked.

His words had also puzzled me. Was it a reference to that old book? To Count Eudes of Burgundy?

Ellen shook her head. 'That's not it. What did he say about me?'

'He said, "There is one who can guide you to the light. You must listen to her."'

'Did he mention my name?' she asked earnestly.

I thought carefully, recalling the old man's last moments. 'No,' I said at last. 'He didn't mention you.'

Ellen nodded her head solemnly.

'It's not me,' she said. 'The messenger is someone else.'

'It has to be you,' I protested. 'I don't know any other…'

'Gifted people,' she suggested. 'It's not me, Thomas. I've sought guidance on the matter. The messenger Edward Lomas spoke of is someone gifted, someone worthy. Someone you would not expect to give you such a message. It is someone you have shared much with. Someone you've been close to. A person you trust.'

I thought about the handful of people who would fall into that category, and a name suddenly forced its way to the forefront of my mind.

'Penny?' I said. 'Penny Blake?'

Ellen was puzzled.

'Katie Blake's mother,' I explained. 'We, well, she found out about me. I told her what happened and we…we're close. And I trust her.'

'I see,' Ellen said. 'You need to bring her here, Thomas. As soon as possible. Take my car.'

CHAPTER 70

It took me fifteen minutes to get to Penny Blake's house, but when I arrived, she wasn't there. I'd borrowed Ellen's car, and returned to the classic Mercedes to wait. I kept an eye on Penny's house while I made a call. It rang out, so I dialled again. On the third attempt, I got through.

'Hello?' Baker said.

'It's Schaefer.'

'I know who it is. You gave me your new number. You'll hear from me when I've got something,' Baker said coldly, before hanging up.

A dead line. A dead relationship, but I wasn't going to lament the loss of Baker; I had bigger things to worry about. I sat outside Penny's house for over two hours before she finally showed up. In the harsh, grey light of day, she looked wrung out. Her eyes were rimmed red and weighed down with bluish bags that even the best concealer couldn't hide. Her face fell when I stepped from the car, and I instantly knew that there was something wrong.

'What are you doing here?'

'I've got a lead,' I said. 'I need you to come with me.'

'What? No. I can't,' Penny replied, avoiding my gaze. She was afraid. 'Marcie's inside. She's waiting for me.'

'There's no one home,' I observed. 'I've been here a while.'

'She's coming,' Penny lied. 'She'll be here any minute.'

She tried to push past me, but I grabbed her arm and held it fast.

'What's happened?' I demanded to know. 'Why are you afraid?'

'Let go of me!' Penny tried to pull her arm free.

'I'm trying to help you,' I protested, holding her firmly. 'I'm the only hope you've got of ever seeing Katie again.'

The slap was sudden and hard, but it didn't surprise me enough to release my grip. She struggled some more, but when it became clear my grip wouldn't break, she stared at me with burning indignation.

'I spent the morning with the police, Schaefer. I went in for an update on their investigation, but almost the whole time was taken up with talking about you,' she said angrily. 'You're wanted in connection with the murder of a policeman.'

I felt a lurch of nausea. The walls were closing in. I was going to be fitted up for Noel's murder. A long stretch this time, killing any hope of finding Amber. Penny was no longer just a potentially valuable source of information; she was also a threat. The moment I released her, she'd phone the police.

'Murder!' Penny spat. 'They told me you're a homeless drunk who goes around beating people up. That you're borderline insane, that you won't listen to anyone who tells you the truth – that your daughter's dead. She's dead, Schaefer, dead!'

Penny was screaming by now.

'She's never coming back! Never! And you've dragged my Katie down with you! Katie!'

She screamed and shouted as she fought to get free, and the first curtains twitched in a house across the road. The neighbours would respond soon.

I felt no anger, merely practical necessity. There was only one solution. I punched Penny square in the jaw. A look of shock flashed across her face for a split second, before her eyes rolled back in her head. I caught her before she hit the pavement, and moved quickly, dragging her to the Mercedes and laying her across the back seat. I got behind the wheel, started the engine, which roared into life reassuringly, and sped away, trying to figure a way out of the mess I found myself in.

CHAPTER 71

I parked the Mercedes in its spot outside Ellen's house, and hurried out to close the black gates. By the time I returned to the car, Bernie was at the front door.

'Did you find her?' she asked.

Her face fell when she saw me lift the unconscious Penny out of the car.

'What happened?' Bernie asked. 'Is she okay?'

I didn't respond as I carried Penny across the threshold. Ellen was fussing over her cats in the pantry at the far end of the hall. Her expression changed from motherly indulgence to thunderous disapproval the moment she saw me.

'What have you done?' she exclaimed.

'How do you know I did anything?' I replied, trying not to look at the purple swelling on Penny's face, which was becoming more pronounced with each passing minute.

'Thomas!' Ellen said impatiently.

'You told me to get her,' I protested. 'She wasn't going to come any other way.'

'Take her upstairs to the Pink Bedroom,' Ellen commanded. 'Bernice and I will look after her.'

I climbed two flights of stairs and crossed a landing that was crowded with fluffy toys and shelves that were covered with more fine china figurines. I took Penny into the second bedroom, which was dominated by an antique double bed, and gently placed her on the soft quilt.

'I'm sorry,' I said quietly.

'She probably isn't that interested in anything you've got to say,' Ellen said tersely, as she entered.

Bernice followed, carrying a first aid kit.

'Leave her to us,' Ellen instructed. 'I'm going to give her a healing, and I don't want you messing it up with your bad energy.'

'Where—'

'Downstairs,' Ellen cut me off. 'You can wait in the sitting room.'

I backed out of the room, as Ellen laid her hands upon Penny. Bernie shut the door on me.

I had been healed by Ellen once, long ago, when I had been at my weakest and most desperate to believe in her power. I hadn't enjoyed the strange sensation of Ellen's hands burning with a cool flame, and couldn't cope with the loss of control that came with the healing. At the time, I had been convinced I'd travelled to a place without space or time, where my sense of self was lost in communion with something far bigger, but now, with the benefit of hindsight, I knew that I had simply succumbed to sleep and experienced some strange dreams. The idea that the body could be healed by the power of another's will was ridiculous, but, given the circumstances, I wasn't about to share that thought. I left them to it and went downstairs.

CHAPTER 72

Three hours into my wait and the clock struck six. The small sitting room was on the same side of the house as Ellen's consulting room. There was a small two-seater sofa, a brass coffee table, a small grandfather clock and some large potted plants. There was a stack of magazines on the table to cater to almost every interest, but I'd ignored them, and had focused instead on how I could get myself out of trouble. It would take some very fast talking to convince Penny not to call the police, and she was bound to share the news I was on the run from a murder charge with Ellen and Bernie. Would they turn me in? Almost certainly. Ellen was alternative, but she wasn't a criminal and had very clear opinions of right and wrong.

I only had two reasons to hope. The first was grounded in very real detective work; Baker would trace the two men who'd posed as MI5 operatives and used me to lead them to Edward Lomas. The second was a more tenuous hope that Ellen was right and that Penny had a message or some guidance that would give something of value.

My phone rang, and I recognised Baker's number.

'Yeah,' I said.

'Ranoush. Seven-thirty.'

Baker hung up without saying anything else.

I checked the clock: 6.15 pm. I had just over an hour to get into central London. I left the sitting room, walked up the second staircase and crossed the long landing to find Bernie sitting outside the Pink Bedroom.

'Ellen's had to go very deep. She says your friend's spirit is badly damaged,' she offered by way of explanation.

'I've got to go,' I said. 'Something urgent. I'll be as quick as I can. If she wakes up before I get back, ask Ellen to give me a call.'

'I don't think she'd want you to go, Mr Schaefer.'

'Probably not, but then I never do what she wants,' I said with a wistful smile. 'I'm going to borrow the car again. I'll let you decide whether you want to tell her that.'

I left Bernice looking deeply troubled, hurried downstairs, grabbed the car keys from the bowl on the sideboard and made a swift exit. I shut the heavy front door firmly behind me, and felt far more confident of what lay ahead of me than what I'd left behind. A lover and client who suspected me of murder and a psychic convinced in messages from beyond were uncomfortable territory.

If, as I hoped, Baker was armed with a couple of names and addresses, I'd be in my element. I opened the gates, jumped in the Mercedes, gunned the engine and headed for the city.

CHAPTER 73

I parked the car in a bay on Portman Square and walked four blocks to Edgware Road, taking care not to draw attention to myself. I had to assume my photo was in the hands of every police officer in London. I also had to assume Baker would be aware the police were after me. That put the decadent man in a powerful position. If he wanted to curry favour with the law, he could turn me in. No overt betrayal needed. All very coincidental; a passing policeman happens to spot me heading to our meeting place, and calls for back-up. I get busted on the way out, and Baker slinks away without me knowing he'd set the whole thing up. After our last meeting, Baker had made it clear he wanted me out of his life, and what better way to get rid of me and avenge the attack on his brother than to send me away for a stretch?

I had stayed east of Edgware Road to avoid the discreet permanent police surveillance operation in force around Connaught Square to protect Tony Blair, the former prime minister. When I reached the corner, I turned right and walked halfway up and down Edgware Road, not once, but twice, checking the rooftops, windows and doorways for any tell-tale signs of surveillance on the tiny café Baker had chosen.

When I was satisfied, I headed for Ranoush Juice, a small *shawarma* bar on the west side of Edgware Road, near the junction with Connaught Street. The place served one of the best sandwiches in London and was Baker's eatery of choice. I'd watched the man scoff Ranoush's signature sandwiches on many occasions. I checked the surrounding shops and restaurants, but there were no obvious threats.

I saw Baker through the window. He was sitting at a table near the back, and was midway through a wrap. He stiffened when he saw me enter. Arabic music played from recessed speakers and the half-dozen or so customers conversed in the same language. The air was rich with aromatic spices and the smell of sweet roasted meat. Like experts in any field, the two chefs behind the counter maintained an air of haughty detachment and didn't even acknowledge my arrival. I joined Baker at his feast.

'I didn't know how long I should wait,' he said between mouthfuls. 'Seems a lot of people want to talk to you.'

So, he knew. I took comfort in the thought Baker wouldn't have raised the subject if he planned to betray me.

'It's a frame-up. Probably the same guys who killed Lomas,' I explained.

'Hey, as long as nobody clocks us together, none of this is my problem.' He shrugged. He took another mouthful of juicy sandwich.

'How's Billy?' I asked.

Baker stared coldly and simply nodded as he chewed his food.

'I'm really sorry,' I said. 'I was—'

'You want anything to eat?' A waitress cut me off. She was in her early forties with a scraggly blonde bob, smoker's lines around her mouth, and sad eyes that had once dreamt of bigger things. 'Sandwich? Chips?'

'Nothing,' I replied. 'I'm not hungry.'

'You have to order something,' the waitress said. 'It's policy. Tables are for customers only.'

'He'll have some chips. And a sandwich,' Baker added as an afterthought. As the waitress hurried away to fill the order, he leant forward. 'They know me here. So, don't embarrass me.'

He started to unwrap his next sandwich.

'I found your people,' he said, producing an envelope folder that he'd kept concealed on his lap. It was thin and contained a few pieces of paper, and some photographs.

'The two fingers belonged to Steve Richards and Joseph Benyon. Not MI5 by any stretch,' Baker said.

I bridled at the ease with which I'd been played. Had they threatened Noel? Or misled him too? Either way, they'd manipulated him into vouching for them, which had convinced me they were with the Security Service.

'Wouldn't have thought they'd be able to get one over on you, Schaefer,' Baker observed.

I didn't reply, but I knew desperation had made me weak.

'Both of no fixed abode,' he went on. 'Both ex-cons. Richards did a four-year stint for GBH, Benyon was in and out, mostly for drugs. Nothing in the past three years; as far as the law's concerned they dropped off the radar. Nothing on the electoral role, no bills, no phones, no nothing. All I got was a bank account for Benyon, which wasn't much to go on. But then I noticed a standing order he's got set up to pay a gas bill on a property. I checked out the address, and it's an old theatre on the Streatham High Road. Only it isn't a theatre anymore. There's nothing online, but I went down there and the place has been taken over. It's now the First Church of the Eternal Light.'

The moment he revealed the name, adrenaline flooded my body.

He drew my attention to a leaflet caught inside the envelope folder.

'I picked that up in the lobby. Proper dodgy place,' he said.

The amateurishly printed, folded document promised redemption, salvation and release from mortal toil. On the back of the leaflet was a photograph of a man I recognised. It was Shark Eyes.

'Pastor goes by the name of Felix Obsidian,' Baker continued. 'That's your man, right?'

I nodded as I studied the photo. Shark Eyes – Obsidian – wore some kind of cassock, his mouth was contorted into a rictus smile, but his eyes were dead and inhospitable. I felt nothing but hatred as I looked at the man.

'I appreciate this, Baker, I really do. Thanks,' I said, getting to my feet.

'Schaefer?' he responded. 'Remember what I said about not wanting to see you again?'

I gave a slight nod.

'I meant it. We're through,' Baker said, before turning back to his sandwich.

I understood. I wished I hadn't treated him and his brother so badly, but I had, and this was the price. I knew it was the last time we'd see each other.

'One more thing,' Baker said, looking up. 'What the fuck did you do with my car?'

'It's in Ross-on-Wye, on Greytree Road,' I replied.

'And the keys?' Baker asked.

'In the glovebox,' I said, before walking away.

I heard Baker mutter curses under his breath as I stepped through the automatic doors onto Edgware Road. For all his flaws and baser desires, Baker had been useful in a tight spot. I would never have described him as a friend, but, like Noel, the man was probably the closest thing I had to one.

People were turning their backs.

Doors were closing.

Walls were closing in.

I was running out of time.

I crossed the busy street and hurried to the car. It wouldn't take me long to reach Streatham.

CHAPTER 74

I staggered along Streatham High Road, playing the part of a tumbledown drunk in order to check the place out. The First Church of the Eternal Light was housed in a Victorian theatre on the corner of Hilldown Road. The building was in a state of disrepair. At some point in time, chunks had fallen from the stonework around the roof, like missing teeth from a rotten mouth. Paint flaked like dead skin and damp rose like a creeping disease. The high windows had been veiled to hide whatever was happening inside. A large red neon sign pulsed with the word *CHURCH,* and cast an eerie glow over the main entrance, which was set into a curved wall that linked the building's street-side frontages. Two men stood outside the entrance. Hard, unwelcoming faces, and cheap polyester suits that shimmered in the red light.

I turned right and walked down Hilldown Road, maintaining the pretence of a lost-cause drunk to check the rear of the building. There was an alley that ran behind the church, and a padlocked fire escape. That was the only other way in, and there was no way of knowing where it led. I was going to have to go in through the front entrance. I just needed to be sure of one thing.

I returned to Streatham High Road, staggered across the busy street and concealed myself in a pile of donation bags in the doorway of a charity shop directly opposite the church. The doorway stank of old vomit and urine, but I got used to the smell quickly and it kept people away. I watched the building for three hours, and far from being welcoming acolytes tasked with seeking new recruits, the two doormen gave any passers-by who showed the slightest interest in their church the same unflinching, cold stares. *Outsiders, they not welcome.* I recalled Leon Yates's words and they most definitely applied here.

Finally, shortly before midnight, a familiar car pulled up, the Mercedes M-Class. No Neck jumped out of the driver's seat and hurried round to open the door for the man I now knew as Felix Obsidian. The two doormen bowed their heads as he approached, but Obsidian didn't even bother to acknowledge his subordinates as he entered the building. I knew what I was about to do was desperate and dangerous, but I didn't have much choice. Obsidian had used me to kill Lomas, and framed me for Noel's murder. This man was my prime suspect in Amber's abduction, and just the thought of that made my whole body tremble with rage.

I couldn't go to the police, and if I didn't act fast, I'd get picked up by the police in the next couple of days anyway and spend a good few weeks trying to prove I had nothing to do with Noel's murder. If I failed, I'd get a life sentence, and Amber would be gone forever. If I succeeded, and managed to walk free, there was no guarantee that Obsidian would still be around.

I leant into my anger. I'd need it for what would come next. This man. This cruel, manipulative man was the closest I'd come to a suspect in my daughter's abduction in ten years. I was not about to let this opportunity slip.

I climbed out of the pile of bags and dodged the traffic as I crossed Streatham High Road. I stumbled for effect as I stepped onto the pavement on the other side to ensure the doormen only saw a shambling drunk. The taller of the two signalled to his colleague and they both smirked at me.

'Can I help you, brother?' the tall one asked, as I drew near. 'You look lost.'

I whipped my fist into the man's face with such force I felt his nose shatter. The shorter doorman was startled by my sudden, violent sobriety, and, as his companion fell senseless, didn't even manage to get his hands up to protect himself as I stepped in to deliver a ferocious head-butt that sent him sprawling.

I shot up the stone steps and walked through the opaque double doors into a dilapidated marble lobby at the bottom of a large atrium, which went all the way up to a filthy round skylight in the roof. An ornate staircase ran round the outside of the atrium to the top of the building. I was immediately greeted by two unfriendly faces. Unlike the men outside, these guys weren't wearing suits; they were in jeans and t-shirts, and judging by the look of them, they weren't hired for decoration. The squat black man and his white, skinhead colleague were covered in tattoos and scars. Both were muscled and looked as though they could handle themselves.

'Who are you?' the squat one asked.

I reverted to my drunk act.

'Wassur, mate. Yer pals ouuside, tell me yer gotta pissoir,' I said as I closed on him.

'Get the fuck out of here!' the squat man said.

He reached out to grab my arm, but I was waiting for the move, and stepped inside his reach to rabbit punch his solar plexus. I followed up by driving my knuckles into his

Adam's apple, and, as he fell back, choking, I clobbered him around the ears with both fists. The squat man went down hard, and cracked his head on the marble floor.

The skinhead crossed the lobby and smashed the glass that covered an old-fashioned fire alarm. I rushed towards him, but he twisted the mechanism before I could get to him, and the sound of a loud, constant klaxon filled the building.

I was in trouble.

CHAPTER 75

I rushed the skinhead and smashed the man's skull against the wall, and his eyes went glassy. I did it again, hard, and they rolled back in their sockets, and I let the big man drop.

Noise echoed around the atrium, and I stepped into the middle of the lobby to look at the staircase. I saw shadows of activity on the landings above me, and heard thunderous footsteps. At the top of the building, looking over the balustrade of the very highest landing, was Obsidian, and I boiled with rage when I registered the man's self-satisfied smile.

I looked round the lobby and saw no weapon or tool I could use to my advantage, so I'd have to use the stairs themselves. The staircase was only wide enough for two people, three at a push. If I met them on the stairs, I'd only have to face two at a time, so I flung off my jacket and hurried to the foot of the stairs. I was halfway up the first curved flight when the vanguard of Obsidian's horde came into sight. Eight men. They sprinted across the first landing and raced downstairs to meet me.

The cohort paired off and descended in twos. I just had to ensure I held firm against the initial onslaught. If their momentum carried me downstairs to the wide lobby, I was finished. The first two were rabid with anger. One was shirtless, the other wore a vest. Shirtless wielded a baseball bat, and Vest had a far more useful, but dangerous, short-handled axe. I sidestepped and let Shirtless's momentum carry him down the stairs.

The bald man following Shirtless was caught off balance by my manoeuvre, and I grabbed his head and pulled him diagonally down, in front of Vest's first axe blow. As the blade buried itself in Bald's back, I twisted the screaming man and hurled him down on top of Shirtless. He fell past me and I grabbed the axe handle and yanked the weapon out of his back. Bald tumbled onto Shirtless and both men fell down the stairs, and collided with the hard marble below. Vest was aghast to see the axe in his enemy's hand, and I worked the advantage. As the man tried to retreat, one of his associates stepped forward and struck me with a short cosh. The blow caught my collarbone and sent me onto one knee. The pain was agonising, but adrenaline overwhelmed it and I lashed out, slashing Vest and his neighbour across the shins with the axe blade. Both men buckled, and I stood to face their accomplices, who were trying to clamber over them to get to me. I kneed Vest in the face and dug my axe into the shoulder of a man wielding what looked like a chair leg. Chair went down, tumbling over Vest and sending both men hurtling towards the bottom of the stairs. In one fluid motion, I stepped out of their way, wheeled round and struck the next man in the ear with the flat side of the axe head. The blow sent him reeling into his neighbour, and I pressed my advantage, pulling the neighbour forward and then pushing him down the stairs. I punched the man I'd hit with the blunt axe head, and knocked him out.

There was only one man left to face in this group. He had fearful eyes, and held a short wood saw in front of him. I was impressed. Not many people recognised the fighting advantages of a domestic saw. The weapon is great for slashing and the serrated edge can cause extremely painful damage in a confined environment. It would be very useful for whatever lay further up the building and I silently thanked the nervous man for bringing me such a useful tool.

Few things are more demoralising than seeing an axe-wielding maniac dispatch an entire gang, and Fearful Eyes did the best he could in the circumstances. As I approached, he made a wild lunge with the saw, but he misjudged the distance between us and the blade swung through the air, throwing him off balance. I took the opportunity to hack at the man's arm with the axe. Two fearsome blows opened up a fountain of blood and sent him into a screaming collapse. I picked up the saw and headed up the stairs.

CHAPTER 76

The first-floor landing was clear and I met no resistance on the stairs up to the second, but when I reached the next landing, I found a group of eight acolytes, each armed with a club, knife or some other handy weapon. I thought about backing down the stairs, but spotted a more advantageous option. I rushed to the edge of the landing and put my back to the balustrade. My position prevented me from being surrounded, but it meant I was forced to fight four men at once as I inched my way to the next flight of stairs.

I used the axe and saw to parry furiously, focusing purely on the defensive, until I felt the first step of the next flight under foot. I slashed wildly with the saw, creating space, and backed up the stairs quickly, forcing my assailants into pairs, and as they came at me, I switched to the offensive. With two weapons and the advantage the stairs gave me in height, I gave these men an education in hand-to-hand combat. The SAS had given me the opportunity to learn from some real monsters, and I passed on their lessons now.

I used the saw to scour the top of the first man's scalp, and swung the axe into his neighbour's gut. As they went down, I slashed at the two men behind them, using the saw to gouge out chunks in one man's neck, and the axe to cleave the thigh of another. I backed up the stairs and allowed the last four to clamber over their convulsing, screaming colleagues.

I sensed danger at the last possible moment and instinctively brought the axe handle up to parry a blow from a baseball bat. Batter, a monstrous man, had crept from above, and was behind me, attacking from two steps up. I didn't like this. Fighting on two fronts would get me killed, so I did the only sane thing and ran up the stairs in a crouch, hitting Batter in the groin with my shoulder. The bat was brought down on my back, but I ignored the blow, grabbed the guy's legs and tossed Batter over my back, into the path of the four men on my tail. As the five men collided and tumbled downstairs, I ran up to the third-floor landing.

The whistling sound told me to duck. A split second later a razor-sharp sword blade skewered the space where my head had been. I rolled and stood to see a tall man holding a samurai sword. The man's grip and stance let me know I was not dealing with an expert, but even in the hands of a novice, one of those blades was bad news. I lunged with the saw, and when Samurai parried the blow, I moved in close, to reduce the advantage of the long-bladed weapon. Samurai punched me in the face, dazing me and bloodying my nose, but I was not about to allow myself to be forced back. I stood my ground and took another dizzying punch. When Samurai brought his fist up for a third, I raised the axe and held it in front of my face. Samurai split his fist open on the blade of the axe, and keeled over in agony. I put him out of his misery by cracking him on the back of the head with the heel of the axe.

I picked up the dropped sword and turned to confront Batter and his four colleagues, who had recovered their senses and made it to the third floor. Baseball bats, clubs and knives were no match for a samurai sword in the hands of someone vaguely proficient. I moved through the men like a vengeful scythe through errant grass, opening up flesh in their arms, legs and torsos. In less than a minute five men lay bleeding and crying at my feet.

I ran up the stairs towards the fourth floor, sweating profusely and out of breath, but I was alive and the old rush of battle was back. I felt as though I could take on another army of these fiends. I was close, so close to finding her, and hope mixed with adrenaline to send me into a euphoria. Old soldiers spoke of berserker frenzy, a battle madness that came upon certain warriors and made them legends, and I felt as though I could be among their number this night.

I didn't even skip a beat when I saw No Neck at the top of the stairs, holding an Ingram MAC-10 that had been fitted with a large suppressor. I heard a series of cracks and saw the muzzle light up, and bullets thudded into the wall by my head. I recognised them as warning shots, but was in no mood to heed them.

I charged up the final few steps and hurled my sword at No Neck. The deadly blade spun through the air, but the big man dodged it. I hadn't intended to hit him, merely distract him while I covered the ground that separated us. I barrelled into No Neck and kept pushing until I felt the butt of the MAC-10 crack against his neck. I stood up rapidly and caught No Neck on the chin, sending the man's head flailing back wildly. I punched him in the temple and heel-kicked him in the knee, snapping it. As the big man fell, I delivered a powerful right cross to his face.

With No Neck out cold, I picked up the MAC-10 and the samurai sword and headed for the double doors on the other side of the landing. I pulled one of the tarnished brass handles and stepped inside.

CHAPTER 77

I entered what had once been the theatre lighting control room. Observation windows set into the far wall offered a view of the main auditorium. The control panels and lighting equipment were long gone, replaced by a large double bed, a sofa and screened dressing area. Candles burnt around an altar area set against the left wall. A carved relief of the mandala that had plagued me was surrounded by other occult images. A goat's skull lay on the floor, encircled by dead weeds. I looked up and saw a large painting of the mandala on the ceiling, and there was no doubt in my mind Obsidian was connected to Amber's kidnapping. He stepped out of the shadows and stood before me in a black-and-red satin robe that matched the sheets on the bed.

'You truly are a thing of beauty,' Obsidian said calmly. 'Come in, Mr Schaefer, we have much to do.'

I moved forward, brandishing the samurai sword.

'You are going to tell me everything you know about my daughter.'

He seemed unmoved by the threat and simply smiled. 'Like so many in the world, you are chasing an illusion. You want your daughter, and that is understandable. But she is not what you need. What you need is the truth. Only then can you set yourself free.'

'I didn't come here to talk riddles. You're going to tell me where she is,' I countered. 'One way or another.'

'What are you going to do to me, Mr Schaefer?' he asked. 'What are you going to do, that I have not done to myself already?'

Obsidian opened his robe and allowed it to drop to the floor, revealing his naked body. I had never seen such extensive scarring and the sight turned my stomach. Below the neck, Obsidian was a hideous mess of disfigured tissue. His torso, arms and legs all bore the evidence of horrific wounds with whips, knives, bullets, razors and other implements that I could not even guess at. Most disturbing of all was that Obsidian had been roughly castrated and dismembered. A ragged stump was all that remained of his reproductive organs. Whether self-inflicted or not, Obsidian had suffered through the most tremendous evil, and his corrupted flesh was a testament to his warped history.

'Can you see, Mr Schaefer? Can you see how beautiful he makes us?'

'Who?' I asked. 'Who are you talking about?'

He roared and ran at me. I couldn't kill this man. He was my only link to Amber, so I dropped the gun and sword and prepared to meet him as he charged. I sidestepped, clasped my hands together and drove the balled fist down into the back of his head. He tumbled to the floor, and, buzzing with charged rage, I kicked him in the face. His eyes lost focus and his arms and legs flailed as he fought the pull of unconsciousness.

'Who are you talking about?' I asked, driving my boot into his ribs. 'Where's my daughter?'

He groaned and tried to protect himself, but I kicked him again.

'Tell me what you know!' I yelled. 'Where is she?'

I kicked him again and again and again, and he gave up trying to protect himself and rolled onto his back. He stared up at me, his bruised and bloodied face contorted in pain.

'I'll tell you nothing,' Obsidian rasped. 'Finish it. Kill me.'

I staggered away from the grotesque man, suddenly aware of the monster I'd become. I'd maimed and killed tonight, and now I was standing on the precipice, ready to torture and kill this man because he stood in my way. He was possessed of the same inner strength as me and the two of us collided in a battle of wills. His turned to evil, mine set on one purpose.

'Where's my daughter?' I cried. I looked down at his horrifically scarred body and my mind raced with terrible thoughts of the ugly things he might have done to my little girl. 'What have you done with her?'

'Even if I knew, I wouldn't tell you.' Obsidian spat a mouthful of blood onto the floor. 'You're too perfect to ruin. Too beautiful, Mr Schaefer. This is your fate. You cannot escape it. He made sure of that.'

He goaded my anger to new heights. 'Then I've got nothing to lose,' I said, reaching down to pick up the sword. 'I'm going to send you to Hell, Pastor.'

I stood over him, and the blade glinted in the candlelight.

'Do it,' Obsidian murmured. 'Finish this.'

I hesitated.

'Do it, Dolor Man,' Obsidian said. 'Think of all the nice things we've done with your girl, and do it.'

The words were like a finger pulling a trigger, and they sparked in me a fury I'd never felt before. He'd just confessed, but refused to relieve my suffering. He deserved to be punished. He deserved to die. It was justice. I focused on his neck and brought the sword down. He shut his eyes as the blade sliced the air above him, racing down towards his throat.

CHAPTER 78

I heard something, and stopped myself at the last moment. The blade froze millimetres above Obsidian's neck.

'Help,' a voice said weakly, between sobs.

'No!' Obsidian said, and he tried to roll clear of the sword, but I kicked him in the head and knocked him cold.

I stood still for a moment, straining to hear where the voice had come from. I picked up the sound of traffic on the high road, and above it the groans and cries of the men I'd brutalised on my way up. I heard movement beyond the double doors, and rushed over and locked them to buy myself time.

I crept through the room as quietly as possible, listening, and then I heard the sound again.

'Help,' a child said, before there were more sobs.

I grabbed the discarded gun, moved behind the three-panel screen that separated the room, and saw a small hatch cut into the wall. I drew back the bolt that secured it, and peered through to find a small attic space at the top of a set of metal fire stairs that spiralled down the building. In the far corner of the attic, bound to a pipe, was a child.

At first my mind played a cruel trick and I thought it was Amber, but the girl was eight or nine, and my daughter would be a grown woman by now. This was Katie Blake, the child I'd been hired to find.

She looked at me fearfully, as I crawled through the opening. I heard men trying to kick the double doors down, so I closed the hatch behind me and signalled Katie to be quiet. I crept over and pulled down the gag she'd partly worked clear.

'Katie, my name is Thomas. Your mother, Penny, sent me to bring you home,' I said.

She nodded and wept.

I cut her bonds with the sword, and eased her to her feet.

'We're going to go down these stairs,' I said, putting the sword down.

On the other side of the hatch, I heard the double doors splinter and heavy footsteps as Obsidian's men entered the room.

'Come on.' I urged Katie forward, and we started down the stairs.

I kept her in front of me, and she sobbed every step of the way as we hurried down the metal staircase. I glanced up regularly and held the barrel of the MAC-10 ready to open fire on anyone who came through the hatch.

We move down, past one landing after another until we reached the ground floor and a fire exit, which was locked. I guessed it was the door that led into the alleyway and recalled the rough position of the padlock.

'Stay behind me,' I told Katie, pushing her to my rear, as I raised the MAC-10 and opened fire.

Katie cried out as bullets chewed through the door, which suddenly swung open to flood the small space with the yellow light of a London night. I grabbed the girl and we ran into the alleyway behind the building. We raced to Hilldown Road and turned right, running away from the twisted church. I saw no sign of Obsidian's men as we made our way to Ellen Ovitz's old Mercedes, which was parked a few streets away.

'Who took you?' I asked as we hurried towards the car.

'The man in the big room,' she replied fearfully.

'Did he say anything about another girl? About Amber?'

She shook her head. 'He didn't talk to me or anything. He just kept me locked in that place.'

I could see she was getting distressed, so didn't press, and we soon reached the Mercedes.

Katie was scared, but she calmed slightly when I helped her into the passenger seat. I stashed the MAC-10 beneath the driver's seat and got behind the wheel.

'Thank you,' she said. 'Thank you for saving me.'

I tried to swallow the lump forming in my throat. I hadn't found my girl, but I'd rescued this innocent from the clutches of evil. I didn't trust myself to reply without breaking down, so I simply nodded and started the engine, and within moments we were speeding south.

CHAPTER 79

It was approaching one in the morning by the time we reached Ellen's house. Her street was deadly quiet and the gates were open when we arrived, so I steered the Mercedes into its spot.

'Where are we?' Katie asked fearfully.

'Somewhere safe,' I replied. 'Your mum's inside. You can stay here while I fetch her.'

She shook her head. 'I don't want to be alone.'

We got out of the car and I rang the doorbell. Soon, the large front door swung open to reveal a bleary-eyed Bernie. She looked from me to Katie and back again and her eyes widened in astonishment.

'Oh my God,' she said. 'You'd better come in.'

I took Katie through the lobby, into the hall, and saw something I will never forget. Penny was halfway down the stairs, with Ellen behind her. Like Bernie, the two women were in pyjamas and had just been roused from sleep. Penny's expression shifted from bewilderment to disbelief when she saw Katie, and a moment later her face lit up with the purest joy.

Tears rolled down her cheeks as she ran down the stairs and rushed across the hallway to gather her daughter in her arms and pull her into a tight embrace. Katie was crying too, the pair of them overwhelmed by the moment and unable to speak.

Penny looked at me over her daughter's shoulder and smiled. She tried to form words, but couldn't. I knew what she wanted to say. I knew how she felt. I knew the relief and ecstasy she was experiencing because I'd imagined it so many times for myself. I watched mother kiss and hug daughter with a painful mix of happiness and envy. I longed for that moment of reunion for myself. I wanted to hold my own daughter more than anything in the world, and I thought tonight would bring me closer to that dream, but if anything it felt further away than ever.

'You've done well,' Ellen said, drawing alongside me. 'You've done very well, Thomas. You should be proud.'

I didn't feel pride. I felt defeat and failure. I'd brought back a child, but it wasn't my own.

'You look exhausted. Take the Grey Room and get some rest,' Ellen suggested. 'You'll not get any message out of her tonight.' She indicated Penny, who was basking in the ecstasy of finding her child. 'Clean yourself up and get some sleep.'

I nodded. I should have been happy for Penny and Katie, but I was numb. I left them all and went upstairs.

I walked along the landing to the Grey Room, one of the smaller guestrooms with a queen bed and grey wallpaper flecked with silver flashes. I closed the door and leant against it with a heavy sigh. A moment later there was a soft knock and I opened the door to find Penny, tearful and smiling. She threw her arms around my shoulders and kissed me all over my face. I stank of sweat and violence, but she didn't care.

'Thank you,' she sobbed. 'Thank you so much. I can't…I misjudged you. I'm sorry.'

'It's okay,' I said. 'I'm very happy for you both.'

I think she must have sensed my pain. 'You'll find her,' she assured me. 'You will.'

I wasn't at all sure.

'I'm going to go to her now,' Penny said, 'but I wanted you to know I owe you everything.'

She kissed me again, this time on the lips, lingering and passionate.

'Thank you,' she said, before backing away.

I watched her go, a once damaged person, now made whole. Would I ever know what that felt like? Not without breaking Obsidian. I shut the door, wondering what it would take for me to find the happiness that now gripped Penny Blake.

CHAPTER 80

Flame.

Heat.

The flickering light of a forge at night.

A man works at an anvil, bashing hot metal into the shape of a sword. Screams fill the air. Now I'm outside, I'm the man. Wield the sword to stave off an attack. Many men on horseback. Swords. Armour. The village is in chaos. A blow. Darkness. The cold chill of morning. Something over me. A roof. The remains of someone's home. Stand.

Search among the bodies.

There, near my home.

Family.

Loss.

Grief.

A pain beyond all.

Years pass. Vengeance. Bloodshed. A quest. Beyond revenge. Twisted belief. Mountains.

A dark castle.

A throne room.

A beautiful queen.

Prostrate at her feet, a plea for knowledge. A black promise. Consummation of a pact. A bedchamber full of depraved lust.

A library.

Many books.

Old, some written in blood.

Knowledge.

A dungeon. Stone walls. A granite slab. A man on the slab. I become the man.

Victim.

Terror.

A beautiful queen and a twisted old man stand beside me. I scream. Torture. Suffering. A dagger.

Two dragons twisted around the handle. Death approaches.

Lightning.

Power.

The transfer.

I am gone.

The victim stands, but I am not him. A smile. Satisfaction. A new beginning.

CHAPTER 81

Warm.

Clean.

Soft.

Pleasant sensations. All unfamiliar. All welcome.

I opened my eyes and found myself surrounded by grey. Grey sheets. Luxurious pillows covered in grey linen that was now flecked with blood. Dappled sunlight was suppressed by a pair of heavily lined grey curtains. I remembered I was in the Grey Bedroom in Ellen's house, and as I stretched, my body ached and cried out for me to remain still in the snug cocoon of the freshly starched sheets, but I ignored it and got to my feet. I'd got into bed naked after my shower and had used a first aid kit I'd found in the bathroom cabinet to clean and dress my wounds. My clothes were in a pile at the foot of the bed, but they were covered in blood and stank. I couldn't put them on. Instead I search an oak wardrobe and found an old Issey Miyake suit, shirt and a pair of boots that were all roughly my size. I dressed slowly, feeling my way around the most tender, raw parts of my body.

As I stepped out of the room, I heard indistinct voices rising from the ground floor. I walked downstairs, surveying the framed family photos that lined the staircase walls. Faded childhood images of Ellen and her husband Michael with their families. A holiday by the beach. A group photograph in the grounds of a country house. A formal studio picture. There were others, taken later in life; Ellen and Michael together, getting married, then later with friends. There were a couple with Dr Gilmore, and the sight of his young face peering out at me was a reminder of what I'd done to betray his trust at Milton House. I felt a pang of guilt.

'Let's give him another hour,' I heard Ellen say, as I reached the bottom step.

She, and whoever was with her, stopped talking when they heard my footsteps crossing the hallway. I entered the dining room to find Penny, Ellen and Katie at the table, and Bernie fussing in the kitchen behind them. Penny beamed when she saw me, and Katie did likewise. Ellen smiled proudly, and Bernie came rushing from the kitchen.

'What can I get you?' she asked. 'Tea? Coffee? Breakfast? We've got—'

'I'm fine, thanks,' I cut her off.

She looked disappointed. 'Let me know if you change your mind.'

'I see you found Michael's clothes,' Ellen said. 'They suit you.' She paused. 'I don't know how you did it, Thomas, but I'm very glad you did.'

'Thank you, Mr Schaefer,' Katie added.

'Yes, thank you,' Penny said. 'The police want to interview Katie about the men who took her. We've made an appointment for this afternoon, but I just wanted to thank you again.'

'Penny and I have had a good chat, Thomas. I've explained why we needed to see her, and why you were so – shall we say – forceful,' Ellen said. 'I've also assured Penny that there is no way you would have been involved in the murder of a policeman. Is there, Thomas?'

'None at all.' I nodded. 'I was set up.' I turned to Penny. 'Can you stall the interview? Say Katie can't face it. Put it off until tomorrow.'

She looked at me in puzzlement.

'I need time. The man who took Katie ordered the murder of Edward Lomas, I'm sure of it,' I explained. 'And I think he was involved in Amber's abduction. I need to work out how to get him to talk.'

'You're usually quite persuasive,' Ellen remarked.

'He's not like anyone I've ever encountered,' I replied. 'Please, just until tomorrow morning.'

Penny nodded reluctantly. 'I'll do what I can.'

'Penny, my dear, you can take your darling child now,' Ellen said. 'Take her home. I'll tell Thomas what he needs to know.'

Penny nodded, and helped Katie to her feet. 'Come on, Kit-kat,' she said, and Katie beamed.

I longed for my daughter to look at me like that, but even if I found her, those years of childhood had been stolen from us, and that was a wrong that could never be righted.

Penny came round the table and gave me a hug, and I choked up a little when Katie did likewise.

'We'll never forget what you've done for us,' Penny said. 'I'll be in touch about your fee.' She looked at Ellen. 'Thank you for everything, Mrs Ovitz.'

'You're welcome, my dear,' Ellen replied.

I watched a slightly dazed and disbelieving Penny lead her daughter from the room. She had been thrust into a world of horror, but I'd delivered her from it before she became trapped like me.

Ellen waited for a few moments until she heard the front door slam shut.

'I could be wrong,' she said in a whisper, 'but from what I sensed, that girl has as much of a gift as this teacup. She is not the messenger Edward Lomas spoke of.'

'So if it's not you and it's not her, who is it?' I asked. 'I'm convinced this Felix Obsidian took Amber. I had him in my hands, and I couldn't make him talk. I need guidance. I need to know how to break the man.'

Ellen's face puckered into a frown of disapproval.

'Your world is becoming bleak, Thomas,' she said. 'I fear your quest will end badly. You're set on a course of self-destruction.'

'This man is evil,' I protested.

'And by associating with him, do you become more good, or more evil?' she asked pointedly.

'I need your help,' I pleaded, my voice cracking at the memory of the horrors of the previous night and the fear I would never experience the joy I'd seen in Penny Blake.

Ellen relented and closed her eyes as she concentrated.

'That's interesting,' she said hesitantly. 'The veil is lifting. The darkness around you is clearing. I'm being permitted to see – what – something. There's something there.'

Ellen frowned.

'I see a place of great knowledge. Lost souls waiting for answers. I see a great book. A man of learning,' she relayed.

'Mathers?' I interjected.

'You haven't been back to see him, have you?' Ellen asked. 'I told you not to go.'

'He's been there for me,' I replied. 'When I needed him.'

'You turned your back on me, Thomas,' she replied. 'Anyway, I think he's the messenger. He's the one Edward Lomas spoke of, but this Mathers has missed something. Something you can help him with.'

'What?' Schaefer asked.

'I don't know,' she replied, trying to feel her way around the problem, 'but it is important.'

I turned to leave.

'The car keys are in the bowl by the front door,' Ellen called after me, as I hurried from the room.

CHAPTER 82

As I drove into Mayfair, I considered how I might have handled things differently with Obsidian, but struggled to think what else I could do to break the man. Find his relatives? Friends? But Obsidian did not strike me as the sort of person who would bow to such pressure. I had to find a way to reach the man. He'd had Katie Blake locked in his lair and there was little doubt, given the connection between the two abductions, that he'd had a hand in taking Amber. I needed to find a way to force him to tell me where she was.

I parked on Albemarle Street and walked two blocks to the Burlington Arcade and Mathers' shop. There was something reassuring about a place that changed so little. Kelvin stood behind his counter near the draped window and nodded at me when I entered. I could see why people would come back to Mathers' shop day after day. Unaltered, it had stood in the Burlington Arcade for decades, like an unyielding rock against the stormy tide of progress. Technology could digest the world into bite-sized chunks to be fed to the soundbite hungry attention deficit generation, but it would never be able to replicate the depth and richness of a place like this. It wasn't just the books, which contained secrets within secrets; it was the experience of holding history. A physical link with a world long gone. Books that had travelled through time and brought with them the notations of their many owners, the intricacies of their journeys, their own histories. Even I could see the magical attraction of such artefacts.

I passed between two bookcases and opened the door to the waiting area. A smaller, but similar collection of peculiar people waited to see Mathers. Lost souls, Ellen had called them, and, as I looked at the strange men and women, I thought it a most appropriate description. There was a sadness about them. Something was missing from their lives and, like me, they all hoped Mathers could help restore it.

'Good morning, Mr Schaefer,' Margot said brightly. 'I'll just see if he can fit you in.'

She looked more beautiful than usual. She wore a tight-fitting black dress that was covered in red poppies. She smiled as she entered Mathers' office and closed the door behind her.

I'd seen the woman with alabaster skin and blood-red lips on a previous visit, and she looked at me and frowned. It was the first time any of the peculiar people had ever acknowledged me.

'You're almost there,' she said. 'He'll help you.'

'Excuse me? What?' I asked in puzzlement.

'Don't worry,' Alabaster said. 'You're on the right path.'

'He'll see you now,' Margot called across the room from the office.

I looked at the woman with the alabaster skin, and she returned my gaze and smiled sadly. These people were even stranger than I'd first thought. The last thing I needed was another psychic.

'Thanks,' I said insincerely. 'You're on the right path too.'

Her smiled broadened and she shook her head, as I followed Margot into Mathers' office.

The small custodian of ancient books was his usual brusque and busy self. He was using a magnifying glass to study tiny text in a large book.

'Where have you been, Thomas? Margot has been trying to get hold of you,' Mathers said.

'I lost my phone,' I said. 'Well, I had to ditch it. I'll give you my new number.'

'Do you want a drink?' Mathers asked.

'No, thanks.'

Margot withdrew and shut the door behind her, and Mathers looked up for the first time and noticed some of the superficial injuries I'd sustained in the fight.

'Good grief!' he exclaimed. 'You look a mess. What happened?'

'It's nothing,' I dissembled. 'It was just something that got out of hand. I'm okay.'

Mathers frowned and let the matter drop.

'I wanted your help. A fresh perspective. I'm afraid I've hit something of a brick wall,' he admitted. 'If you've been through the papers I gave you, you'll see there's plenty of evidence to suggest that the Totus is real, but who they are—'

'I think I've found them,' I interrupted.

'Really?' Mathers asked. Then it dawned on him. 'The thing that got out of hand?'

I nodded.

'And your efforts yielded no fruit?'

'No.' I shook my head. 'I also hit a brick wall.'

'I can't see a way beyond it, Thomas.'

'We've missed something.'

'How do you know?' Mathers asked.

'Someone told me,' I replied.

'Someone?' Mathers said, but he immediately let the question drop when he saw the look on my face, which suggested that it was better he didn't know. 'What have we missed?'

'I don't know,' I admitted. 'But I was told I could help you. Where are the photographs I took?'

Mathers rooted in one of his desk drawers for the photos I'd given him of the interior of Leon Yates's house and his nest at the tower block. He handed them to me, and I laid them out across his desk. Four rows, twelve images in each row. A collection of illuminated symbols from within the house, and occultism disguised as graffiti from the corridor of the tower block.

'What are we missing?' I mused. 'What are we missing?'

We concentrated on the images, scouring them for clues. Satyrs, Latin inscriptions, pentagrams, a blur of signs and symbols, and then I saw it.

Four images, two from the house, two from the tower block. I pulled them out of their rows and set them together to form a rectangle. Where the four photos joined, what seemed like disparate, incomplete symbols in each one became a coherent, complete insignia: the familiar mandala of the Totus. But this one was different; it had text written within the circle that surrounded the three overlapping triangles.

'Do you see it?' I asked Mathers.

The bookseller nodded in disbelief, as he read the Latin text.

'The Summoning of Carmichael. Fifth word,' he said excitedly. He hurried over to one of the large bookcases in his office and searched the shelves.

'What is it?' I asked.

'The Summoning of Carmichael is an old book of black magic,' Mathers replied. 'Those fearing persecution by the Inquisition would conceal the true darkness of their books by burying their meaning within a broader text. "Fifth word" is an instruction to read every fifth word. Ah, here we are.'

He pulled a small, leather-bound book from the bookcase and returned to the desk. He put on a pair of white fabric gloves and opened the unassuming tome. The yellow-brown paper was bone dry, and the hand-inscribed ink faint with age. The book's title page offered no author's name, but featured the image of a malformed demon with its tentacle-like arms wrapped around a young boy. The boy looked into the hideous creature's eyes with an expression of love and respect. Mathers moved on, and turned to the first page of text. He began to translate the Latin, falteringly at first, and then more fluidly as he grasped the rhythm of the encoded message.

'The...constraints...of human life can be...defeated. For those...willing to tread...the dark path, death is not absolute. For those that can find her, Astranger can teach the secret of recurrence. Only by following the tenets of the Totus, and submitting to the will of Astranger, can one attain the secret of immortality. Take heed of her instruction on the preparation of an innocent. The transference. The defiance of death. Darkness must reside in darkness. Evil must make its home in evil. Only then can the veil be lifted.'

Mathers turned the page to reveal an illuminated image of a man lying on a large stone slab, a woman on one side of him, an old man on the other. In the old man's raised hand was a dagger that had two dragons wrapped around its handle.

'I've seen that knife, that place,' I said suddenly. 'In a dream.'

Mathers closed the book and turned to face me.

'Thomas,' he said sadly, 'you are caught up in a great evil. Legend has it an ancient queen discovered the secret to immortality. She came to be known as Astranger. It is clear the Totus regard her as their leader. Her name is only spoken in connection with terrible evil. The utter corruption of good. The destruction of the innocent. Astranger does this to extend her life beyond its natural term. The victim is subjected to such torment they willingly sacrifice themselves. The surrender must be by consent; only then will the sacrifice nourish Astranger. If they have taken Amber in her name...'

Tears filled my eyes as Mathers trailed off. I looked at the bookseller in despair, choked by my emotions. Unable to take the horror, and desperate for revenge, I nodded at Mathers and headed for the exit.

'Leave this, Thomas. It's over,' Mathers called after me. The horror of what we'd found had marked the bookseller's voice so it sounded cracked and scratched like an old record.

CHAPTER 83

Was that it? I thought, struggling to see through my tears. *Was that how I learnt my daughter was dead? From some old book written about demons and the nutters who worshipped them?*

I'd resisted accepting her death long after everyone else had given up on her, but how would I ever find closure if I didn't have answers? Real answers. Not from a book, but from someone who was undoubtedly involved in her disappearance. I didn't need guidance to break Obsidian. I just had to be prepared to go further than him. And if Mathers was right and my daughter had been sacrificed to appease some eternal demon, what did I have to lose? If Amber really was gone, there was no reason for Obsidian to live. I would either learn the truth or avenge my daughter before turning myself over to the police.

I wiped away a steady stream of tears as I headed east. A storm of emotions raged so powerfully I was afraid it would overwhelm me, and I almost crashed Ellen's beautiful car at least half a dozen times as I drove south towards Streatham High Road, but the angry shouts and blaring horns barely registered as I left a trail of near misses across London.

By the time I arrived in Streatham, the afternoon sun had turned the city into an oven. I parked on Hilldown Road and reached beneath the driver's seat for the MAC-10 submachine gun I'd hidden there the previous night. I got out of the Mercedes and concealed the gun beneath my jacket before heading towards the First Church of the Eternal Light.

When I turned the corner and joined Streatham High Road, I saw the front door was open, but was surprised to find no one outside. The absence of a police presence suggested Penny Blake had succeeded in postponing Katie's interview, and Obsidian and his men were hardly likely to call the law themselves, given their criminal activities.

I clasped the submachine gun tightly as I entered the building. The lobby was also deserted, and all signs of the previous night's mayhem were gone. I heard the sound of chanting coming from the auditorium, and the idea that people might be hoodwinked into believing the people running this church were pious angered me beyond measure. This was a foul place, riddled with evil.

I stepped towards the double doors that led into the theatre, and inched one open slowly and quietly. I saw forty or so men facing the stage, standing in a large open space where the stalls had once been. They were in some kind of trance, chanting softly in Latin. On stage, the disfigured Obsidian ministered the ceremony, carrying the fresh swellings and wounds I'd given him the previous night. He sat in an ornate gilt chair and read Latin incantations from a large book on a lectern. I stepped forward and quietly closed the door behind me, before moving towards a pillar and taking up a firing position. I lined Obsidian in my sights and steadied my aim.

'Obsidian!' I yelled. 'Tell me where my daughter is, or you die!'

He looked in my direction, utterly unfazed, and I realised the reason for his confidence too late.

A sound came from behind me, and I turned to see four men. A baseball bat caught me in the face, and there was the sound of a wild gunshot, as everything went black.

CHAPTER 84

Life was catching up with me.

I came round to a stabbing pain in my neck. The complex web of ligaments had been twisted and torn by the force of the baseball bat's blow, and the gentle slap Obsidian delivered to rouse me sent searing pain up and down my spine.

I snapped out of the grey space between waking and unconsciousness, my pain making me even more alert than usual to the realities of my miserable life. I was on the church stage, with Obsidian's disfigured face directly in front of me. Two sets of strong hands held my arms, and a third pair was on my shoulders, keeping me on my knees. Behind Obsidian, a mass of faces, some of which I recognised from the previous night – battered and bruised, eyeing me with the same kind of hatred I had for them.

'Thomas Schaefer, you do not disappoint,' Obsidian said, his voice distorted by his missing teeth and swollen lips. 'You came back exactly as he said you would.'

'Who said I would?' I asked.

I ignored the pain and tried to get to my feet, but the heavy hands pushed me down and someone delivered a punch. I heard a cry, and realised it had come from me.

'Speak when spoken to,' one of my captors said.

'What did you do with my daughter?' I asked through the agony.

The question earned me another punch.

'We give thanks to the great darkness,' Obsidian announced to his congregation.

'We give thanks,' the men replied in unison.

'What did you do to her?' I asked again.

Another punch, and the world swam. I couldn't take much more.

Obsidian drew close. 'It is not your daughter you should be afraid for; her fate is sealed. You should turn your thoughts to your wife and son.'

I roared with horror at his words.

'What have you done to them?' I yelled.

'Did you think you could invade the sanctity of my church and go unpunished?' Obsidian countered. 'Your fate is ordained, Thomas. As is theirs.'

'I'll kill you,' I shouted.

I struggled against the men holding me, and pain coursed through my body, but it only served to agitate me further. Suddenly there was another punch, this one a hammer blow to the top of my skull that sent me spinning to the edge of consciousness.

Somewhere in the distance I heard Obsidian's voice saying, 'Take him to them.'

I felt myself flying, but I was no angel. Hands lifted me and my feet remained connected to the mortal, imperfect ground and scraped along behind me as I was carried onwards. I was dazed and disorientated, but my family didn't need the weak man who allowed himself to be a puppet in the arms of these men.

Snap out of it! The voice in my head was insistent. *Save your pity for later. Wake up!*

There was no room for negotiation. I recognised the uncompromising tone that had driven me on in the face of seemingly insurmountable adversity for years. It was the rock solid core of determination that forced me to do things others considered impossible.

I came round to find myself being carried down a set of dark, dank stairs into a miserably lit, derelict corridor. I heard footsteps behind me, but was unable to see who or how many followed.

I was dragged into the monochromatically tiled men's toilets, where a huge man with a machete stood in front of Sarah and Oliver. My wife and son cowered in the corner of the room, huddled together against the black and white tiles, mortal terror, shock and anguish writ large upon their wide-eyed faces. They were both crying.

'Tom,' Sarah said. Her broken voice betrayed her fear.

'The Totus took your daughter, Mr Schaefer,' Obsidian said, leaning over my shoulder. 'Now we have the rest of your family, Papa Boya will grant us the gift of eternal life.'

I could feel the man's hot breath against my ear. I looked over at Sarah and held her gaze. Full of despair, her eyes told me everything I needed to know – I had to get our son out of that room. My family was counting on me. This would hurt, but I was no stranger to pain, and consoled myself with the knowledge that my suffering would be a shadow of those holding me captive.

CHAPTER 85

I lifted my right foot and kicked down with all my force, snapping the shin of the man to my left. He tumbled to the floor, screaming, and let go of my arm, which allowed me to drive my left fist into the face of the man on my right. Ignoring the searing pain that came from moving my head, I snapped it back into the nose of the man directly behind me.

Someone tried to grab me, but I had already moved out of reach, and sprinted towards the huge man with the machete, who squared up to me. The machete whistled through the air and I dropped to my knees and slid along the tiled floor. The wild slash caused the huge man to overbalance, and there was nothing he could do to protect himself from the punch that I thumped to his groin. As Machete doubled over, I jumped up and drove my forehead into the man's chin. The blade clattered to the floor as the huge man fell. I picked it up, and in one fluid movement turned to confront those behind me.

Obsidian rushed forward, closely followed by the three men who had dragged me into the toilet. The machete was a slashing weapon, engineered to hack through thick jungle, and I put it to good use, swinging at Obsidian, who tried to back away. He was too slow, and the blade sliced through his left forearm, which had been raised in a desperate attempt to parry. Obsidian's hand fell away just below the wrist, and the screaming man dropped to the floor, clutching the gushing limb.

Sarah and Oliver were screaming behind me, but I had to ignore their cries – the three men closing in on us needed to be dealt with. There was a new hesitancy to the men's movements as they considered their screaming leader and the bloody blade in my hands. I didn't wait for them to find their courage, and rushed forward. I dropped to the floor and slashed with determined clarity at the men's legs. One of them lost some fingers in a vain effort to fend off the blows, but within moments all three were lying on the floor, clutching at terrible wounds in their calves and shins.

'Come on!' I yelled at Sarah and Oliver.

I grabbed Sarah's hand and pulled her forward. She held on to Oliver, and the three of us hurried from the toilet. I heard footsteps coming down the stairs; more of Obsidian's followers, attracted, no doubt, by the chorus of screaming men.

'This way!' I said, pulling Sarah and Oliver away from the stairs.

There was terror in their eyes, and I knew they were right to be afraid. We had one chance at escape. After what I'd done to Obsidian and his men, recapture would be an ugly and horrific experience for the three of us. I pulled Sarah and Oliver along the corridor towards a dark, unlit area. I slowed, trying to give my eyes time to acclimatise to the darkness.

'What are you doing?' Sarah asked frantically. 'We've got to get out of here.'

'Quiet,' I instructed. 'They're coming.'

Behind us a gang of Obsidian's followers spilt down the stairs and crossed the corridor into the men's toilet. I led Sarah and Oliver further down the dark corridor, praying my memory of the building's layout was accurate; the darkness would only conceal us for so long.

'Find them!' I recognised Obsidian's voice even though it was horribly distorted by pain.

Men emerged from the toilet, and one of them shouted instructions to others who had come down the stairs. 'The Dolor Man has escaped,' he said. 'They're somewhere in the building.'

The men spread out, and I saw a group of seven heading up the dark corridor towards us.

'Move,' I said quietly.

I pushed Sarah and Oliver forward, but after a few paces we collided with something solid.

'What was that?' a distant voice asked.

The seven men increased their pace.

I looked to my right and saw the spiral staircase Katie Blake and I had used the previous night. I probed the obstruction and was relieved to feel the familiar metal bar of a fire escape. This was the fire door I'd shot open. I pushed the bar down, but the door didn't open. It had been locked again.

'Thomas,' Sarah said fearfully, 'they're coming.'

I could hear footsteps, no more than fifty feet away, and felt for the end of the bar and found a chain that bound it to a metal loop embedded in the wall. A tiny gap between the door and frame provided a narrow column of light that enabled me to see an old, rusty padlock and chain.

Forty feet.

Concealment was no longer an option; we were trapped against a locked door in the darkness, with seven angry hunters coming rapidly towards us.

'Stand back.' I pulled Sarah and Oliver out of the way.

Thirty feet.

I swung the machete and hacked at the chain ferociously. The footsteps started running.

'They're here!' someone yelled.

More footsteps from further down the corridor.

I hacked at the chain.

'Thomas!' Sarah screamed.

'Dad! Please don't let them get us!' Oliver pleaded.

Few sounds had ever given me so much joy as the noise the chain made when it snapped. I kicked the door open, flooding the corridor with light, and hurled Sarah and Oliver into the alleyway beyond. I turned to face our pursuers, and hacked at the first three men, slicing open a shoulder, severing an arm at the elbow, and cleaving a thigh. The violence caused the other four men to hesitate, which was all I needed. I backed through the doorway, slammed the door shut, and slid the machete through the door handle and a latch to create a makeshift bolt.

The door shook as the men on the other side tried to batter it open, but it held fast. There was a sudden clatter of cracks, and bullets peppered holes in the door.

I grabbed Sarah and Oliver and dragged them away. I rejected the dangers of Hilldown Road, and instead led my ex-wife and son further along the alleyway, behind the buildings that lined Streatham High Road.

Angry shouts bounced off the buildings, echoing behind us. Hurried footsteps pounded against the crumbling tarmac. Sarah was exhausted and Oliver was on the verge of collapse. I picked up my boy and ran on.

'Come on!' I told Sarah. 'We're almost there!'

I spun round to see shadows on the alley wall. Obsidian's men were closing. I pushed my legs harder and faster. I could see the next street along, and barely felt the burden of my son as we flew along the alleyway.

Sarah and I hurried onto Heathdene Road, and sprinted round the corner onto Streatham High Road. I saw some of Obsidian's men racing towards us, picking their way through the pedestrians on the busy high street. I glanced round to see another group of men heading along Heathdene Road. I looked desperately for escape.

Then I saw it.

I stepped into Streatham High Road in front of a black cab, which was forced to screech to a halt. I didn't give the driver any time to get angry, and ran round and opened the rear passenger door. Oliver, Sarah and I fell into the cab.

'Drive!' I yelled. 'Get us out of here!'

The cabby was no fool. He saw the two gangs of men converging on his vehicle and understood the urgency of my request. He put his foot down and, as the cab sped south, I looked out of the rear window and saw Obsidian's men curse me as they receded into the distance.

CHAPTER 86

I snagged the curtain to create a gap just large enough for me to look out of the grimy window and see that Calthorpe Street was quiet. We were in the middle of a Georgian terrace that mirrored the one on the other side of the road. Further up the street, closer to King's Cross, the old buildings gave way to modern office blocks and hotels. A cab pulled in at the Holiday Inn at the other end of the street, and two businessmen in cheap suits jumped out. They'd be staying in relative luxury compared to the shithole that housed me and my family.

The King's Cross Grand Hotel was anything but. Four terraced houses knocked together to create a perplexing warren of bedsits and two-room apartments. Stained carpets, dirty sheets, old, infested mattresses and a building that was permeated with the stench of misery and failure. The one thing the meagre establishment had in its favour was its old-fashioned view of anonymity. No credit card for incidentals. No proof of identification. A false name and a bundle of cash suited the owner perfectly well. I'd occasionally hidden clients here before taking them down to Gilmore and was on nodding terms with the greasy reprobate who owned the place, a former pimp called Tosh.

He'd insisted on giving us his biggest deluxe suite. Two rooms, one double with a bed that sagged in the middle, and a living room that doubled as a second bedroom. I stepped away from the window as Sarah entered the living room and shut the bedroom door behind her.

'He's asleep,' she whispered, as she switched off the small black-and-white television. I'd been surprised to see such an ancient monochrome set, but it was in keeping with the rest of the place. An old re-covered sofa bed, paisley carpets from the early eighties, heavy curtains that looked even older, and dusty black-and-white prints that clashed with the faded floral wallpaper.

'Thank you,' Sarah said.

She was calmer than she had been when we'd arrived, but I could see she was still shaken. Tears welled up unbidden, only to be wiped away by a trembling hand. I went over to her and placed my hands on her shoulders to pull her close. The tender safety of my comforting embrace was too much, and Sarah began weeping freely. We stood silently for a few moments, her shuddering in my arms.

'Who were they?' Sarah asked at last, pulling away from me.

'They belong to a cult known as the Totus,' I replied. 'They were the ones who took Amber.'

'Why?' she sobbed. 'Why us?'

'I don't know.' I shook my head slowly.

'We should go to the police.'

'I think they might have people in the police. And the Security Service. We can't trust anyone,' I said. 'They've already fitted me up for a murder.'

'I know. The police came round asking questions,' Sarah revealed. 'This can't be happening.'

'It is. They killed Noel, that policeman. And I saw them murder two others,' I said, referring to the officers killed at Yates's house.

'Is this it then?' Sarah indicated our meagre surroundings. 'Do we have to live like this for the rest of our lives? On the run?'

I wasn't sure how to respond.

'I've seen what this life has done to you, Tom,' she continued. 'I've seen you put everything on the line and I've seen the toll it's taken. You've lived in the dark, in the shadows with these people. I can't do that. So, whatever you have to do – whatever it takes, you get us out of this. You hear me?'

Sarah's tears were replaced by a steely resolve.

'This isn't about Amber anymore. This is about us. This is about keeping me and your son safe. You do whatever it takes. Do you understand?' she said. 'Whatever it takes. I want our lives back.'

I nodded. She was right of course. The only way to remove the threat was to destroy the Totus, but in order to do that, I needed intel.

'Then I'm going to need you to do something for me,' I said. 'The man who lost his hand; his name's Felix Obsidian. They won't have treated that kind of injury in the field; he will have been admitted to hospital. Call every hospital in a ten-mile radius from the church. Say you're his sister. When you've found out which one he's in, phone me on this number.'

I scribbled my new mobile number on a hotel notepad.

'Don't open the door and don't leave this room until you hear from me,' I instructed. 'If they find us, these people will kill us.'

Sarah nodded.

'Thomas,' she said, as I started towards the door, 'be careful.'

I smiled and then was gone.

CHAPTER 87

I left Sarah and Oliver and took a cab to my storage unit in Hackney Wick and told the driver to wait. Max, the security guard, let me into my lockup, and when he was gone, I opened up one of my tea chests. Hidden at the bottom were some weapons. I took a sawn-off shotgun and a box of twenty-five size two cartridges, which were the kind used to bring down geese. I emptied the box and split the cartridges between my trouser and jacket pockets. The shotgun went into an old leather satchel, along with a black, tactical switchblade. I'd just finished packing up, when my phone rang.

'Yeah,' I said, answering.

'It's me,' Sarah replied. 'He's been admitted to St George's. Room 361, D Ward.'

'Thanks.'

'Please be careful,' she said.

'I will,' I assured her.

I closed the tea chest, and a few minutes later was back in the taxi, heading for Tooting.

The journey took us an hour in the late evening traffic, and the driver, a taciturn man, spent the entire time listening to a pirate drum and bass radio station. My anticipation grew with each passing mile, and I knew Sarah was right. If I didn't neutralise this threat, none of us would be able to return to our normal lives. Or normal in their case, abnormal in mine.

By the time we reached Tooting, my heart was hitting 160 beats-per-minute in time to the fast drumbeats. I asked the driver to drop me near the public car park, and paid the fare.

St George's Hospital was one of the largest in South London, a sprawling complex of modern buildings. D Ward was in the main building, a squat red brick structure at the heart of the hospital. I set off from the public car park with my satchel slung over my shoulder and walked towards the main building.

The vaulted hospital lobby reminded me of a cathedral. A few visitors crossed the polished floor, talking in hushed tones about the prospects of their nearest and dearest. I wondered how many people had prayed for miracles in this building, and how many of those prayers had been answered. The hospital was winding down. The computerised self-service check-in terminals were unused, a handful of hospital staff gathered at one end of the lobby for a gossip, and there was the general air of a busy organisation taking a breather before the next day of frantic activity. I followed signs to D Ward, which lay on the north side of the building.

The notice by the ward door said visiting hours were from 8.00 am until 10.00 pm, which gave me twenty-five minutes. I pressed the buzzer and waited.

'Hello?' came a voice through the intercom.

'I'm here to see Felix Obsidian,' I offered in harmless tones.

The door buzzed open and I went into the quiet ward. I nodded a smile in the direction of the duty nurse, but she was too busy with paperwork to give me anything other than a cursory glance in return. I checked the room numbers and saw 361 a few yards away.

Obsidian stirred as I entered. I shut the door behind me, and turned to see the injured man, struggling to prop himself up against his pillow. His arm was bandaged at the wrist, and I was pleased to see they had not been able to reattach this evil man's hand. Obsidian tried to reach for the call button, but I raced across the room and snatched it away.

'You made a big mistake coming here,' Obsidian leered. 'Papa Boya told me desperation would lead you back. You want your girl so, so bad.'

I didn't reply and instead walked to the end of the bed and calmly put my satchel on his meal tray. I reached into it and took out the switchblade, which I opened.

'Who gives you orders?' I asked, moving towards his bandaged arm. 'Who's Papa Boya?'

'He is the Totus,' Obsidian replied.

'I thought Astranger was the Totus,' I countered, teasing the top of his bandage with the tip of my blade.

He watched it nervously.

'They are two sides of the coin,' he replied. 'We are all Totus. We shape the world according to our wish. Everything is known to us, friend.'

His words struck me like blows. Derek Liddle had said the same thing, and I recalled them from the case of patient Jones in the book by Dr Alfred Stern. Had Liddle and Obsidian been indoctrinated by the Totus in the same way?

'They took you off the street, didn't they?' I asked, and immediately saw from the flash of uncertainty in his eyes that I'd struck home. 'They tormented you. That's where you got the wounds. The Totus made you suffer.'

'No!' Obsidian yelled. 'Deceiver! They gave me truth. And love beyond love.'

'They gave you Hell,' I told him, 'and left you with a Devil. Answer my questions or I will drive this knife into your arm. I'll grind this blade against bone and make you suffer like never before.'

I didn't want things to have to get ugly, but I had to keep my family safe.

'I am beyond you, Dolor Man,' he countered defiantly.

'Dolor Man,' I remarked. 'Let's start with that. Why do you keep calling me the pained man?'

I pressed the knife into his wound, and blood started to colour the bandage.

He cried out in pain and moaned. Then, in an exhibition of self-control, Obsidian turned to face me and smiled. 'Do what you like to me. I serve a power greater than you can ever imagine. He said you would come, which is why my people have been watching the hospital since I got here. You're a wanted man, you know?'

I had a terrible sinking feeling and rushed towards the door.

'You cannot run!' Obsidian called out from his bed. 'The Totus is everywhere.'

I opened the door and ran into the path of four suited men. The first, clean-shaven with a crew cut and a square jaw, produced a warrant card.

'Thomas Schaefer, I'm Detective Sergeant Simon Lucas. I'm placing you under arrest for the murder of David Noel,' he began.

I didn't wait to hear my rights. I pushed the man away and started to run in the other direction, but I didn't get more than a couple of steps. I felt a sudden stabbing pain in my back, followed by searing agony. My body started to spasm violently, and as I dropped to the floor, convulsing, I caught sight of the police-issue Taser in Lucas's hand.

A moment later, the world went dark.

CHAPTER 88

Failure.

I drifted at the edge of consciousness. I was moving. Travelling a great distance at some speed. I had no sense of time, but could sense whispered voices at the edge of my hearing. I tried to open my eyes, but they refused to oblige. It felt as though they were pinned down by boulders.

I lay in darkness, reflecting on the failure my life had become. I knew sooner or later every man had to face the fact he had failed. As a father. A son. An employee. A boss. A friend. A husband.

For some, recognition came early in a life that was defined by an angry, destructive response to failure. For others, recognition arrived late in life in the form of regret. I thought about all the choices I'd made in life, and how any one of them might have led to a different path. My ruination had left me hollow and empty, devoid of hope. My daughter would never come home, and my family would always be in danger.

Failure.

I felt a certain inevitability, that I had been doomed to fail, that I had only succeeded in prolonging the day of my defeat. Even if I could avoid going down for Noel's murder, I'd struggle with the other charges I'd have to face. Obsidian would be bound to press charges, and might even try to implicate me in the Lomas murders. I couldn't bear to think of Sarah and Oliver waiting for me in that dingy hotel. My one permitted phone call would have to be to them. I would ask her to go and stay with her mother until I got out.

Failure.

'Listen to me,' I heard myself saying.

I finally managed to open my eyes, and was blinded by harsh light emitted by a single bulb. A few moments later and I was able to focus on three suited policemen seated in the back of the van. I lay on the flatbed at their feet, my eyes wet with tears.

Failure.

'The man, the man in that hospital room, he took my daughter. And another girl, too. Katie Blake. I rescued her,' I said. 'I'm innocent. I only hurt people who deserved it. Not the good. I don't hurt the good. Just the evil.'

That didn't come out how I meant it to, and I realised I wasn't thinking straight. I sounded unhinged.

One of the men, Lucas – I recalled his name with a strange pride – leant forward and said, 'Save your breath, Schaefer.'

'The Totus. They're evil,' I countered rapidly. To some, my speech might have sounded like gabbling, but I knew it was a temporary side effect of the Taser. 'They take children and twist them. Sacrifice them. Do evil with them. You have to believe me. They've done terrible things. Papa Boya. Astranger. Look them up. Look them up. They have my daughter. They're going to kill my family. Trauco. Trauco.'

Lucas rolled his eyes at his colleagues. 'Looks like we were right.'

'Right about what?' I asked. I tried to sit up, but my body wasn't taking orders. 'What were you right about?'

Lucas leant forward again. 'Right to send you for psych evaluation. What you did to Noel marked you out as a nutter. The doctor's waiting for you, Schaefer.'

The words *psych evaluation* filled me with fear. These people thought I was insane, and my hurried babbling wouldn't have helped convince them otherwise. If they sectioned me, I wouldn't be granted recourse to traditional legal rights until a qualified psychiatrist said I didn't pose a threat to myself or others. That meant no lawyer, no fixed period of custody and, worst of all, no phone call.

I railed against the prospect. 'I'm not mad. I'm not. Forget about the Totus. And Papa Boya. They don't exist. Take me to prison. Charge me. I did it. I did all the murders. Don't send me for a psych test. Please don't!'

'Shut up!' Lucas commanded.

I couldn't let them do this. I started thrashing around the flatbed, but my motors weren't working properly and all my efforts to sit simply translated into violent convulsions.

Failure.

I looked back at the accusations I'd made about the Totus and Papa Boya, and realised that these men had every right to think me insane.

I pleaded, 'Okay, okay, okay. Please, I see that I was wrong. I'm okay. Don't take me to the doctor. Take me to prison. I'm fine. There's nothing wrong with me. I need my fucking phone call. My wife and kid. Sarah and Oliver are in danger. I need to warn them. Please.'

'I'm not listening to this all the way there,' Lucas said as he produced the Taser from his pocket.

'Please don't,' I said pathetically. 'Please.'

Another searing blast of pain and everything went dark.
Failure.

CHAPTER 89

I opened my eyes.

I was lying down.

The ceiling wasn't familiar, but when I turned my head, I recognised the painted door and flush wood-effect inlay around the small glass portal. Beyond it I could see the mesh reinforced windows on the other side of the corridor.

I was in Milton House.

I was in the custody of Dr Gilmore.

I tried to stand, but was unable to do so. My arms and legs were tightly restrained. I knew the drill; they considered me a danger to myself and others. I would be restrained for the foreseeable future.

I lay back. I had seen this play out dozens of times, and promised myself I wouldn't give in to the madness my situation engendered. There were those who pleaded, begging for the opportunity to prove their sanity. Others ranted and raged against a system that was so myopic as to be blind to their perfect and unique clarity of vision. Some sobbed and wailed for release, while the remainder withdrew into their minds to keep company with whatever warped thoughts had led them here. I decided I would be rational and reasonable, and, at the first opportunity, I would ask Gilmore to intercede.

The image of Lomas lying dead in the duck pond invaded my mind again. Why? And why now? Uninvited and unwelcome. It was evidence of a mind not fully in control. Lomas had told me I was gifted, but had I imagined it? Was there a Lomas at all? Was there an Amber? I'd been on the trail for so long, how could I be sure I wasn't just pursuing an ideal? Is that why everyone else had given up? Because they hadn't cared to begin with? Because she wasn't real?

'I remember her,' I yelled, and my voice died against the soundproof walls. 'I remember her,' I repeated more quietly. 'I will get out of this, and I will find her.'

It's the hope that kills you, I thought.

No matter how bleak our circumstances, we will always find hope, but it was the hope of finding Amber that had brought me to this locked room and left me bound to a bed. Maybe hope was dangerous?

I once heard a story of three sailors whose boat had been caught in an ocean storm. The vessel had capsized, but the three men had found an air pocket in one of the compartments in the upturned hull. As the waves buffeted the boat, water seeped into the compartment, and it became clear the men were going to drown. Two of the men accepted the inevitable and used a waterproof camera to record messages for their families. The third man refused to do so, and instead spent his final moments diving to other sections of the boat in a desperate effort to find another air pocket. When the boat was discovered many days later, the recalcitrant man was found near a hatch that had been marked and scored by his fingertips, which were worn to the bone. His family had no message. No goodbye.

I was the recalcitrant man, and I'd left my family with nothing.

What was it Leon Yates had said? The Dolor Man. Obsidian had said it too. The pained man.

I continued scrabbling in an ever-decreasing pocket of air, drowning but refusing to acknowledge the fact. Clinging to hope, however vain, however false. Because it was preferable to the alternative, to the acceptance of defeat. To the acceptance of death.

Failure.

We all die, there is no avoiding that fact, but we can create the illusion we're winning. The false edifice that tells the world we are a glorious success, that we will be victorious…

'You'll never beat me!' I shouted. 'I'm still here!'

My words were met with silence.

'I'm still here,' I whispered, but now I wasn't so sure.

Maybe I wasn't here at all?

CHAPTER 90

'I'm gonna fucking kill you all!' I yelled at the world. 'Let me out of here!'

They're watching you, I told myself, *testing you. Don't blow it.*

'I'm sorry,' I said. 'I'm not going to kill anyone. If I could just have my phone call. Or speak to Dr Gilmore. He'll vouch for me.'

I sounded as though I was slurring, but I felt completely lucid. I wasn't sure what drugs they had me on, but time had lost all meaning. I seemed to skip from moment to moment, an orderly here, a nurse there. I'd dream of Amber and wake up to find I'd been bathed and changed into fresh clothes. I'd dream about being in my cell, only I wasn't restrained, I was free to wander. I discovered my cell was part of a huge stately home and spent a long time in the library reading books. But when I woke up, I was always back on my bed, strapped tight, unable to move.

'Please call Dr Gilmore,' I said, but was I continuing my conversation? Or had days passed? I was struggling to keep track. The sun seemed to rise and fall far more erratically than it did in the world beyond the walls of this place.

Why are you here? I asked myself, and I couldn't really respond. *To find Amber*, seemed to have been the answer to every question I'd been asked in the last ten years, but lying in this bed wasn't helping me get any closer to her, so how had I ended up here? I couldn't really put my finger on one thing.

Many people had told me I needed help. Maybe this is what happens when a person ignores the warning signs.

'Let me out of here, you fucks!'

I was angry again, but I couldn't believe I'd lose control so soon after I'd told myself to be calm. Was this a different day?

'I'm sorry. Please. Please. Please.' I was crying now. 'Please tell Dr Gilmore I need to see him. I need help. Please.'

Sobbing.

Howling.

Screaming.

I was losing my grip. In my more lucid moments I found myself obsessing over whether Amber had two missing teeth when she was abducted or three. If I couldn't remember something as fundamental as the number of teeth in my girl's mouth, how could I trust myself on other things? How did I know anything I remembered was real?

'No!' I yelled at myself. 'Don't do this.'

I was losing my frames of reference. Robbed of external stimuli, my mind was turning in on itself, and the drugs I was being given weren't helping. But it's one thing to recognise a problem, quite another to solve it.

I tumbled further and further into my own little weird world. I tried to hold on to time. Days could come and go, but what about hours? Minutes would be virtually impossible. Unless I started counting. Seconds. Yes, seconds. If I could hold on to seconds, I could build from there. I ran my thumb over the tops of my fingers, recalling the counting method I'd learnt in the regiment. Each time my thumb bounced over all four fingers, a second had passed. The proper way to count, as Amber had always reminded me. I passed my conscious moments counting, and felt better for it. It was good to have a purpose and control over my destiny. I was a counter, but while my actions made sense to me, any uninformed observer might have been concerned to see a man furiously tapping his fingers and muttering as he racked up numbers. I even started counting them in my sleep, and it became harder than ever to separate my dreams from waking because when I shut my eyes, I saw myself strapped to the bed, tapping my fingers. The real and unreal were becoming one.

CHAPTER 91

The noise was so unfamiliar I didn't realise what it was at first. It wasn't until the door started to move that I realised it had been the sound of a lock.

How long had I been in here?

As the door swung open, I saw darkness through the windows on the other side of the corridor.

Night. The word had lost meaning for me.

I stopped counting out my seconds, and felt blessed relief. Tears came to my eyes when I finally saw two faces I recognised. Gilmore entered, and Charlie, the young nurse, shut the door behind him.

'We tapered your meds, so you and I could have a chat,' Gilmore said, taking a seat at the end of my bed.

'Why haven't you been to see me?' I asked.

My throat was hoarse. Had I been screaming again?

'I've been to see you every day since you got here,' he replied.

'No you haven't. That's not possible.'

'It is,' Gilmore assured me. 'You've not been well. This path. It's been hard on you.'

'Oliver. Sarah,' I said.

'Safe,' he replied. 'Don't worry about them.'

'When can I leave, Alvin?'

'Soon, Thomas, soon.'

'Please don't hold what I did to Derek Liddle against me,' I said. 'I'm not a threat to others. Or myself. I could go now, and I'd be no trouble.'

'Yes,' he replied. 'I believe that's true, but unfortunately that can't happen.'

My heart sank. I thought my friendship with Gilmore might get me preferential treatment, but he knew better than most just how damaged I was.

'I would like to tell you a story, Thomas. I think it will help you. Would you like to hear it?'

'Will it help me get out?' I asked.

'Undoubtedly so,' he replied, so I nodded emphatically.

CHAPTER 92

'The year was 912 AD and Edward the Elder was on the throne, but this story does not concern kings and queens and the intrigue of court. It is the tale of a simple blacksmith called Wenden, who lived in the village of Aston in Shropshire. He had a beautiful wife called Emma and two children, Alfred and Sweyn. Both boys were smart and strong and they liked to help their father in the forge. Emma kept house and learnt medicine from Gunhild, the local wise woman. Part philosopher, part psychic, Gunhild taught Emma the secrets of herbs and tinctures that could cure most ills.

'They lived, the four of them, in a house near the brook that gave Aston its water and they were very happy. In summer, Emma would sit outside the sweltering forge preparing her tinctures on an old millstone, while Wenden and the boys worked the red hot iron. Life was as good as anyone could hope it to be, but in the winter of 912, Emma fell ill.

'She caught a fever, and her lungs filled with a brown fluid that was expelled with each hacking cough. Wenden and the boys sat outside her room, listening to Gunhild tend her, but with each day her health declined, her beautiful blonde hair became like grey straw and her skin turned parchment white. Wenden pleaded with Gunhild to do something, but she said the sickness was beyond her power. He knew she had more to say and forced her to reveal what was on her mind. The wise woman who'd taught Gunhild had told her of a witch called Astranger who had unlocked the secret of eternal life.

'I see you recognise the name, Thomas. This is why I thought the story would be useful.

'Wenden left his boys in the care of Gunhild, and traded all his work and wealth for a horse and supplies. He set off in search of this Astranger, and travelled across the shire, braving storm and blizzard to try to save his wife.

'He finally found her in what we now call Wales. She was living in a fort she'd acquired, practising her dark arts. Wenden pleaded with Astranger to return with him to save his wife, but her putrid heart was unmoved. He threatened her, and was rewarded with a glimpse of her power that almost drove him mad. Finally, after days of trying, Astranger said she would ride with Wenden. She said he had a gift few possessed, that her power should have killed him. She said he was like her, a person with potential, someone who might rise to power, but Wenden wasn't interested. All he wanted was to cure Emma of her sickness.

'When they arrived at Aston, Wenden found Emma's freshly dug grave. He raged against God and all holy things when he realised his sons were gone too. Taken by invaders who'd raided their village. Gunhild and many of his friends had been slaughtered.

'Reeling from the death of his wife and the loss of his sons, Wenden asked Astranger for help tracking those who'd taken his children. She had long searched for an equal. A companion who had her otherworldly gifts, and she agreed. They travelled the length of England for two years, searching for the boys, and then took their quest to foreign shores, to what is now Denmark, France, Germany and beyond, but they never found Wenden's sons.

'Twenty years passed and, now old, and reaching the end of his natural days, Wenden apologised for wasting much of Astranger's life, but she told him their journey had just begun. She taught him the secret Gunhild had spoken of, the secret of eternal life. It was a secret that could only be used by those with a powerful gift, and Wenden was such a one. To extend beyond one's natural days, a person had to offend the laws of nature and God beyond breaking. One had to find another person with a powerful gift, a younger person, and torture and torment them until their mind and body were prepared to take a corrupt and dark soul. When they were ready, a ceremony would be performed, expelling their soul and transferring the new one into their body.

'Wenden made his first transfer in 940 AD, taking the body of a nobleman from Wiltshire, and Astranger took her new host in 945 AD.'

CHAPTER 93

'How does this help me?' I asked. 'Why are you telling me this?'

'The truth is always hidden in plain sight, Thomas,' Gilmore replied, and I raged against my restraints.

That the river card. Show he face. Leon Yates's words before he leaped to his death.

Gilmore moved along the bed and stroked my hair.

'Shush,' he said. 'Struggling will do you no good.'

I was too full of sedatives and grief to fight my bonds for long.

'I never did find Alfred or Sweyn,' Gilmore said. 'And many years later, Astranger told me she'd paid mercenaries to ransack Aston and take my sons. Even she didn't know what had happened to them.'

'You killed her,' I responded.

'No. Why would I do that? She was my queen by that time and she had taught me how much beauty there was in darkness. My sons would have understood.'

I struggled again. 'You're sick.'

'No,' he replied. 'I'm pure. I know what I am. We founded the Totus to feed us suitable candidates. People like you and I are rare, Thomas. Gifted people. And as my queen and I age, our power becomes greater and greater and we must find more and more gifted people, so our hosts become rarer still. I knew you were right for me, the moment you brought your sister here.'

'That's what this has been about?' I asked. 'That's why you took my little girl?'

'You have to be prepared for me,' he said. 'My soul is powerful and dark, and so you must suffer darkness and torment so your body and mind can cope with what will enter it when your soul is expelled. What better suffering than what you've endured?'

I spat at him and called him every foul name I could think of. I screamed at this horror made flesh and fought my bonds, but it was no use. He had me in his trap.

He'd had me years ago.

When I was finally too exhausted to fight any longer, I wept like a child.

'And Amber?' I said through my sobs.

'Fated to suffering beyond anything you can imagine,' he replied. 'My queen needs a new host.'

I shouted until my voice was hoarse, and when I could only whisper, I said, 'Do it. Just do it. Get it over with.'

He leant over me. 'Not yet. You're not quite ready.'

CHAPTER 94

I cried.

    I yelled.

        I raged.

I finally understood the extracts from the old books Mathers had given me. They were tales of these two and their acolytes tormenting people through history, looking for hosts, recruiting familiars. All so Astranger, the queen, and her king, Wenden, Trauco, Papa Boya, could live their eternal lives.

Failure.

The word really meant something this time. It hit me like a punch in the gut, knocking the wind from me. I was a failure. All this time the man who'd taken my daughter had been using me to find others. He'd been right there, in front of me. I felt sick. I'd brought young adults rescued from cults into the arms of the vilest creature, identifying those who were vulnerable and easily led and presenting them to his 'hospital'. I wondered how many people I'd inadvertently recruited to the Totus.

Failure.

This was why Ellen had been encouraging me to give up. My desperation to find Amber had brought me here. It had propelled me further and further into a world of shadows. I'd been a hero once, a soldier, a defender of the weak and scourge of the wicked, but ever since her abduction the line between right and wrong had become increasingly blurred, until I no longer understood the concepts. The only thing that mattered to me was whether an action would get me closer to or further away from my daughter. I'd been played for a fool, dragged deeper and deeper into the darkest reaches of the world, enduring suffering that only served one person: Gilmore.

My cell was dark and I was alert. For the first time since I'd arrived at this infernal lair, I was thinking clearly. He hadn't sent anyone in to dose me after he'd left, and my mind was racing with thoughts of escape. I had found him. After years of searching, I'd found the man who'd taken my daughter. He'd said she was being prepared for his queen, Astranger, which meant she was alive.

Amber was alive.

There was a sound at the door, so I lay still and shut my eyes. The door opened and I heard someone creep into the room. The bonds around my ankles were loosened, and then the one around my left wrist. Did they think I was still out?

I opened my eyes to see Charlie, the young nurse, working the straps that held my right wrist in place. She hadn't noticed I was awake.

This was my chance.

I reached up, grabbed her by the throat and squeezed. She looked at me with wide, terrified eyes as she tried to choke down breaths.

'Da…' she said, clawing at my arm.

I did not relent. Amber's life was at stake.

'Dad,' she wheezed.

I was startled and released my hold immediately, and she doubled over in pain, gulping down air.

'Amber?' I asked.

She glanced at me and nodded, and a broad smile accompanied a flood of tears.

'Amber,' I said, releasing the final restraint. 'Amber,' I repeated, rolling off the bed and hugging her. 'Amber. Oh my God. Amber.'

'Dad,' she said.

'I found you, Amber,' I remarked in disbelief. 'I found you.'

CHAPTER 95

I was terrified this was just a dream, but this young woman, my daughter, was as real as my own flesh. I was so overwhelmed I could hardly breathe, but she had her wits about her.

'Come on,' she said quietly. 'We don't have long.'

She led me out of my cell, and we hurried along the corridor. I guessed it was very late, because the other cells were silent. Amber, my daughter, Amber – I would never grow tired of her name – used her pass to get us through the security doors.

'Why didn't you say anything?' I asked, as we hurried along one of the inner corridors towards the main lobby.

'He said he'd kill you,' she replied. 'He said if I so much as looked at you the wrong way, he'd kill you, Oliver and Mum.'

I don't know why, but I was pleased she knew about her brother. He'd be thrilled to meet his big sister for the first time. I kicked myself for not trusting my instincts. I had suspected she might be my girl, but hadn't the courage to ask.

'All those times we saw each other,' I remarked.

'I was in such pain, Dad,' Amber responded. 'But I knew what he'd do to us all. Now, we have nothing to lose.'

I nodded.

'He has such a hold over people,' she said. 'He promises them reincarnation. Greater power and a new life. His followers believe if they serve him well, they will be blessed with a more satisfying life when they are reborn.'

That explains Leon Yates, I thought. Why would people believe such a thing without any proof? Yates had taken his own life because a monster had brainwashed him into believing something better lay on the other side of death. What a waste. But it did explain the fervour with which people served the Totus.

'People are easily fooled,' I said.

'No,' she replied. 'He told you his story. He isn't human. Not anymore. He's somewhere between god and man. He has incredible power. I believe he can grant this gift.'

'No, Amber,' I said, pulling her to a halt. I looked her square in the eyes. 'No. No one has that kind of power, and to believe they do is very dangerous.'

She nodded. 'Of course, Dad. I'm sorry.'

I felt such joy when she called me that. I smiled and she returned the expression before we carried on. We raced through the silent, deserted building until we reached the corridor that led to the lobby.

'I'll take care of the security guard,' I told her, moving to the front.

We kept low as we approached the door, and she reached up and swiped her key card. I heard the lock click and pushed the door open, and we crept into the lobby.

I felt sick to my stomach the moment we entered the large, vaulted space. Gilmore was waiting with a dozen orderlies. Obsidian stood behind him, alongside many of the men I'd attacked at the Church of the Eternal Light. They rushed us, and I tried to fight them off, but I was overwhelmed.

'Dad!' Amber screamed as they took her captive.

'Don't you hurt her!' I yelled, struggling against the men who held me. It was no use; there were too many of them and I'd been weakened by the sedatives I'd been given.

'Take them,' Gilmore said. 'It's time for us to be born anew.'

CHAPTER 96

Amber and I were dragged through the building by Gilmore's orderlies and Obsidian's men. We both struggled and shouted, yelled and wailed, but it was no use. I'd fought impossible odds over the years, but these were too much even for me. I roared and raged, but in the hands of so many men, I was as helpless as a newborn, and through bitter tears I looked over my shoulder to see my daughter, only a few feet away, weeping and terrified. I'd failed her in the most profound way possible. Everything I'd done, all the suffering I'd endured, was for nothing. Gilmore and Obsidian walked behind Amber, calm and unaffected by all their evil. I burnt with such hatred for them I thought my body might catch fire, but all my frustration, hatred and rage were useless. We were dragged further into the building.

We burst through a set of double doors and were carried into the middle of a room I'd never seen before. It looked as though it had once been a grand ballroom, but now it was to be the scene of terrible sacrifice. There were hundreds of candles set about the space and in their flickering light, I saw dozens of faces I recognised. Orderlies from the hospital, patients; the lewd Farah, prim Jane, haunted Anna, insolent Haley, weeping Hodda and dozens of others. There were more of the people from the Church of the Eternal Light, and many others I didn't recognise. This was the Totus, and they'd been assembled for high evil. That much was clear from the pentagrams, mandalas and Latin inscriptions that had been daubed on every surface around the vast room. I recognised some as foul incantations. Others were so ancient and rare as to be beyond me. Above us, a beautifully painted fresco depicting a hideous scene covered the ceiling. It showed two devils tormenting a sea of people whose faces were contorted in suffering.

'*Et huc venietis,*' Gilmore commanded.

Bring them here.

The crowd parted and to my horror, I saw Sarah and Oliver dragged from an antechamber by a gang of men. They were both weeping, eyes wide in terror.

'Let them go!' I yelled, but no one paid me any attention.

'*Affer mihi inquit cultro,*' Gilmore said.

Bring me the blade.

Obsidian opened a case on a stone altar and reached inside for an ancient black dagger with two dragons twisted around the hilt. I recognised it from my dream and the illustration Mathers had shown me. Obsidian carried the knife like a holy relic and delivered it to Gilmore, who studied the blade as he walked towards Amber.

'Thomas!' Sarah called. 'Help us.'

I struggled against the men who held me, and wept at the futility of my efforts. I'd failed them all.

'Alvin,' I pleaded. 'Wenden. Remember the love you had for your wife. For your boys. Don't do this.'

'It's been a long time since anyone has called me by that name,' Gilmore replied. 'It means nothing to me now.'

'Please,' I begged. 'Take me, but leave my family alone.'

He smiled. 'I told you we need you both, but your daughter betrayed her part in this. She still has hope that we can be defeated. She is still defiant. Surrender of the host must be absolute and by consent, and without it a body is useless to us.'

He raised the dagger and plunged it deep into Amber's chest. I wailed at the sound of her scream, as he drove the blade until the hilt touched her chest. The men holding her released her grip and our eyes met as she fell to her knees. Blood spread from the mortal wound, soaking her uniform in slowing pulses. He'd pierced her heart.

I fought and raged, and was crying so much I could hardly see, but there was nothing I could do. She died looking at me. He'd taken my little girl from me.

She was gone forever.

CHAPTER 97

I grieved for my daughter for what seemed like an age, and through floods of tears I saw Sarah and Oliver were similarly distraught. Had they known the beautiful young woman was Amber? Or were they simply crying at the murder of an innocent?

She lay on the floor, blood pooling around her body. Mine shuddered and shook with a sadness more complete than anything I'd ever experienced.

I became aware of a figure approaching. Gilmore. I raged against my captors anew, but I couldn't reach him. He wiped the tears from my eyes and looked at me sympathetically.

'There is a way to end your pain, Thomas,' he told me. 'Surrender. Give up willingly, and your soul will be evicted from this body. You will join your daughter in the afterlife, and your wife and son will be spared. I know how much they mean to you.'

I was reeling from Amber's death, but was sufficiently in command of my wits to understand what was being offered. My life for theirs. I caught Sarah's gaze and she looked at me pleadingly.

'It's over, Thomas,' Gilmore said, drawing my attention to Amber's body.

Fresh tears fell, and I shouted curses at him, but he remained calm in the face of my tirade.

'This is the last of your resolve leaving your body,' he told me. 'Give up, Thomas. It's time to accept defeat.'

I knew he was right, but hope is a seductive drug. I pictured myself twisting free of my captors, grabbing the black knife, plunging it into Gilmore's chest, rescuing Sarah and Oliver and setting the place on fire as we made our escape.

'Kill the boy. That will convince him.'

My heart sank when I registered the voice, and the crowd parted to reveal Ellen Ovitz. She walked into the room, trailed by Bernice.

'I told you this body was failing,' she said to me.

A stranger, I thought, and everything became clear. She was Gilmore's queen, the ancient and foul creature who'd taught him. The two of them had manipulated me for years, dragging me further and further into torment.

'I trusted you,' I said pathetically. 'I trusted you both.'

'Kill the boy,' Ellen repeated, as though I hadn't spoken.

Gilmore started to move towards Oliver.

'Stop,' I said, and he froze.

This is it, I thought. *The end of the road.*

'I give up,' I said between choking sobs. 'Do whatever you want to me.'

Gilmore smiled as he drew close, and behind him Ellen began muttering an incantation in Latin. I looked at Sarah, who wept incessantly, and then at Oliver, the son I'd neglected and endangered in pursuit of folly. I smiled at them both. If my sacrifice did this one good thing and saved their lives, it would be enough.

I felt a strange power build between me and Gilmore, as though we were connected at the heart of a storm. All the candles in the room flickered simultaneously, and I felt my captors loosen their hold of me. I was reigned to my fate. I closed my eyes, so I didn't see whatever horror came next, and my mind filled with memories of Amber. Feeding the ducks. Running in the garden. Playing hide and seek. I tumbled into a pit of despair that seemed to have no bottom, and just as I felt I would be lost in the void, Lomas's words suddenly came to me.

When all seems lost, keep your eyes open. Look for the count.

Hope is addictive. It is tenacious. And even in the void, I could feel its warm tendrils reaching down to me. I opened my eyes and glanced around the room, trying to make sense of what Lomas had said. And then I saw it, and everything became clear.

There is one who can guide you to the light. You must listen to her.

I'd only had one guide for the past ten years: Amber. And she was guiding me now. She was the messenger Lomas had spoken of. The one who would show me the truth and she was showing me now.

Almost unnoticeable. Directly opposite me, the heavily sedated girl with the brown eyes and red hair: Anna. Her thumb was dancing across her fingertips, counting out the seconds exactly as I'd taught her. They'd dyed her hair, and had likely used contact lenses to change the colour of her eyes. I don't know whether it was my connection to Gilmore, desperation, or the fact I was seeing clearly for the first time in years, but I recognised my daughter in that tiny gesture; it was Amber.

Hope came flooding afresh. Charlie, the nurse, must have been one of their gullible sacrifices, promised reincarnation if she played her part as my daughter to rob me of hope. Astranger needed Amber as a host, so they would not have killed her. She was there, drugged, brought to watch me die. I tried not to think of all the horrors they might have inflicted on her in this place, of all the times she'd seen me over the years. Had they told her they'd kill me if she spoke? Or was she simply too drugged? They would break her spirit with my death and probably threaten her mother and brother's life in order to get her to surrender in the same way I had.

Only I wasn't about to surrender. The defeat that had sapped all my energy was swept away by a tidal wave of hope. I thought I'd lost my girl forever, but there she was, within my reach.

All I had to do was kill the monsters that had taken her from me.

CHAPTER 98

'Wenden,' I said to Gilmore.

He was lost in a trance, as a strange power built between me, him and Ellen.

'Wenden!' I yelled, and this time he registered the word and looked at me. 'I do not surrender.'

He hesitated.

'I am not willing and I do not consent to the abomination you would make me. My spirit is not broken, and hope lives within me. You will not take this body,' I yelled.

I twisted free of the men around me, and reached for the knife in Gilmore's right hand. He tried to step back, but I lashed out with my foot and caught his ankle, and he fell over.

'Stop him!' Ellen cried out, and the men who'd been holding me lunged in my direction, but they weren't fast enough.

The knife clattered free when Gilmore hit the marble floor, and I raced to grab it before it spun out of reach. The twin dragons felt familiar as I curled my fingers around them, and I suddenly understood my dreams. Others had tried to kill these monsters and failed, but they weren't me.

I turned and used the knife to slash at the men coming for me. Blade met flesh and sliced new wounds, giving me the space I needed to reach Gilmore. He was trying to get up, and I kicked him back down.

'Stop!' Ellen yelled, and I turned to see her summoning the dark energy she'd used to kill the lily.

I felt a sudden sickness, and saw the veins in my hands blacken, but I was not going to be defeated by this evil. My girl was there, and my family, now whole, were counting on me. I was driven by the purest, unassailable love, and as I thought the word, I felt relief from the foulness that assaulted me.

Ellen gasped and fell back as though I'd struck a blow.

I leapt on Gilmore, who was trying to rise again.

'You made me,' I told him. 'You put me through hell. But the strongest steel is forged in the hottest fire.'

I plunged the knife into his heart, and he howled with a force that shook the room. Hundreds of years of evil were thrown into his cry, and he made sure the world knew a monster had perished. I pressed the blade further and further into his dark heart, and he looked at me with eyes that blazed with hatred.

Then they went blank.

A murmur went round the room and there were cries of grief and despair. I knew I wouldn't have long before shock and dismay turned to anger. I had to get my family out of there. I pulled the knife from Gilmore's chest and got to my feet, but before I could move, I heard an unwelcome voice.

'Drop the knife,' Ellen said.

I glanced in her direction to see Obsidian holding a blade to Amber's throat.

'Drop it or she dies,' Ellen told me.

'She's your host,' I replied. 'Whatever horrors you've subjected her to were years in the making. You can't kill her. It would leave you without anywhere to go.'

Ellen realised her mistake. She'd made an empty threat, and her eyes turned to Sarah and Oliver, but I wasn't about to give her the chance to correct her error. I flipped the knife so I held the bloody blade and hurled it at the old woman. The knife spun through the air and embedded itself in her throat.

She made a terrible shrieking sound as she clawed at the wound, and her twisted followers gasped, as I raced across the room to grab the hilt. I pulled the knife from her throat and buried it in Obsidian's collar. He fell away from Amber, clutching at the hilt, trying to pull it out. I went after him, kicked him onto his back, and reached down to take the weapon from his body.

When I turned around, Ellen was on the floor, crawling towards Gilmore's corpse. She was crying, but none of her people could help her. I ran over and drove the knife into her back, twisting and pressing until she stopped wailing and fell still.

Her followers looked on in stunned silence. Whatever secrets, whatever power, whatever promises they'd been offered, had all died with these two. I kicked over a candelabra and hot wax and flame spread across a huge rug. The sight of fire stirred the members of the Totus, and some started running for the exits. I grabbed Amber, Sarah and Oliver and shepherded them to the nearest door to escape into the cool night.

EPILOGUE

The sun shines through the trees. Leaves cast dappled shadows on the dry grass as branches sway in the gentle breeze. I am barefoot, and my feet crunch the brittle summer earth into dust as I move towards the table in Sarah's garden.

Life will never be what it was, but that doesn't mean it can't be good.

Amber sits at the table, her contact lenses gone to reveal her sapphire blue eyes, the red dye washed out over the weeks to bring back her natural blonde. I still can't believe my daughter is home. Like me, she's different, changed by her years of suffering. They'd kept her drugged and put her through hell, threatened to kill me and her brother and mother if she ever failed to comply. She'd tried to reach out to me through the fog of sedation, and had been punished for her efforts, but she's getting better now. She started therapy some weeks ago and is beginning the process of healing.

So am I.

I don't know whether to believe Lomas. To accept that Amber and I are gifted. Alvin Gilmore and Ellen Ovitz, or the creatures that had taken their bodies and their names, seemed to think so and they had gone to great lengths to possess us. One day I might explore the road Lomas walked, but not today. Not now. Now is a time for family, for healing.

A few days after the fire burnt down Milton House, when I knew my family were safe, I surrendered to the police. I explained what had happened, leaving out the more fantastic elements of the story. I painted Gilmore and Ellen as the leaders of a dangerous cult that abducted children, and Penny Blake and Baker were able to corroborate my story. Obsidian was identified as Noel's murderer, and after I'd told my story a few times and they were satisfied any violence had been in self-defence, the police turned their attention to hunting the remaining members of the Totus who'd been implicated in Noel's murder and the other crimes I'd described. I was released as a free man, and in the eyes of my family, a hero.

Sarah emerges from the house, carrying a big salad. Oliver is behind her with the plates and cutlery. She smiles at me, her gratitude still palpable. We've decided to try to give our relationship another go. The horror that broke us is gone, and I know I never stopped loving her. The look in her eyes suggests she never stopped loving me either.

I take my seat as they put the food and plates on the table, and Amber leans over and takes my hand. For a moment I see my little girl, ten years old, vulnerable and innocent, and tears come to my eyes. I haven't been able to stop crying whenever I see her, but these are tears of joy, not grief. She looks at me, her eyes similarly shimmering. We're a family again, but only she and I can truly understand what we've been through, and our shared suffering has brought us closer than ever.

I smile and nod at my daughter, and she smiles back. I found her and brought her back, and that's all that ever mattered.

She's home.

ACKNOWLEDGEMENTS

I'd like to thank my family for continuing to support and cheerlead my writing. I'd also like to thank Alice Rees for copy-editing, Victoria Goldman for proof-reading, and Mark Swan a.k.a. Kid-Ethic for the cover design.

If you've enjoyed this book, please do let other readers know it's worth their time by leaving a review.

ABOUT THE AUTHOR

Adam Loxwood lives with his wife, their three children and two dogs, and loves telling stories.

Printed in Great Britain
by Amazon

36288166R00219